Autumn 2015, Issue Number 33, www.DarkDiscoveries.com

DISCOVERIES

FICTION

FEATURES

COLUMNS

REVIEWS

Publisher
JournalStone Publishing, LLC

Editor-in-Chief and Art Director
Aaron J. French

Contributing Editor
Vincenzo Bilof

Assistant Editors
Russ Thompson (Senior Submissions Editor)
Stuart Conover (Assistant Reviews Editor)

Layout and Design
Paul Fry

Contributors

Vincenzo Bilof, Laird Barron, Chris Kelso, Phil Differ & Gavin Boyle, Hal Duncan, Colleen Wanglund, Cameron Pierce, John Palisano, Max Booth III, MP Johnson, Mary A. Turzillo, Shane McKenzie, David Agranoff, L. Andrew Cooper, Mike Davis, Donald Tyson, Robert Morrish, Richard Dansky, Peter Emshwiller, Jeff Noon, Ardi Alspach, Colin Dunsmuir

Founding Publisher and Editor
James R. Beach

Special Thanks
Laird Barron
Chris Kelso
Phil Differ & Gavin Boyle
Hal Duncan
Colleen Wanglund

Contributing Artists/Photographers
Henry Stampfel (cover photographer)
Denise Daniel (cover art)
Steve Santiago (pg 17 & 25)
Greg Chapman (pg 31, 45 & 77)
Luke Spooner (pg 57 & 69)
Ardi Alspach
Colin Dunsmuir

DARK DISCOVERIES
(ISSN 1548-6842) is published (Qtrly) by JournalStone Publications
439 Gateway Dr., #83, Pacifica, CA 94044

Christopher C. Payne
JournalStone Publications
439 Gateway Dr., #83, Pacifica, CA 94044, U.S.A.
christophercpayne@journalstone.com.

Editorial

Updates From

Hello and welcome to our Bizarro themed issue (#33) of *Dark Discoveries*. This is a very special issue in that it marks our second time around with a featured author gracing the cover. That lucky author is Laird Barron, a man who has been working diligently over the years and consistently producing quality dark fiction. He really needs no introduction. Laird has recently joined the DD team as a new columnist; "The Black Barony" will recur every issue. We're very excited about it!

With our Bizarro theme, we explore all the mayhem, violence, sex, and wackiness that's come to be associated with this subgenre. This issue is bloody, crazy, and a whole lot of fun—but most of all it's intelligent. Just because bizarro tropes seem mindless doesn't mean the practitioners composing them aren't thoughtful and insightful artists; quite the opposite. Bizarro is a complex and newfangled region, sometimes hard to get a *firm grasp* on (please expect this kind of punning throughout the issue), and so for compiling the content this time I am indebted to Vincenzo Bilof, a wonderful poet and author in his own right, who co-edited the issue. Vincenzo edits the Bizarro Pulp Press bookline from JournalStone Publishing, some of the authors of which appear here. I'm also indebted to Chis Kelso for assisting with some interviews. If you've been impressed with the recent look of the magazine lately, that's because Paul Fry of Short, Scary Tales Publications has been laying out and designing the issues, and he's been doing a fantastic job. We're very pleased to have him on board. Our regular stable of story illustrators includes Greg Chapman, Luke Spooner, and Steve Santiago. Be sure to check out their work outside of DD; you won't be disappointed!

2015 was the first full year I worked as editor-in-chief of *Dark Discoveries*, and it's been a lot of fun and quite a ride. I enjoyed working with James Beach and Jason V Brock, but doing this on my own has given me the freedom to come up with themes and seek out authors I personally resonate with. It's been a blast to do that. I hope the DD readership has enjoyed the content this year as much as I enjoyed putting it all together. We've got many more big things and cool stuff lined up for 2016, so please continue this journey with me! Cheers to 2015. I sincerely appreciate all of your support and interest in the magazine.

Now, to enter into this idea of bizarro fiction and art one must truly become quite mad. It makes me think of the sign above the door in the wall of Hermann Hesse's *Steppenwolf* (1925), which reads: "For Madmen Only!" Such a disclaimer might do well applied to the cover of many bizarro books. And mad women, too! As new weird sought to present scenarios in which the world-as-weird

was taken for granted, so bizarro presents the world-as-fucking-crazy as a given. Its images and characters are gritty, real, and irreal. After you've finished this issue, I'm sure you'll be itching to bash your brains on the asphalt. Let's get on with it!

And so it is my dissenting pleasure to bring among you readers of DD a new full-length interview with the cosmic juggernaut of weird fiction Laird Barron, which was carried out by myself and Chris Kelso. A *ménage a trois* of mouth-trash verbiaging! Bizarro frontman Cameron Pierce serves up a fishy tale of woe and incertitude; the great John Palisano shows off his plant copulations; Max Booth III reveals the hidden supernatural of weirdness; Nebula Award winning author Mary A. Turzillo recounts the bizarre nature of twins; and finally, the king of gore Shane McKenzie lets this whole issue have it.

For our nonfiction, we have an interesting piece by Donald Tyson chronicling the progression of modern horror. L. Andrew Cooper presents an irreverent breakdown of the current trend of the bizarro field. We've got an excellent new interview with legendary and eccentric author Hal Duncan, as well as a look at David Agranoff's new bizarro punk rock book. There's a bizarro comic strip and an unusual piece of bizarro nonfiction from yours truly.

Finally, this issue's theme is tackled by our stable of columnists, including a new piece "The Golden Age of Dread" by Laird Barron. The editor of the very popular *Lovecraft eZine* has joined the current lineup of regular columnists with his "Weird Reflections." Colleen Wanglund penetrates the esoteric symbolism of two Alejandro Jodorowsky films, and she will be returning each issue to do more esoteric film analysis. And Robert Morrish delivers an enjoyable interview with horror author Thom Metzger.

Come now, put on your Mad Hatter hat, wring the neck of the March Hare and get yer slow asses to the tea-party table. It's time to have some fun...

—Aaron J. French
Editor-in-Chief

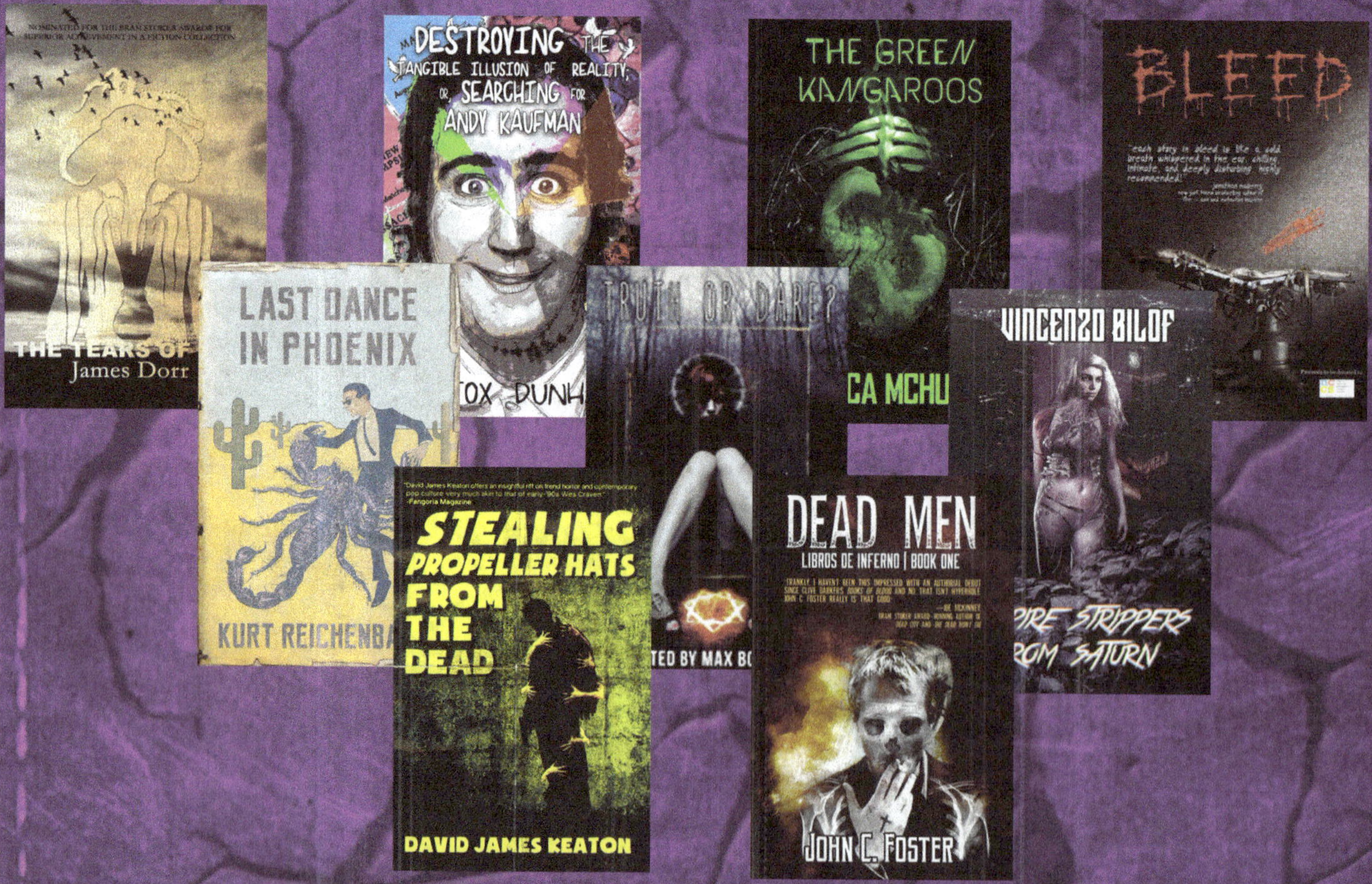

Chris Kelso: Hi Laird. I felt that *The light Is the Darkness* was a bit of a departure for you, I'm sure most of your fans will agree. Is this the start of a new direction for your fiction, perhaps you'll delve into the SF or crime fiction you grew up reading and enjoying? I suppose I'm really asking if you see yourself gravitating away from cosmic horror and, if so, have you fallen out of love with the genre? (I thought your story "The Cyclorama" in the Bond anthology was wonderful, by the way.)

Laird Barron: I wrote that short novel five years ago. *The Light Is the Darkness* is a departure in tone, but it slots into the kinds of characters and themes I've explored from the beginning. The story is part of an epic narrative. At the moment I'm working on a series about a pair of teen boys set in the 1950s—a pulp throwback that pays homage to serials such as Doc Savage, The Phantom, The Shadow, The Hardy Boys, and so forth. It ties heavily into *The Light Is the Darkness*, among other things.

Yes, I enjoy science fiction and crime, among other genres, and I've written a number of stories anchored in noir and psychological horror. There was a moment, probably around 2009 or so, where I considered walking away from cosmic horror completely.

That didn't happen for several reasons. Mainly because

Master of the Weird: An Interview with Laird Barron

By Aaron J. French & Chris Kelso

my personal life collapsed. 2010 to 2013 were dark ages. I lived the worst kind of country and western song, face down in the dirt existence. But I kept writing. I became relentless. Locked myself in a room and wrote two collections and three novels. And I broke through. As a consequence, I've stepped back from the zero-sum cliff. I made a decision to embrace everything I could, to be reckless. There's no reason to abandon cosmic horror. It's not a fixed point, it's not an antiquated artifact.

The question of where to go next is ongoing. I've written and sold around half a million words these past four years. You'll still see cosmic horror/Lovecraftian work in novellas such as *X's for Eyes*, "Don't Make Me Assume My Ultimate Form," and "Fear Sun." My Jessica Mace stories veer into occult and psychological horror, and another series about Rex, a cyborg war dog's adventures on a post-human Earth, are science fiction to the hilt. Instead of tossing aside the old canvases, I'm working on bigger ones.

CK: You're good friends with another writer I greatly admire, John Langan. Can you tell me how you guys got to be so close? Have you ever thought of collaborating?

LB: John and I made our professional debuts within a month or two of one another back in 2001. This was in the *Magazine of Fantasy & Science Fiction.* We corresponded for a while, hit a few conventions together in the mid to late Aughts, and eventually became good friends. I share commonality of interest with John—we read a lot of the same authors as kids, read the same comics, enjoyed the same movies. Our execution differs, but we share a philosophy of horror as a literary mode. Lately, people have decided we're part of the weird lit movement, and fair enough, "The Weird" covers a lot of ground and it's part of what we do, but the core of our identity has always been in-the-trenches horror authors. I don't see that changing anytime soon.

The subject of collaboration is an ongoing notion. We've threatened to co-write a novella. The right project simply hasn't materialized. Unofficially, we collaborate often. If you read carefully, we've shared characters and plot points, and phrases and titles. My broken ring symbol of Old Leech has its genesis in a line from John's "On Skua Island." The Black Guide from *Mysterium Tremendum* was originally conceived at the ReaderCon bar circa 2007. Paul Tremblay was there too. All three of us have worked the BG into various projects, although, like the best ideas, it constantly mutates.

CK: You have a real talent for infusing your stories with this unique sense of dread and foreboding—the only other example of something similar in tone and execution (that springs to my mind, at least) is some of T.E.D. Klein's work. Do you consider yourself a happy person or does your fiction reflect your own dark sensibilities? I realise you can have a happy person with bleaker tastes but usually we're attracted to the shadows because we identify with something deep within them.

LB: T.E.D. Klein's *Dark Gods* is a bible. *Koko* by Straub and McCarthy's *Blood Meridian* are two more. Klein and Straub taught me how to manipulate characters in a physical sense—how to stage them, move them around, and most importantly, how to present large group interactions.

I suffer acute depression. It is a lifelong affliction that affects my productivity, personal relationships, and ability to interact with the world in general. Depression looms mountain-sized on my internal landscape. It is a fact of my existence. So, when I can, I mine it for inspiration and source material. When I can't mine the mountain, I go around it, over it, or bore through it.

These points notwithstanding, depression isn't a compelling factor regarding why I choose to work at the dark end of the spectrum. For many years I wrote pulp fantasy and science fiction. I enjoy horror, and am good at it. Experience has given me the reason, nature the tools.

Aaron J. French: Your story in the new JournalStone anthology *The Gods of H.P. Lovecraft*, edited by yours truly, features the Tooms brothers, and it's the first half of the longer novella *X's for Eyes*—which is also coming out from JournalStone. Could you tell us about these projects and how the Tooms brothers differ from some of your other work?

LB: The Tooms brothers inhabit a counterfactual universe. A universe where Elvis recorded multiple albums by 1956; a league of corporations make good on Illuminati-style conspiracy theories; Doc Savage and The Shadow are viable career choices; flying cars and jetpacks prototypes are on the way; and humanity is manipulated by a vast alien intelligence who is quite smitten with the Lovecraftian Mythos. With "We Smoke the Northern Lights" and the complete novella, *X's for Eyes*, I went for a dryer and more tongue-in-cheek delivery than usual. It's more satirical and makes use of absurdism in ways I've not attempted prior to this novella. Pulp and Golden Age of Science Fiction references are overt. Readers who follow my work will discover that these stories stand alone, but tie into *The Light Is the Darkness*, among others. Ultimately, if there's a demand for these, I've plotted a sequence of novellas that will fit together in a sprawling saga.

AJF: Let's talk about Lovecraft. How do you see his work as important to your own writing, given some of the controversy surrounding his views and his bust being retired as the World Fantasy Award and everything? Where is Lovecraftian fiction and weird fiction going, in spite of all this?

LB: Lovecraft was a visionary. I respond to that vision more than I respond to the nuts and bolts mechanics or execution of his prose. He basically pointed toward the outer dark and said, Look! And some of us looked.

His literary influence upon the weird as a whole is undeniable; his influence upon my own work is equally undeniable. "Hallucigenia," "Shiva, Open Your Eye," "The Forest," "The Broadsword," and "Vastation," are stories of mine that are heavily indebted to HPL and his visionary cosmic horror. However, Lovecraft is but one figure among giants, he is but one inspiration among hundreds in my mind. I acknowledge the influence of Clark Ashton Smith, Lord Dunsany, and the Old Testament to varying degrees.

Lovecraft also held personal beliefs no sane or decent person can sanction. The retirement of his bust from the WFA was a long time coming. This change doesn't signify censorship nor diminution of his accomplishments as an author and mentor. Retiring the bust was foremost a nod to decency. It was also a rational decision amid an often irrational furor. Ongoing slap-fights surrounding this decision aren't a good look for involved combatants. The signal to noise ratio between narcissistic dancing on the grave celebrations by the anti-Lovecraft hardliners and the proprietary hysteria among the orthodox Lovecraft apologists is poor. David Nickle recently wrote a fine essay on the subject that seems to be the definitive word on the subject so far.

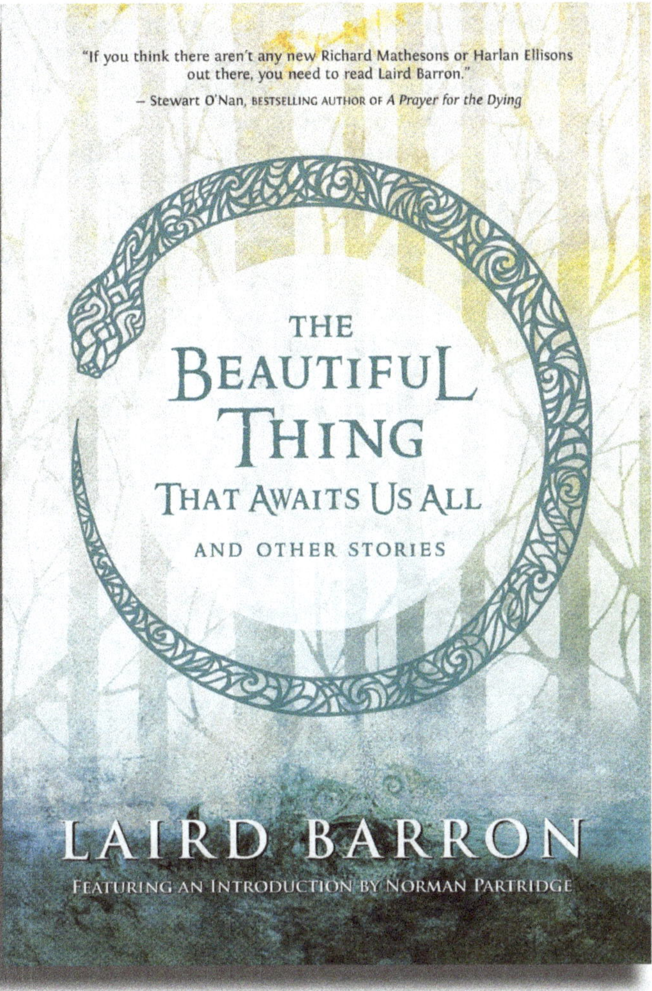

I imagine Lovecraft pastiche will continue while well-written, literarily ambitious cosmic horror will exist in unicorn-scarcity, as ever. Weird fiction was around for ages before HPL made the scene. It will persist well beyond his current popularity and associated tempests.

AJF: Some of your work, along with fellow weird fictionists Simon Strantzas and Richard Gavin, often includes elements of what I might call the esoteric and occult. Lovecraft certainly intimated at these things, though he never took a personal interest. What is the extent of your own interest in these areas, and how do you see the occult and esotericism influencing weird fiction and horror today?

LB: My fascination with the occult has waned since its zenith during my early to mid-thirties. I researched heavily during that era and that research infused some of my early stories. Now I'm more fascinated with the fascination that people have historically indulged. The contemporary Western Weird canon seems too enamored with the facile or apocryphal aspects of occult tradition. I have at least one foot firmly planted in that graveyard—the pop culture visage of the occult gleaned from mass market novels and Hollywood films. Matt Cardin and Richard Gavin are two writers I'd cite as exceptions. Both approach the subject in a scholarly fashion. Cardin's essays are some of the most thoughtful examinations on the topic. His site, *The Teeming Brain,* is a treasure trove of articles and interviews. Richard Gavin's upcoming treatise *The Benighted Path: Primeval Gnosis and the Monstrous Soul* will doubtless prove informative.

AJF: You have talked some about this before, but I'd really like to know which authors exactly inspired your unique approach and style when it comes to writing? If you had to list them and point out their individual contributions, what would that look like?

LB: Roger Zelazny taught me that when it comes to description, less is usually more, *in media res* is a good beginning, and humor should be sharp as a honed knife; from Peter Straub I studied the fine art of verisimilitude and meaningful digression and how to move characters through time and space; Charles Simic imparted the blood-soaked brutality of prose poetry; Martin Cruz Smith showed me where characters are vulnerable, even the toughest of them, or especially them.

CK: So who are the rising new weird fiction writers today that nobody has heard of yet? Or, which authors should readers be keeping their eyes out for?

LB: None of these writers are unknown per se, they simply aren't household names: Kristi DeMeester, S.P. Miskowski, Matthew Bartlett, T.E. Grau; Michael Wehunt; Frank Duffy, V.H Leslie, Mike Griffin, Orrin Grey. Some of these people have a collection or novel under his or her belt; some are approaching that debut book; each of them represents a data point of the weird and the horrific. There are so many more popping up every week. The emergence of skilled new writers feels exponential.

AJF: You've worked with Mike Davis of *The Lovecraft eZine*, with myself, and now with *Dark Discoveries*—and we're extremely glad to have you! What are some of the best markets for weird fiction these todays, and how do you find things in relation to mainstream horror and even sci-fi and fantasy?

LB: As I mentioned, back in the Aughts I came up through *The Magazine of Fantasy & Science Fiction* and SCI FICTION and the occasional anthology. Excellent writers such as Kelly Link, Dale Bailey, John Langan, Charles Coleman Finlay, and M. Rickert did the same. These days I primarily work by commission. I haven't cold-subbed short fiction for years, so I may be behind the curve regarding the trending markets. Focusing on short fiction? As a reviewer, awards jurist, and occasional editor, I can tell you where I reliably find top notch work that features a spectrum of voices—*Nightmare Magazine, Dark Discoveries*, Datlow, Lockhart, Guran, and Adams anthologies. *Tor.com* and *Tachyon* are developing fantastic novella series. Some of the best fiction is coming from Canada, specifically *Chizine Books* and *Undertow Press*.

Infrastructure is an important part of succeeding as a professional writer. Ralan and Duotrope are good databases to research editorial needs. The economy took a hell of a hit seven years ago and publishers received a double dose of punishment. There was a subsequent contraction that meant fewer books were being picked up. Borders went under, which certainly didn't help matters. Making a living in my neck of the woods isn't easy, and likely never will be, but there seems to be more optimism and more success stories of late. I hope the upward trend continues.

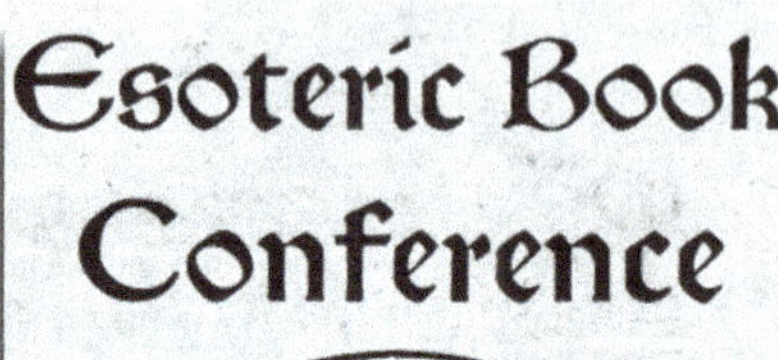

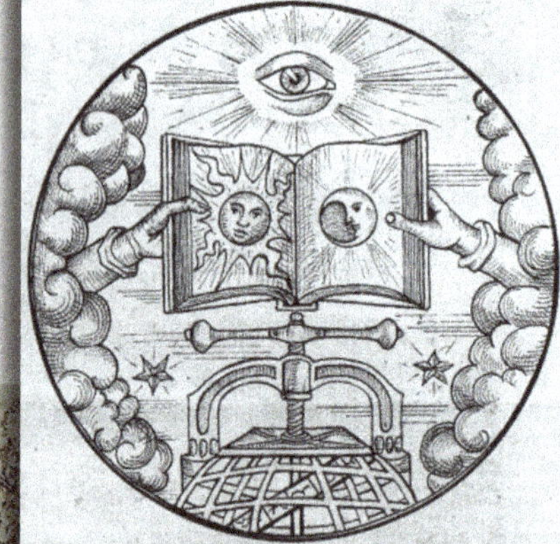

AJF: *NecronomiCon Providence: An international conference and festival of Weird Fiction, Art, and Academia.* You've gone; I've gone; we got to chat there, and that was awesome. Tell us a little about this particular convention and what you find intriguing about it, or hell what you don't like about it, if that's the case. Why might this convention be important?

LB: It's a great convention. Niels Hobbs and his team did a tremendous job in 2013 when I was there. Great attendance by a rogue's gallery of industry people. Much kibitzing occurred and whiskey flowed. There were excellent panels and some less so. It's one of the few major conventions that caters to weird fiction and horror professionals, and thus is valuable to those of us who care for such things.

Some have floated the notion Providence in 2013 marked a critical mass in the so-called Weird Renaissance. On a personal level that may well have been true for individual authors. For some it was their first major convention, or their first collaboration with like-minded artists. The resurgence of weird fiction and horror, abetted by the independent and small press, was in full swing long before 2013. At the time of this interview, it's late autumn 2015. Perhaps, years from now, history will regard NecromiCon 2013 as a sort of Concordat of Worms. But let's not get ahead of ourselves.

AJF: Have you ever heard of The Esoteric Book Conference in Seattle? It's mostly non-fiction, but is that something which might be of interest to you as a writer/reader?

LB: Sorry to say, this is the first I've heard of the convention. The literature of the occult—who writes it and who reads it—fascinates me, as I said earlier. I enjoy research. If the stars aligned, I'd quite happily book a trip to the Emerald City to participate.

CK: Speaking of reading, are you able to read anymore given your current schedule? If so, what are you reading?

LB: Reading has always been a vital component of my life; I find ways to fit it into my schedule. I devote several hours a day reviewing materials for *Locus Magazine* and as a World Fantasy Awards judge. Lately, I've seen terrific work by Paul Tremblay, Mike Allen, Gemma Files, Adam Nevill, and Anna Tambour. *A Head Full of Ghosts* by Tremblay and *Experimental Film* by Files are standouts.

AJF: Ten years from now, how has your writing developed? How much crime fiction, psychological horror, or even science fiction elements have worked their way into your stories?

LB: Cosmic horror still grips me. There's a lot more to do in other genres and time keeps slipping away no matter how much I write. I've maintained a relentless schedule since 2010 and it still isn't enough because there's simply too much to do. I love straight crime, straight science fiction, and high fantasy. Ten years from now it would be nice to have sold a handful of books about a semi-retired mob enforcer I've worked on since 2012. I'd like to pen an epic fantasy novel. There are screenplays to be written and a volume or three of essays on writers I admire—especially Michael Shea and Roger Zelazny.

Recently I put together a new collection called *Swift to Chase*. It has a different feel, the beginning of a new direction. The stories are set in, or strongly reference, Alaska. Several follow the journey of professional final girl, Jessica Mace. A couple of the pieces verge upon cosmic horror; the rest inhabit different intersections of horror—psychological, science fiction, slasher, and thrillers. We'll see how it's received; I anticipate doing more in this vein. I also have a hunch you'll see a string of novellas (in addition to the Tooms brothers saga) from me in the near future. The novella is my favored format and I may have an opportunity to more thoroughly explore that facet of my work.

AJF: You spoke earlier about depression. What about your stress level, your mental well-being? Does writing increase or alleviate stress for you? You're not as bad as Tom Ligotti, are you? Does drinking alcohol help with stress build up? Does it help with writing? Do you drink alcohol?

LB: Twin scourges of depression and hypertension run in my family. It's a struggle and one that many people endure in all walks of life. Things were worse during my teens—all those hormones compounded with my parents' bunker mentality probably brought me closer to the edge than was necessary. Sometimes I say that I didn't leave Alaska, but rather that I escaped.

These conditions and their history inform my writing, although it's more a case of working around a problem rather than directly benefiting from one. Writing satisfies my need for expression and writing pays the bills. Writing doesn't alleviate stress; it generates stress, except for rare occasions. It's something I step away from and regard with pride. Certainly, while writing is primarily a job, it's my dream job.

I'm a scotch man. Glenrothes, Glen Livet, and Auchentoshan are my preferences. Sometimes a nice bourbon is my choice—Hudson Baby Bourbon is amazing, but a shot of Maker's Mark is never a bad idea. I drink socially—and yes, I've written blind drunk. The myth of privation, mental illness, and alcoholism being conducive to art is bullshit. If one can repurpose negativity into something positive, hurray. As my life has stabilized during its second act, so has my ability to produce consistent quality art.

AJF: Who's the best editor working in the genre right now? Wait; don't answer that.

LB: Determining the best is definitely an enterprise fraught with peril. Plenty of editors, from Ross Lockhart and Gordon Van Gelder, to Paula Guran and Michael Kelly, routinely produce anthologies, collections, magazines, and novels of merit. Any of these editors is capable of snagging one or more of the year-end literary accolades the industry bestows. It has been my honor to work with these folks and a dozen others. I can't say who the best is because it's a moving target and this is a what-have-you-done-lately business. Nonetheless, Ellen Datlow is the gold standard when you're talking about horror/weird fiction editors. She's worked slicks, major online publications, and scads of anthologies. Her secrets, beyond an affinity for literature, are adaptability and diversity. She changes her approaches and her stable of authors. Look back over her career and you'll see that progression. She's always in motion and never satisfied to repeat prior successes. You want to take home the blue ribbon, more often than not, you'll have to go through Ellen to claim your prize.

AJF: Who has better weird fiction, Britain or America? Or another geographical locale? At the very least, how does it differ?

LB: Yes, let's stick with "different." And for the record, I tend to lump Canada and Australia into the British contingent when it comes to literary sympathies and trends. In broad strokes, North American (USA) horror and weird fiction tends more toward bombast and rugged individualism. Especially in US literature, we solve problems with guns, swords, fists, and good old fire. Characters stuck in a US horror story tend to argue, fight, and otherwise resist to the bitter end. British horror tends more toward the miserabilist. Protagonists resist the notion that anything too weird is happening; after all, daily life is an existential morass, a horror from beyond is simply another escalation. When ye lively awfulness does eventually manifest, the stiff-upper lip set either faces it down with flashlights and sober resolve, or glumly accepts what fate decrees.

Frankly, I enjoy both brands. Brian Keene is an exemplar of the hands-on North American horror philosophy, as are Norman Partridge and Jonathan Maberry. On the British and Canadian side of the aisle, I point to Simon Strantzas, M. John Harrison, and the late great Joel Lane. Naturally there are brilliant exceptions—Nathan Ballingrud specializes in the emasculation of tough guys while Michael Marshall Smith is no stranger to hard cases and violent ne'er do wells. Gemma Files (Canada) and Kaaron Warren (Australia) are also reliably brutal.

CK: What should writers and editors in the weird fiction and horror genre be thinking about as the field develops? What are its strengths, its weaknesses? What should we be doing differently, or how much should we adhere to tradition?

LB: The greatest threat to art is stagnation. Stagnation is tricky because it presents in different guises—pastiche and homage are the most obvious; contemporary authors aping masters from bygone eras down to monocles and top hats. The more insidious form of stagnation occurs when styles of the classical canon are updated for modern consumption but don't really branch off into a separate line. This more sophisticated form of aping is often smooth, it is often entertaining in its own way. Unfortunately, such recursion doesn't advance the cause of art, it merely repeats stories better told the first time around. As I've said in the past, the world doesn't need Poe or Lovecraft 2.0. We need new blood and new ideas that honor tradition and more importantly, contribute to the canon. Perhaps even make improvements.

There are plenty of people doing it right—Livia Llewellyn, Joe Pulver, Paul Tremblay, Kaaron Warren, Gemma Files, Nathan Ballingrud, Karen Tidbeck, and Adam Nevill, for starters. I could cite scores. We've said it for a decade, at least—this is a golden era for the macabre and the strange.

CK: As far as future projects go, is there anything you're particularly excited about that you can tell us about?

LB: It's a busy time. My next collection, *Swift to Chase*, should appear in 2016. Around twenty original stories are slated between now and the end of next year. I'm particularly happy that several of these are novellas. *Rex Versus* follows the adventures of a cyborg war dog on a post-human Earth. Another is *X's for Eyes* and concerns the Tooms brothers. Dad is reminiscent of an evil version of The Shadow and his kids are negatives of the Hardy Boys and Johnny Quest. I'm also working on a novel that expands upon events of "In a Cavern, in a Canyon," which I wrote for Christopher Golden's *Seize the Night* vampire anthology.

Murmurs in the Dark: THE PROGRESSION OF MODERN HORROR

BY DONALD TYSON

For a long time, horror didn't change very much. Pliny the Younger (61-113), a Roman who lived during the first century, related in one of his letters a story of a ghost who appeared late at night at a house in Athens, moaning and groaning and dragging his chains. For this reason the house got the reputation of being haunted.

> In the dead of the night a noise, resembling the clashing of iron, was frequently heard, which, if you listened more attentively, sounded like the rattling of fetters; at first it seemed at a distance, but approached nearer by degrees; immediately afterward a phantom appeared in the form of an old man, extremely meager and squalid, with a long beard and bristling hair; rattling the gyves on his feet and hands. (Pliny the Younger, *Letters*, b. 7, letter 27)

Why was the ghost dragging chains? Because he had been murdered, and his body was wearing manacles and leg irons when buried.

Now jump ahead to the Victorian Era, and *A Christmas Carol* of Charles Dickens, which was published in 1843. The main character, old Ebenezer Scrooge, is visited at his house by the ghost of his late business partner, Jacob Marley, who died exactly seven years earlier. And how does Marley's ghost appear?

> Marley in his pigtail, usual waistcoat, tights and boots; the tassels on the latter bristling, like his pigtail, and his coat-skirts, and the hair upon his head. The chain he drew was clasped about his middle. It was long, and wound about him like a tail; and it was made (for Scrooge observed it closely) of cash-boxes, keys, padlocks, ledgers, deeds, and heavy purses wrought in steel. His body was transparent, so that Scrooge, observing him, and looking through his waistcoat, could see the two buttons on his coat behind. (Dickens, *A Christmas Carol*, Stave 1: Marley's Ghost)

The explanation Dickens gave for Marley's chains is more fanciful than Pliny's account of the chains on the ghost in Athens. Marley is being punished for all the customers he cheated in business during his life. Yet the appearance of the ghost in Pliny and in Dickens is substantially the same—the transparent figure of a groaning, bristling old man who drags chains behind him. This terrified the Romans in the first century, and it equally terrified readers of Dickens' book in the 19th century. The object of horror is unchanged for eighteen centuries, because the taste of readers for horror remained the same for this period of time.

Two Factors In Traditional Horror

Traditional horror in Western nations consisted largely of two factors—fear of death and everything connected with it, such as ghosts, vampires, the grave, corpses, physical corruption, and premature burial; and fear of damnation, which included witches who traditionally were believed to have signed a pact with the Devil, werewolves who were believed to change into wolves because they were cursed by God, demons from hell, possession by demons, familiar spirits assigned by the Devil, and the Devil himself who sometimes came to snatch away damned souls.

For centuries this was enough to terrify Western readers, whose tastes in horror remained the same from generation to generation because the underlying moral code of society remained the same. What was considered evil in Pliny's day was still considered evil by the Victorians. In literary fiction there were boundaries that simply could not be crossed without provoking universal outrage. Occasionally a writer would cross them. The sexual horrors described by the Marquis de Sade in his unfinished novel *120 Days of Sodom* (written in 1785) transgressed these boundaries by a wide margin. But the mores of Western society prevented such horrors from becoming widely read or celebrated.

There were ups and downs in the moral behavior of Westerners from one century to another, and from one social class to another. The aristocracy was apt to be less censorious toward forbidden ideas than the working class. This allowed such amusements as the various "hellfire" clubs that were formed in England and Ireland during the 18th century for the purpose of mocking Christianity. Membership in these clubs was strictly limited to gentlemen. The most infamous of these clubs was that headed by Sir Francis Dashwood, active in London from 1749 to 1760.

Nonetheless, the general moral tenor of the West remained remarkably stable for the better part of two thousand years, as the conservative nature of horror literature demonstrates. This was due to the pervasive—some might say oppressive—authority of the Christian churches, which imposed a unifying and stabilizing code of thought and behavior on the common people. During all this time, the peoples of Christian nations attended church on Sunday and were informed by priests and ministers what they were permitted to do and believe, and what was forever forbidden to them.

Scientific Horror

That began to change in Europe during the Victorian Era, when the rise in science challenged the eternal and immutable tenets of the Church. As society changed, horror changed with it, for the two are inextricably woven together and cannot be separated. We see the beginnings of scientific horror in such works as Mary Shelley's *Frankenstein; or, The Modern Prometheus* (1818) and in Robert Louis Stevenson's *Strange Case of Dr. Jeckyll and Mr. Hyde* (1886). Science, with all its wonders and possibilities, is able to push horror to new levels of fear. It can literally create horrors that never before existed, or were even conceived.

Notice that in these 19th and early 20th century works, the science that gives rise to the horrors is always decried by the writer as imprudent or not worth the danger it provokes. Those who seek to transcend the laws of God and nature are punished for their hubris.

On a cruder intellectual level, this trend toward scientific horror showed itself in the strange alien races and gigantic monsters that began to appear in early works that would later be called science fiction. It is science that enables the horror.

For example, in Jules Verne's 1870 novel *Twenty Thousand Leagues Under the Sea*, Captain Nemo is forced to fight a giant cephalopod only because his masterpiece of scientific invention, the undersea craft *Nautilus*, has been able to descend to the depths where the monster dwells. It is the advanced science of a monstrous alien race that enables it to devastate and conquer the world in H. G. Wells' 1897 novel, *The War of the Worlds*.

Cosmic Horror

Horror arises from the microscopic level, or descends from the stars, or enters through dimensional gateways opened by machines. At its best it becomes the "cosmic horror" defined by H. P. Lovecraft—a horror from beyond the common experience of human beings. In his essay, *Supernatural Horror in Literature*, which he finished in 1927, Lovecraft wrote:

> The true weird tale has something more than secret murder, bloody bones, or a sheeted form clanking chains according to rule. A certain atmosphere of breathless and unexplainable dread of outer, unknown forces must be present; and there must be a hint, expressed with a seriousness and portentousness becoming its subject, of that most terrible conception of the human brain—a malign and particular suspension or defeat of those fixed laws of Nature which are our only safeguard against the assaults of chaos and the daemons of unplumbed space. (Lovecraft, *Supernatural Horror in Literature*)

Cosmic horror can only exist in a culture that has begun to shrug off the yoke of religious dogma. In the 19th and early 20th centuries we see not only the rise of science, with its scepticism toward anything that cannot be weighed and measured, but the rise of atheism, which rejects the very existence of God. On the social level, atheism took the form of communism. Communism has always been the enemy of Christianity. Beginning with the writings of Karl Marx and other atheistical thinkers, it gathered strength during the late 19th century in England among writers and intellectuals, such as dramatist George Bernard Shaw and sexologist Havelock Ellis, and soon spreads itself across much of the Western world.

Atheism, expressed in philosophical works of the time such as Nietzsche's *Thus Spoke Zarathustra* (1883-5), represented a rejection of Christianity's unchanging and rigid moral code of belief and behavior. It is in this book by Nietzsche that the following famous passage appears:

> "When Zarathustra was alone, however, he said to his heart: 'Could it be possible! This old saint in the forest hath not yet heard of it, that GOD IS DEAD!'" (Nietzsche, *Thus Spoke Zarathustra*, Zarathustra's Prologue)

Upon such a foundation of doubt Lovecraft, who was a declared atheist from early childhood, was able to build his concept of cosmic horror, which at its heart requires a fundamental uncertainty about the very nature of reality. When we start to suspect that the things we have always taken for granted as true and eternal are mere illusions, the fear that arises from this uncertainty is the essence of Lovecraft's cosmic horror. Nothing in life is stable, nothing is fixed, nothing is to be trusted, for when it is examined it falls to dust.

Cultural Decadence

As a consequence of casting away the stabilizing influence of Christianity, Western culture laid itself open to a progressive and increasingly rapid decadence. By decadence, I mean the easy indulgence in studies, appetites and urges that were formerly forbidden. This did not occur all at once. A society is a kind of collective creature of habit. It continues to fulfill various traditional forms and customs even when the reasons for doing so have been forgotten, and only gradually lets these ancient habits slip away as they fall under strident criticism from its more radical element.

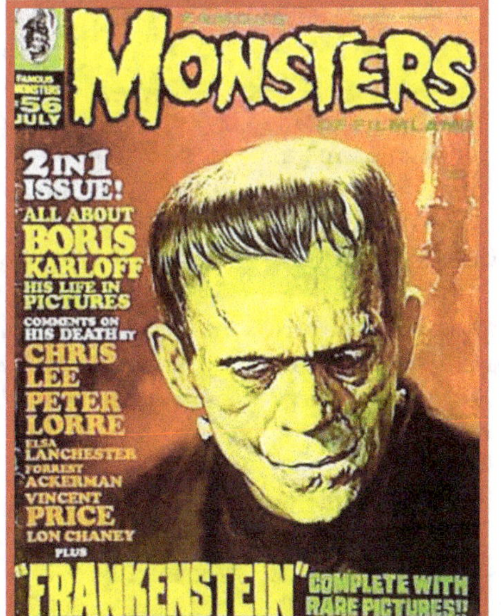

Decadent societies are fun to live in. In many ways they are the best of times. All the constricting taboos that held people back in previous generations are successively stripped away. The sense of freedom is intoxicating. People are permitted to do things they could not do, say things they could not say, even think thoughts they dared not think. During decadence, literature and drama tend to become exaggerated. This is necessary to keep the attention of the increasingly jaded audience, which always seeks for new thrills.

The downside with decadent societies is that they contain the seeds of their own destruction. They are inherently unstable and do not long endure. The descent of social behavior down a moral ladder proceeds in only one direction, and eventually it reaches the bottom.

We see the great shift in horror fiction occur in the decade of the 1960s, which also marked the flowering of the Hippie Movement. The Hippies evolved out of the Beat Generation of the 1950s. Freedom was the rallying cry of this period—free sexuality, free artistic expression, freedom to experiment with mind-altering drugs, freedom from past guilt and future fear. What began as a relatively slow social transition during the 19th century and the first half of the 20th century suddenly accelerated, even as new discoveries in science were seemingly accelerating at an exponential rate.

The Hippie Movement, in its essence, was astonishingly brief. It lasted from about 1965 to 1967. What happened during the last years of the 60s and early years of the 70s was merely its residual echoes. But we are still living with the consequences. The last of the clinging habitual observances of the old Western moral code were cast off by a large portion of the population—the most influential portion, the young, who presently are running the Western world.

During this modern period, we must talk not only about horror literature, but about horror in film. Movies became more influential as a medium of horror than books. As cultural restrictions were stripped away with ever-increasing speed, horror became more explicit, more extreme, more bizarre. What would have been rejected as perverse and corrupting by film censors and shunned by the general public during the 1950s became permissible in the decades that followed.

The Decadent Cycle

Horror, both in books and movies, began to go through a frantic cycle, the speed of which ever quickened. That cycle is: *forbidden, condemned, decried, accepted, embraced*. Western society was experiencing the same cycle with regard to cultural norms and moral behavior. Horror fiction is a part of Western culture, and cannot be separated from it.

The practical consequence of this cycle was the necessity for horror writers and film makers to introduce progressively more severe shocks to entertain increasingly demanding audiences. Events that caused moviegoers of the 1930s to faint with horror—for example, the mere sight of Frankenstein's monster in the 1931 film *Frankenstein*—were viewed with polite amusement by movie audiences in the second half of the 20th century.

I remember very clearly seeing the makeup for the monster in a photo in Forest J. Ackerman's magazine *Famous Monsters of Filmland* when I was a young boy, and being both terrified and fascinated by it. That was around 1960, and I was probably among the last of those to experience the monster as the filmmakers intended. By the next decade makeup and special effects in film had progressed to a such a degree, his face was no longer horrifying to a more jaded generation of children.

In the 1960s and 1970s, blood and gore became the main ingredients of successful movie horror. This trend was lead by Hammer Films of England, who began to make their horror movies in full color so that the blood would show more convincingly.

They still relied on the stock characters of horror literature—the vampire rising from the grave, the mummy or walking dead, the witch damned by her Satanic pact, the werewolf cursed by God, demons from hell, the Devil himself—but there were apt to be more sadistic scenes of murder, torture and mutilation, and also sexual acts that would be considered deviant for the time.

Deviant sexuality was not unknown in horror literature of the Victorian period, but its physical aspect was usually understated. For example, in Joseph Sheridan Le Fanu's novella, *Camilla*, published in 1871, there is a sexual relationship between an older female vampire and a young woman, but it is never explicitly stated by the author that the vampire is a lesbian. In the Hammer horror of the 1970s lesbian scenes and also nudity became common features.

Can't Trust No Body

The following decade of the 1980s expressed a transition to a new kind of horror that was an extension of Lovecraft's cosmic horror. This is the horror of being unable to trust one's own body, and takes such forms as alien parasites that consume the flesh of living human beings from within, horrifying diseases that mutate and degrade the human shape beyond recognition, and the genetic monsters produced by science or inbreeding.

Who can forget the scene where the alien in immature form bursts through the chest of crewman Kane of the spaceship *Nostromo*, in Ridley Scott's 1979 movie, *Alien*? In this same year, David Cronenberg released the chilling film *The Brood*, in which a woman is able to project the fear, anger, and hatred of her subconscious mind into the forms of ectoplasmic semi-human dwarfs that are birthed from her womb. This is scientific horror of a psychological kind.

In John Carpenter's magnificent film, *The Thing* (1982), we see the evolution of horror when we compare the changes that were made in this remake to the original 1956 classic, *The Thing From Another World*. In the earlier film, the monster is conventional in the sense that it is a giant physical being whose form is fixed. This, by the way, was a departure from John W. Campbell's 1938 forward-looking novella, *Who Goes There?*, upon which the film was based. Carpenter always maintained that his film was not a remake, because it was based on Campbell's novella, not on the 1956 movie.

Carpenter returned to the original literary source and created a monster that had no form of its own, but was capable of imitating any living thing to the smallest detail, including a human being. The amorphous horror of the monster when it creates forms of nightmare that bear no relationship to anything that lives on the Earth echoes the horror of Lovecraft's shoggoths, which are large globular creatures similar to the amoeba that can modify their gelatinous, transparent substance to bud forth such things as eyes, ears, and other appendages at will.

The most chilling aspect of the monster in Carpenter's film is its ability to mimic not only the appearance but the personality of human beings, in effect supplanting and becoming them. Again, the horror arises from our inability to trust the integrity of our own bodies, or the bodies of other human beings.

We saw the seeds of this horror of having both our bodies and our identities stolen from us in the 1956 film, *Invasion of the Body Snatchers*, which was based on the 1955 novel *The Body Snatchers* by Jack Finney. This dread at having not only our bodies but our minds stolen away as we sleep is very much a part of Lovecraft's concept of cosmic horror. Neither our bodies nor our minds can be trusted in a chaotic world where natural laws are broken and there is no God but science.

The Zombie Plague

No overview of the progression of modern horror can avoid touching on zombies, which are a remarkable phenomenon in the history of horror cinema. Before the rise of the zombie craze, a zombie was generally understood to be a corpse taken from the grave and reanimated by Voodoo magic to serve as a slave. The first zombie film, the 1932 *White Zombie* starring Bela Lugosi, featured a woman placed into a death-like trance and buried, who was unearthed and enslaved by an evil Voodoo master, played by Lugosi. In the end, the master is killed, the spell broken, and the woman, who was never dead, returns to her normal condition.

The innovation of George Romero's ground-breaking 1968 film, *Night of the Living Dead*, was to have all the dead rise from their graves at the same time and shuffle around, seeking to consume human flesh. Romero's dead were truly corpses in varying stages of decay. They were not very quick. It was possible to simply walk away from them. But they had a disturbing gift for sneaking up on the unwary from behind.

The very slowness of the zombies in Romero's original film contributes to their horror. They are like the unstoppable things that pursue us in our dreams—no matter how slow they approach, we somehow cannot seem to flee fast enough to escape them, and as we stumble and run into things, they keep drawing nearer and nearer. This same horror theme was used to good advantage in the

1984 *Terminator* movie, which has a wonderful nightmarish quality.

As the zombie meme in film progressed, and audiences began to get bored by it, the zombies gradually became quicker and quicker, until in later zombie films they are actually faster and stronger than living human beings. They also became more sly in their behavior, and in some films overtly intelligent and able to talk.

This zombie subgenre was so popular with audiences, yet became so familiar, that writers were forced to disguise it in various ways, in order to present more zombie product while seeming to be giving fans something fresh and new. Thus we got humans reanimated from death by toxic government waste, or by a mysterious virus, as in such films as *Resident Evil* (2002) and *REC* (2007). Twists were put on the theme. In Sam Rami's *Army of Darkness* (1992) corpses are reanimated by possessing evil spirits. In *Re-Animator* (1985), which was based on Lovecraft's story "Herbert West: Reanimator," the dead are turned into insane, homicidal zombies by the deliberate injection of a serum. And let's not forget Stephen King's 1983 novel, *Pet Sematary*, where dead pet animals, and some human beings, are reanimated and made into zombies by an ancient and cursed Indian stone circle.

The love for zombie films may go hand-in-hand with the increasing tendency in modern Western culture to view other human beings as objects. When a person has been reduced to the level of an object, they can be played with, tortured, or even killed without remorse. Or, the zombie subgenre of horror may have arisen from the prevailing feeling of helplessness and lack of control over their own lives that, at present, haunts the people of Western society.

Tentacle Sex

Another aspect of modern horror that would have been considered too bizarre only a couple of decades ago, but which has gradually moved into the mainstream as our society continues its progressive cycle of decadence, is what is known as tentacle sex. An example may be found in the 1981 movie, *The Evil Dead*, in which a woman who wanders into the forest at night is raped by animated tree roots. In general, tentacle sex in horror is any scene in which a young woman is sexually violated by an inhuman monster that uses tentacles for the purpose of penetration.

This has become a popular sexual fantasy for some women, and probably for some men as well. It would have been considered so repulsive prior to the 1960s that few at that time could even have imagined it would become a mainstream horror theme in its own right, but today it scarcely raises an eyebrow, so easily are we conditioned to accept and even to embrace progressively weirder and more horrifying behaviors as the norm.

Related to tentacle sex as a horror theme is the somewhat less common theme of robot rape. In the 1977 film *Demon Seed*, a self-aware computer decides that it needs to make a baby with a character played by Julie Christie, and rapes her. This was a very common theme in earlier horror, but it was usually a demon from hell or Satan himself who did the rape and engendered the child. For example, in the 1953 novel by Dennis Wheatley, *To the Devil, A Daughter*, which was made into a movie by Hammer in 1976, or the 1968 movie *Rosemary's Baby*, based on the 1967 book by Ira Levin.

In the age of science, the satanic principle may be embodied in a machine. Echoes of this embodiment in cinema go as far back as the silent 1927 German film, *Metropolis* and the silent 1915 German film, *The Golem*. Technically the Golem is not a robot, but nonetheless he is a thing made by human intelligence that has overstepped its intended bounds.

Where are we going in our race to present ever more shocking and grotesque concepts and images for the amusement of a bored reading and movie-going public? What are the recent trends in horror currently working their way through the cycle from forbidden to embraced?

Torture Porn

One obvious trend is sometimes referred to as torture porn. This is not necessarily overt pornography, although sexual scenes can become explicit, but rather, it is the use of sex to render torture erotically exciting. It's a very old trick of advertising to use sex to sell a product. If you want to sell a car, drape a scantily clad woman over its hood. In horror, sex is being used to make scenes of torture, brutality, mutilation, and murder not only palatable, but enticing and attractive. Much of the horror is derived from the tension between attraction and repulsion created in the audience.

The Saw movie series may be mentioned in passing in this context, along with the *Hostel* movies, and the *Human Centipede* franchise. Sex of a kind that a few decades ago would have been labelled as perverse, or at the very least extreme, is adroitly mingled with torture and cruelty. The inevitable result is to render torture and cruelty less repellent in the minds of the movie audience. Familiarity breeds contempt, but also comfort. Repetition takes away the shock value of such scenes, leaving only their sexual titillation.

This mingling of sexual excitement with torture and cruelty is a prime component in the book I mentioned earlier by the Marquis de Sade. In writing *120 Days of Sodom*, it was de Sade's purpose to corrupt the morals of his readers, and make them question their religious faith. To accomplish this, he cleverly combined sexual stimulation with descriptions of torture. In this way he made torture sexually exciting for his readers. It is the same approach being used by the makers of torture porn movies, but whereas de Sade used it to promote his atheistical philosophy, modern movie makers use it to sell tickets.

Body Mutilation

Another contemporary trend I've noticed, which not long ago would have been completely rejected by the public, but which now is gradually being accepted by them as they become acclimatized to it, is horror deriving from the mutilation of the human body.

In the ground-breaking 1993 movie *Boxing Helena*, a mad surgeon uses his medical skills to amputate the arms and legs of a woman, so that he can keep her in a box as his sexual plaything. The director and writer of the screenplay, Jennifer Chambers Lynch, has a *Dallas* moment at the end of her film, when it is discovered that the surgeon did not really cut off the arms and legs of the girl, but only dreamed of doing it.

Today, *Boxing Helena* seems dull and rather quaint. Simple mutilation has given way to self-mutilation, in scenes where the victim himself is forced to cut or burn or otherwise harm his own flesh. Usually the compulsion takes the form of a threat on the life of his wife or children. Part of the horror lies in the terrible choice he is forced to make—will he mutilate himself in some horrifying way, or do nothing and allow his loved one to be killed? The *Saw* movie franchise has exploited extensively the horror of self-mutilation.

I've noticed that even in regular everyday movies where there is no intention to horrify, scenes of self-cutting are creeping in, and it is often presented as a normal, or at least a common, activity. That illustrates how easy it is for the general public to become desensitized to what formerly shocked or repelled them.

Is There Any Limit?

The question must be raised, is there any limit to how far horror can go in books and movies? Should there be a limit? Stephen King evidently believes that there is a limit. In 1977 he published a novel titled *Rage* under his penname, Richard Bachman. It involves a Maine high school student who is expelled, and then gets a gun from his locker, shoots a couple of teachers, and holds his fellow students hostage.

In 1977 Michael Carneal shot eight students at a prayer meeting in Kentucky. The novel *Rage* was found in his locker. It was not the first such incident, nor the second, nor the third. This prompted King to direct his publishers to take the novel out of print.

From this we may conclude that there is a limit to the progression of modern horror, at least in the minds of some writers and some publishers. But at the same time other writers, other filmmakers, will be striving to push that limit as far as they can go, in order to excite their increasingly indifferent audiences, who have read and seen everything that is available and want something more twisted, more intense, more visceral and compelling. And so the cycle goes on.

ASSEBLIEF

BY CAMERON PIERCE

We used to think our dark nights of the soul could save us all. We'd wake in the late afternoon, a stolen road construction sign in the living room, piss on the floor because Theo forgot to use the outhouse again. There'd be holes in the ceiling and shell casings scattered on the floor from rounds we'd shot off in the night. I don't know where all the guns came from or how none of us ever got shot. Like the time Theo played William Tell with a mannequin we'd stolen from a department store. He'd eaten a couple tabs of acid and railed half an eightball of cocaine then struck up a conversation with the mannequin. After a while, I guess it started talking back. That's when he shot it in the head. He spent the rest of the night in the bathtub, naked and shitting himself, shrieking for God.

When he sobered up the next day, we learned that he thought the mannequin was a real woman (as if any women would ever hang out with us) and that he'd murdered her. But Theo is dead now. He overdosed alone while the rest of us were digging mud shrimp to sell to bait shops.

Our lives are different than they were back then. We'll still light up a zule on the beach or knock back a couple beers, but we have no solutions to this life's struggles. We were confident in those days. Not so much anymore. We live in the same beach house where Theo died, without running water or indoor plumbing, near the mouth of the Great Fish River on the Indian Ocean, but we've moved up in the world. We don't dig mud shrimp for a living like we used to. We're fishermen now. We catch the big fish. Lately, we're mostly after sharks.

It's another wet and sweltering day in February. The days are hot, but the nights are cold. Last night, the sky turned purple and lightning lit up everything so bright, we could see Bat Cove in the distance. Hail the size of fists came down on us, and we were beaten and bloodied. We retreated indoors and laughed about the storm over cheap rum. But outside the lunacy of night, it is no laughing matter. We've caught no sharks for seven days, our longest streak of bad luck. Money is running low and the rum is all we have for nourishment.

It is sometime in the afternoon. We own no clocks or other time-telling devices. We're sitting on the floor in the one room of our house, passing the rum, waiting for the tide to come in so that we might change our luck somehow.

Watkin suggests that perhaps the ragged-tooths have already headed north.

"Ja, maybe I'll fish for grunter today," Zane says, in Afrikaans.

"Raggies always hang around through April," I say.

"Every year is different," Watkin says.

"They would not move so early," I say.

"If I caught a grunter today, I don't think I would sell it. I would eat it myself," Zane says.

"I would eat a grunter too," Watkin says.

Zane nods. "Then I will go for grunter at the river mouth."

"There will be sharks off the point," I say.

"You've said that every day," Zane says. "I'll take my chances with grunter now."

"The raggies will not let me down this time," I insist.

"There are three of us and many fish in the river and sea," Watkin says. "You keep your faith in the sharks. We will search the river mouth for something to feed us."

As the sun begins its long descent and shadows creep across the afternoon, the rain also dissipates, giving way to a calm, cool evening. We gather our gear and march down to the beach. Hundreds of iridescent plough snails crawl in spirals above the surf, scavenging the shore for flesh. Sea birds feast on shrimp and baitfish. Everything is waking up after the storm.

"You sure you want to go for raggies?" Watkin asks.

I nod. "I have too much faith."

"How about you come down to river mouth with us? If nothing happens in two hours, we'll go fish the point with you."

The dark will not be here for several hours, but it is not preferable to fish alone here at night. There are poachers and thieves, and also those who are worse. If I hook a large ragged-tooth, I will need someone to gaff it when it is in close.

The tide will continue rolling in for hours. There is no harm in fishing the river for a while. To a fisherman, two hours can pass in the blink of an eye. Besides, raggies tend to come in close at high tide.

"Okay, but only for two hours," I say.

We walk along the water's edge on the hard sand toward the mouth of the Great Fish River. There's no one else around. There rarely is this time of year, except for the poachers and other shark fishermen, who mostly come out at night. With the slow bite, no one else will come around for sharks, meaning it'll likely just be us and poachers. In the morning, maybe there will be an angler out in pursuit of musselcrackers, but with the spotty weather, I don't know. The diversity of fish life around here is pretty much endless. It's the hazards that keep some people away. Upriver, you've got hippos. Down here at the mouth, anything can happen. We've never run into trouble, but we stick together and know when to duck our heads.

We cast out mud shrimp into the river, which is muddy following the storm. "It's blown out," I say.

Zane and Watkin share a look of annoyance then return their gazes to their lines.

I should mention now that Zane and Watkin are twin brothers. Their parents ran a produce stand in Grahamstown until they were hit by a drunk driver on N2 while returning from Port Elizabeth with a truckload of peaches. My friends lived with their grandmother from that point forward, until the old lady died. Then they came and lived out on the beach with me and Theo, rest his soul.

Sometimes I feel outnumbered, living with Zane and Watkin. With Theo around, there was balance. The twins are so much alike, they even dream the same dreams most nights. Or so they say.

"Fish on," Watkin says, his rod arcing into the beautiful shape of a horseshoe.

"It's a good one, ja?" Zane asks.

Watkin nods. "Ja, very good."

The fish makes a powerful run downriver toward the ocean mouth. Watkin calmly tracks it along the shore as line screams off his reel. Zane and I set down our rods and follow. We bring the gaff along in order to snatch the fish when it comes in close. But the fish surges out of the river mouth into the surf with ease. It shows no sign of slowing.

"This does not feel like any grunter," Watkin says.

Zane and I nod solemnly, already lamenting the potential loss of this great and mysterious fish.

Watkin tightens down the drag. The fish slows down some and begins to turn back toward the shoreline. "Give in," Watkin says, as if the fish can hear him. "You are brave, but it is time to give in."

Violet light wilts on the horizon, but the fish remains way out past the surf, doing whatever it thinks it must to reclaim its freedom. We give in to silence out of respect for this great battle. The darkness comes.

Bats are taking over the night by the time the fish surrenders. Zane wades into the surf with the gaff. He has been ready all this time.

We have yet to see the fish on the other end of the line, but we know it will show itself in the surf any moment now. And whatever it may be, it will be glorious. Unless it is an enormous sand shark. There's hardly any meat on sand sharks. To hell with them.

We glimpse a pale, spiked back followed by a scythe-like tail cutting through the dark surf. The fish must be six feet long.

Zane stalks out further into the water, up to his waist, gaff raised above his head. The waves push the exhausted giant into the shore and Zane stabs the gaff down into the fish's back. It does not protest as he drags it onto the beach. This fish is not a creature known to us, and I have fished here my whole life.

The white flesh is translucent. We can see its heart and other organs pumping with life. We can see its tired blood.

My initial estimate was incorrect. The fish is about nine feet in length with its tail. However, it is slender like an eel. The tail resembles that of a thresher shark and makes up nearly a third of its total length.

The fish's head is uncomfortably human. Its blue eyes gaze up at us with sadness. Bloated lips part to reveal a mouthful of molars. The fish's purple tongue runs over its teeth as if to clear its mouth of something, so it might speak. From its chest extend two pathetic baby arms.

"*Asseblief...asseblief...*" the fish croaks.

Please...please...

Zane beats the fish over the head with a stone and

its eyes go cloudy. Upon the second and third strikes, blood of the fish spatters across Zane's face and chest. He does not relent until the fish's hideous face is no longer a face at all. Zane throws the bludgeoning stone into the sea and marches away. Watkin cuts his line, leaving the hook somewhere in the fish's ruined skull, and follows his brother.

I'm left alone in the gloam, staring at a still body that ends in a constellation of teeth and blood, the purple tongue like a distended sun in the center of it all.

I consider chasing after the twins, but it would be a shame to leave the fish to waste, especially after it waged such an impressive fight. I take my knife and fillet it right there on the sand. It is a strange fish unlike anything I have ever seen before, but the flesh is white and firm. We can pass it off as kingklip and sell it for a fair price, if nothing else. I take up the fillets, which are generous and heavy, along with all of our gear, and leave the carcass to the creatures of the night.

Back at the house, I find the twins asleep in their bed. I salt down the fillets, decide to cook some up fresh for dinner. It is a weird fish, but I am curious. If it happens to be exceptional, perhaps we can sell it for a high price.

I start a small fire outside. As the fire comes to life, I cut a palm-sized fillet from a larger piece. I rub the fish with spices. Our catches have been poor in recent times and we have gone to bed hungry on more than one night, so despite the strangeness of the fish, I anticipate the meal greatly. I set the fillet on a large flat stone at the edge of the fire. There's still some rum left over. I drink from the bottle while the fish cooks. Alone like this, I am at peace. The hardest thing in life is not getting along with other people. It is getting along with yourself that proves most difficult. At times I do not believe myself to be up to the task. I stare at the ocean longingly, ready to give myself up to the sharks I so love to catch. Someday I'll probably do it too. For now, I'm holding out hope that someday a person might love me in the way I can never love myself. I can see leaving this beach life behind, settling down in a two bedroom house in Port Alfred with a good woman and a child. Maybe we'd open a restaurant popular with tourists. The twins could supply me with fish in exchange for the deed to the beach house. For now this is all a dream. I'm older than I used to be, but not an old man yet. I'm holding out hope.

Rum, fish, night. It'll do. It always has.

The strange fish grills up flaky and opalescent. A buttery odor mingles with the scent of the sea as the fish's fat melts from the meat. I slide the fish onto a broken tile that we use as a plate.

The fish is surprisingly dense, like tuna, but the flavor is richer, coppery and sweet.

I devour the fillet and consider cooking another piece. I resist, thinking of what some restaurant owner will pay for it. There is still time to fish for ragged-tooths tonight. And yet, exhaustion overcomes me. Whether it is an effect of the rum or the fish, I do not know. Perhaps even I drank too much last night and am still paying for my indulgence. Whatever the cause for my tiredness, I polish off the rum, smother the fire, and retire to my hammock.

That night, I dream of the human-faced fish, and in my dream, the fish is God.

"*Asseblief...asseblief...*" I beg, but no matter how I ask forgiveness, God condemns me.

His purple tongue slides over his teeth and he tells me, "Yours will be a life of suffering."

"*Asseblief...asseblief...*"

When he closes his blue eyes and turns his head away from me, I understand that my sentence has been writ. I am a condemned man.

I climb onto God's spiked back and weep into his translucent flesh. Where my tears fall, his flesh erupts in rainbow blotches, as if my tears are oil and my sorrow is corrupt.

I awake to screaming. At first I think we're being robbed. I leap from my hammock and find Zane in bed, shrieking inhuman shrieks, holding Watkin's lifeless body. Watkin has died in his sleep.

I help Zane bury Watkin with his fishing rod in the sand dunes. We lay bricks over his grave and stand over the burial, not knowing what to do or say. We did the same thing when Theo died. Burying friends doesn't get easier, I guess.

I tell Zane about the meat of the strange fish. "Maybe we should eat it," I suggest, "to celebrate your brother and his glorious kill."

Zane solemnly agrees, so we start a fire and cook more of the strange fish. Salted for a night, it is different than when eaten fresh, though still very good.

Over our last jug of rum, we discuss fishing the night tide in honor of Watkin. Halfway through the bottle, the tide is in and we're ready to hit the beach when a freak storm unleashes fist-sized hail and sends us retreating into the house for cover. We share a laugh and curse the strange fish for bringing ruin down upon us. Cursing the fish causes me pain in my heart, but I'm feeling drunk and desolate. Zane seems in good spirits as we proceed to polish off the rum, so it's a surprise when I awake the next morning, head throbbing and full of cotton, to find him hanging in the kitchen, rope around his neck.

I cut the rope and drag him outside. I bury him in the sand dunes beside his brother. "Dear God, please forgive these brothers. Please understand that our faith in the sea is just another form of faith in you. We fishermen are true believers. Please do not condemn us."

I give this prayer to the strange fish we'd slaughtered. If the flesh of the lord is in me now, I hope he sees the goodness in my heart.

The day is hot. I spend most of it lying in my hammock, silently weeping. As the sun sinks into the sea and a full moon rises in the sky, I take up my shark rod and make my way down the beach to the jetty. I skip over tidepools full of urchins and snails. The night becomes cold very fast. The small creatures do not seem to mind. I do not mind the cold either. What else can I feel besides pain? Ja, let the cold freeze my aching heart and reeling mind.

Asseblief...asseblief...

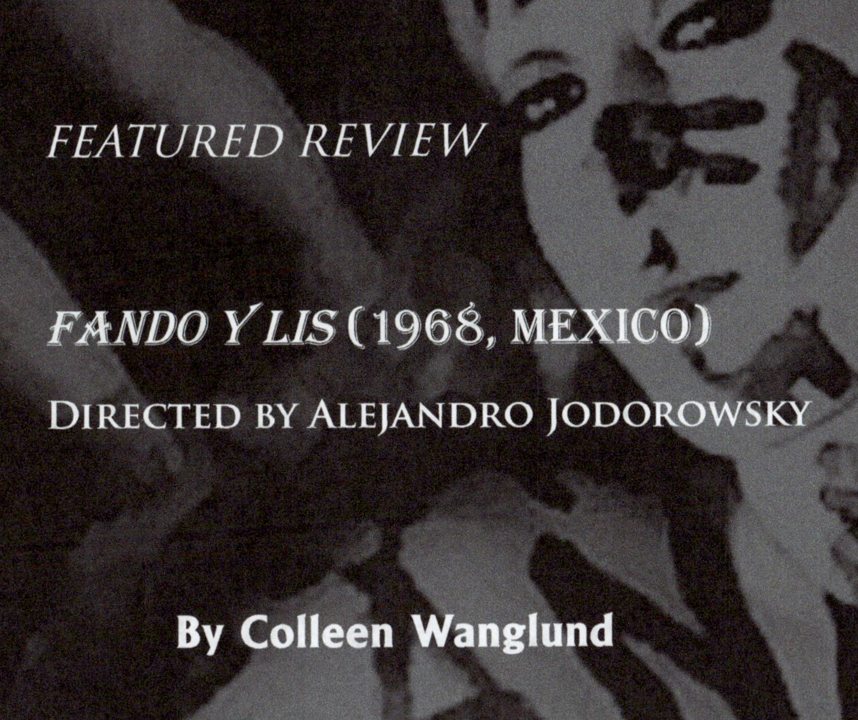

FEATURED REVIEW

FANDO Y LIS (1968, MEXICO)

DIRECTED BY ALEJANDRO JODOROWSKY

By Colleen Wanglund

Fando Y Lis is Alejandro Jodorowsky's first feature-length film, based on a play of the same name by Fernando Arrabal. When it premiered at the Acapulco Film Festival in 1968, a riot broke out over what was perceived to be its blasphemous nature and the film was subsequently banned in Mexico.

Filmed in black and white and with a very low budget, the film follows Fando (Sergio Kleiner) and his paraplegic lover Lis (Diana Mariscal) as they make their way through a grim post-apocalyptic landscape searching for the town of Tar. The mythic town is rumored to make all of your dreams come true. Along the way, they meet up with a very strange cast of characters. They come upon a ruined town where the women try to lure Fando into sex games and Lis is forced to fend for herself. Other scenarios involve people bathing in mud, where Fando leaves Lis to stand on her own for a while; a group of cross-dressers who dress Fando and Lis in each other's clothing in a surreal gender bending scene; and a rather unsettling scene where Fando undresses Lis and allows strange men touch her naked body. One sequence in particular involves four old women playing cards, with the winner of each hand getting up close and personal with a young, buff man. I can't say why, but for me the depravity of this scene had a similar disturbing feel to Pier Paolo Pasolini's *Salo, or the Hundred Days of Sodom,* which wasn't released until 1975. By the time the film reaches its conclusion, Lis has been transformed into a Christ-like figure.

I have to say at the outset that I love Jodorowsky's films. I find them surreal and beautiful and quite spiritual, and *Fando Y Lis* is no exception. While Jodorowsky is usually known for his use of bright colors and psychedelic dream-like sequences, the black and white employed in this particular film only accentuates the bleakness of the landscape, and the temptations that our protagonists are subjected to throughout their journey. What was initially ascertained as blasphemy by the rioters in Mexico is, in my opinion, Jodorowsky's loving interpretation of Christian beliefs. I feel the post-apocalyptic landscape is a metaphor for Purgatory and the legendary town of Tar that the couple are trying to find is, in fact, Heaven. It is reminiscent of Dante's *Inferno* and his description of the nine circles of Hell. At times Fando is abusive toward Lis, threatening to leave her alone to fend for herself, which she cannot do. Lis is fragile and quite helpless without Fando. This treatment calls to mind Peter's denial of Jesus Christ, and even Judas' betrayal.

There are some flashback scenes of Fando and Lis' traumatizing childhoods. Fando's in particular begins with a meeting with his dying mother and then takes him back to his time as a child when his mother was revered as celebrity. These sequences are almost a precursor to Jodorowsky's much later film *Santa Sangre* (1989). Lis' transformation into the Christ-like figure begins with giving her blood to feed a stranger they happen upon in their travels, and completes itself with a group of people feeding on small slivers of her skin as she lays dying. This is obviously a reference to the consumption of the body and blood of Christ from the Last Supper and the Eucharistic ritual performed during the Catholic Mass.

The stunning direction by Jodorowsky and dream-like cinematography of Rafael Corkidi—who also worked on *El Topo* (1970) and *The Holy Mountain* (1973)—combine to make this film a surreal but beautiful homage to Christianity and a statement on modern society's moving away from spirituality and embracing of hedonism and materialism. However, others will surely have a different interpretation, as I'm sure is the director's intention. If you've never seen a Jodorowsky film, *Fando Y Lis* is a good place to start as it is more accessible in tone than some of his later, more bizarre movies.

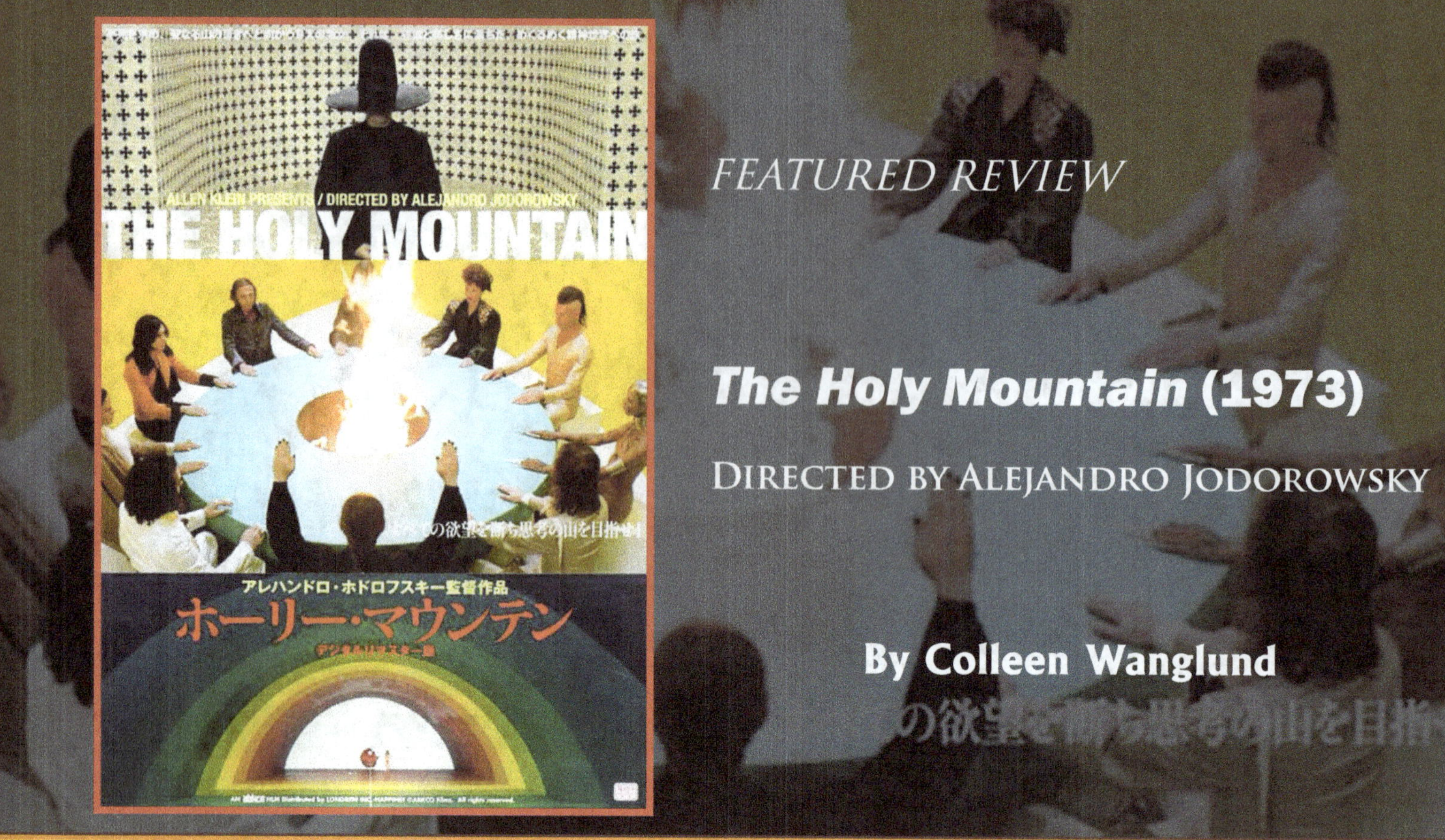

FEATURED REVIEW

***The Holy Mountain* (1973)**

Directed by Alejandro Jodorowsky

By Colleen Wanglund

I love Jodorowsky's films. The man knows how to use bizarre satire and black comedy to get his messages across. I've seen *The Holy Mountain* no less than six times on the big screen and more on DVD and have always wanted to write about it. I've been writing about movies for years but this particular film intimidated me. I was always unsure about my ability to do it justice. So when I got the opportunity to write about bizarre and cult films, I jumped at the chance and immediately decided I would finally write about *The Holy Mountain.* Keep in mind, this is a film wide open to interpretation and my opinion and observations might be different from yours.

At its most basic level, the film is about discovering how to live a better life in a world full of greed, materialism, war, and depravity. It attacks religious and governmental authorities for their corruption and attempts at social engineering. But *The Holy Mountain* is really so much more than that. Jodorowsky incorporates his personal experiences and search for enlightenment to create a surreal and psychedelic admonition that life is more than the things we possess and crave, and our own self-absorption.

The film's prologue, accompanying the opening credits, introduces the Alchemist (Jodorowsky) as he performs a ritual cleansing on two women. This film is all about rituals. It then moves to the Thief (Horacio Salinas) and his ritual stoning and crucifixion by children, establishing him as the Christ figure. We follow the Thief and his limbless dwarf companion into a nearby town, where the viewer is subjected to scenes of senseless violence, oblivious tourists, and a bizarre reenactment of the Spanish conquistadors wiping out the Aztecs played out with lizards and frogs in full costume.

The Thief comes upon a tall tower where a large hook has been lowered with gold and he rides the hook up to the opening high in the tower's façade. There he meets the Alchemist (this time dressed in white) who performs another ritual cleansing and turns the Thief's excrement into gold, representing the inanity of his pursuits to this point. He becomes the Alchemist's first disciple on a quest to climb the Holy Mountain, where there resides nine immortals. The Alchemist claims to know their secrets and that they can be replaced, with the new disciples becoming immortal and godlike. He introduces the Thief to the other disciples explaining "They are thieves like you, but on another level." Each of the disciples display one or more aspects of the Seven Deadly Sins, creating products or rendering services on their respective planets that drive materialism, greed, hedonism, and war.

As they begin this transcendental quest for immortality, the Alchemist explains that they must stop being individuals if they hope to attain what it is they want. He tells them "burn your money", and they do it. He also has them burn the wax effigies of themselves as a symbol of the destruction of their former selves. They proceed on their journey and it is rife with more rituals, tests, and temptations but they do eventually reach their destination. The end is a brilliant and beautifully done "gotcha" and the film really couldn't have ended any other way.

Jodorowsky peppers *The Holy Mountain* with occult and religious imagery and stresses the Roman Catholic Church's role, in particular, in spreading the ills of modern society because it was the religion of his childhood, though he does not mock Christian beliefs. In one scene, the Thief, in his obvious Christ-like incarnation, finds the Pope in bed with a statue of the crucified Jesus representing the Church's hierarchy embracing the cult of death and profiting off of it. He also chases a man dressed as a nun and his cohorts, dressed as Roman soldiers, out of their "temple" after seeing that they created a plaster cast of him while passed out drunk and turned out hundreds of likenesses of the Thief in order to make money. There is one shot reinforcing the Thief as Christ that mimics the famous Pieta, the statue of Mary holding her dead son Jesus. Another scene has a prostitute who comes upon the Thief and cleans the statue he is carrying as well as the Thief's feet, calling to mind the Biblical Mary Magdalene.

One of my favorite scenes, though I do find it quite grotesque, is a recreation of the Spanish conquistadors decimation of the Aztecs performed by lizards and frogs while a German sailing song plays in the background. It is probably meant to represent the many conquests and subjugations of one race of people over another throughout history, usually in the name of progress. At one interesting point at the end of this elaborate recreation the Thief hops around the carnage grunting like an animal. To me, this speaks to man's primal urges, including the urge to make war. Another powerful image in *The Holy Mountain* is the juxtaposition of a fascist military gunning down unarmed civilians in the street with gaudily-dressed tourists looking on and taking photos, oblivious to the senseless slaughter around them. It shows a lack of empathy on the part of the wealthy and well-off to the struggle of those less-fortunate and oppressed by an authority seeking nothing less than power. Jodorowsky uses iconography to stress that all religions and occult practices can give people the spiritual guidance they may need, even though the hierarchy may be corrupt.

The entire film is satire and black comedy, using repeated rituals, metaphor, and a bit of the burlesque to get its point across. The cinematography of Rafael Corkidi and direction of Jodorowsky combine to produce what amounts to a lucid, dream-like state for those watching. Jodorowsky himself has stated that he and the crew were taking LSD during the filming, and I don't doubt it. The movie is loaded with weird and colorful imagery. At the time, the director was studying with a Zen master and a disciple of George Ivanovitch Gurdijeff. Gurdijeff's philosophy stated that due to what he considered the abnormal conditions of life, people no longer functioned in a harmonious way. He stressed working on ourselves using writing, music, and other mediums to bring out the latent possibilities in our beings and how we can live our lives in a more meaningful way. Jodorowsky's film is about the journey of living a good life, not about the destination, and he uses his own experiences and spiritual journey as inspiration. He doesn't rule out religion. On the contrary, he states we should look inside ourselves for God, not without. It explains that people should look within themselves for inspiration and live as well as possible without being encumbered by materialism, consumerism, and judgment of others. Life can be beautiful when lived fully for ourselves and those we love.

The Other One

By Mary A. Turzillo

When Gino and I were a tiny thingumabob of limbs and heads, my mother kissed us each in turn as she lugged our body to our crib. She loved us equally, and I should love Gino, my brother, in the same spirit. Each day of my life, I have orchestrated my movements to coordinate with his. His ear presses against mine as we pay our bills; we have married two women and used the same penis to impregnate them.

They call us the man with two heads, which makes me wince. He always just laughs.

You might wonder how we managed to stand, walk, run, even play tennis (though those days are over). But it's the old sack race trick: as long as I can remember, we have moved together like dancers, like figure skaters careening across tricky physical and social spaces.

I once heard from my aunt that our mother was given a choice when we were born (cut from her body like troglodytes trapped in a collapsed cave, more like). A tricky operation could sever him from me. I was the leftmost twin, and since my head always seems to stick out at an odd angle more than his, I think I was the one to be sacrificed.

The surgeon was sure Gino's brain would take over the governing of the left side of our body. They did MRIs and angiograms to prove it. One twin would be saved, the other sacrificed. Sacrifice Tony that Gino may live a normal life.

She said no. She did not fear the risk, it wasn't that. But she loved both of us, normal except for our conjoined bodies. Two arms, two legs, count the little fingers, count the tiny toes, all normal, except—two heads.

And we grew, uneventfully, our health mostly good.

We became adults. A lot of speed-bumps. Two driver's licenses; that took a lawyer to accomplish.

We have chosen different careers; a hardship since how can we go to different buildings to work? But he worked (before the present troubles) in the evening, a bookkeeper for a small tobacco shop, though the smoke from the other employees' obligatory fume-breathing bothers my eyes. I work in the daytime as a hairstylist. And I wonder, though he never did, whether my customers came mainly for the thrill of being shorn by a freak. He helped with the right hand so I could cut without stabbing my customers in the ear with the scissors. He resents this. Says my work is boring, though he can watch TV while I earn half our living.

I wore contacts for a while, until he rebelled against putting them in. All that hand-washing, he said, made our hands chap in the winter. And the left hand washes the right, you got that right, Shakespeare, or whoever said it. So no more contacts, though I think I look better without glasses.

My grown son says Gino's mistreated me and condescended to me our whole lives. My son says as the older, I should insist on more deferential treatment. My wife agrees, though she's more amiable. Gino hates my wife's perfume, Poison. So she even stopped wearing it so it wouldn't stink up his nostrils.

And now my twin is slipping. Yes, the words that come out of his mouth—he can't remember the names of simple objects. Yesterday he wanted the bath towel and called it, "that thing you, you know, get the water off with." He can't balance his checkbook and asks me to do it. He no longer plays bridge, which is a mercy because I found the whole process boring. He forgot his wife's birthday, his own two children's birthdays, and asked plaintively what day it was, Easter or Christmas, when he found the table set for a feast for our two families.

I ask him not to drive. Did I mention I can doze a bit while he tends to his affairs? He drives (or used to) with his right hand (the gear shift is handier for him than me;

I must seek his help), and uses his right foot on both pedals. Only twice in our whole lives have we erred by my applying the brake while he tried to accelerate to avoid a collision. A narrow miss. Our wives wept and begged us both to stop driving then, but that was years ago, and we have a perfect record since, not even any speeding tickets. Until this year.

His driving has gotten worse. I have to stay wide awake now, because he gets lost, asks me what street signs mean, can't find the right freeway exit. The last time I nodded off he got lost three miles from our house (we share a house; the wives like each other and it's been great for the kids).

He's taken to asking me if I love him. If I love him! He goes into rages about losing things (the keys to his car, the keys to mine, his glasses, his blood pressure pills, the TV remote). He took my computer apart last week, trying to "fix" it because he'd crashed it—don't ask me how—and wanted to retrieve his e-mail. E-mail from our dead mother, who never used a computer in her blessed days.

And then, rage over, he tries to bend his neck to kiss

my cheek. He should know after fifty-seven years that his neck is conjoined to mine and that his lips will never touch my face. He loves me. He loves his wife, his son and daughter. He loves my wife. All this, all day, except when he's half-comatose in front of a television drama he fails to understand. "I love you. I love you." As we were renewing his Aricept prescription last week, he told the pharmacist that he loved her.

Our mother died young of stroke. Her blood pressure, her cholesterol readings, passed on to us. The doctor says it's a miracle we've lived so long. His minister speaks of God's blessing, never mind my forbearance and cleverness at letting him have his way so often.

This morning the results came from the tests I insisted upon. MRIs at the beginning of our life, and at the end. He has had a stroke, maybe several strokes. Multi-infarcts, said the doctor. Perhaps he will recover some use of his mind. Perhaps he will dodder along, making less and less sense, relapsing finally into confused silence, unable to control his arm or leg. We will know then which of us controls the bladder, a topic we have debated for fifty years.

The doctor insists modern medicine can arrest the process. The infarcts are the result of years of rich living, coupled with heredity. I cruise the internet, going to a site called Medline, while he dozes, sometimes interrupting me with fractious questions about how I'm wasting our time, or what video game is this that has so many gray words floating on the white screen.

The doctor is so young, so full of hope. He reminds me of the doctor who predicted a long and happy life for my mother if only she'd follow the special diet and exercise, and quit smoking. It was too late for her. I told this young doctor that, and he said we have time. My brother might even improve some, he said.

So lucky he is, says this doctor, that he has a wife, a sister-in-law, children, nephew, to care for him. He even has a devoted brother who not only can, but must insist that he takes his medications, not wander the street in his bathrobe, eat whole grains and carotene-rich vegetables. Fact is, I can eat these for him, but I can't stop him from stuffing potato chips and donuts in his mouth.

And can I wait? Must I be tied to this dying animal, searching for signs of disgust in my wife's eyes as I slip into her bed on Sunday morning? When I sleep, he awakes and drags us into the kitchen, searching for sweets and knives, leaving the refrigerator door ajar, trying with his strong hand to turn on the gas flames.

My mother chose to let me live. The law did not protect my life; a head is not a baby. But I have grown into more than a head sprouting like a riotous stump from my twin's thick neck. I am a man. I have survived and tolerated this half-life for over fifty years, since I first realized that not all little boys must waltz through life attached to another grudging, riotous boy who grabs with his right hand the fragile toy in my left.

I wish I could go back and warn her. Not that I wished to die. I am grateful even for this demi-life I've endured. Take him, I would say. Take the ungrateful one who intrudes and usurps, because he is destined someday to become less than a man, less than a human being.

I have purchased surgical books from internet sites. I have set up mirrors and an operating arena in our basement. I will not need the help of his right hand. I will trick him into letting me inject him with Novocain. I will do it when our wives are at church, when my son is with his new in-laws. I will send his children on a trip to Niagara.

If I live, I will be whole for the first time. It will be a new birth.

BIZARRO WORLD GOT ME DIRTY AND WET

BY L. ANDREW COOPER

Upon first entry into Bizarro World, I greeted supremacy of men, not in comics form, but as THE SORROW KING, who held before him SISYPHUS, doomed to Rolling Rock forever. ALBERT CAMUS met SIS-FUSS when *almost* feeling his flattest, which he felt later when he got smeared beneath an ever-rolling boulder (Camus rolled to vehicular death in 1960—too soon?). Yet while this tale of youth and questionable self-slaughter holds up the Ka-moos and Cough-Kas, not to mention the RAGE of another KING, and it seems to stand in front of THE CURE, like the LOST SOUL of NOTHING in POPPY Z. BRITE, who may have once *stood on a beach* with Ka-moo and sucked on a BANANAFISH (bone… like a suck on a gun) made Goth-horror after J.D. SALINGER quit the rye. It got too crowded so I turned my heels around in the sand, stepped forward.

And ran into a WALL OF KISS.

Since I was naked and pressed against the wall my nipples got hard immediately. The wall, rough like sandpaper, spotted with filth at the level of my crotch, beckoned, and my tongue slid along it, lips puckering in circles. He was everything a woman might need, I realized, self-consciously, thinking I should step away, knowing **cock is irrelevant**. Overcoming my POLANSKI-danski REPULSION at the thought of being hurt again, I gave into my DJUNA BARNES and Fucked the WALL, sliding against it until I felt an ecstasy unlike anything ever before. The wall glared back at me, Stoic. I grimaced, reached for a hammer that I noticed beside me—

And the hook of a giant wire clothes-hanger appeared and yanked me downward, through a trap door, down a canal into the ABORTION ARCADE, where I realized (I realeyes 3-d) I want 2-d (I 1-ah) *play*! As the voice of MORRISSEY echoed, I recalled the case of PLANTS v. ZOMBIES and thought seriously about fucking my mother right there in the soil. Trouble is I wanted No Children [Novella One], and a *queer* feeling came all over me as I saw brains turn into trees.

The hall was again HIGH SCHOOL [Novella 2, The Roadkill Quarterback of Heavy Metal High], where the TEEN WOLVES roam. One drove over the grassy hallway at me with a TALKING CHAIN SAW, so I dove beyond a musical hell, into a Destroyed Room [Novella 3].

Whence I fled the ARCADE, and fell into the hands of the WARRIOR WOLF WOMEN OF THE WASTELAND. They did things to me, these McDONALDLANDIAN BITCHES.

Carrying me before a crowd of their own parasite-infested kind, they stripped me. Sex, sex, and sex: each fuck, even rape (her fault), brought each BEAST BITCH closer to low class fangs and whiskers. Beyond the WALLS, they could be free to deep-throat my EXTRA LIMBS. One did. My eyes fixed on the bare breasts and belly that stood out from her otherwise DIANE ARBUS beauty, and she guided my penis into her hungry vagina. Let us not speak of THE HAUNTED VAGINA [different book] sprung from the same source [author] as these WARRIORS.

In order to take revenge after my experience with the WOLF WOMEN, I learned HOW TO EAT FRIED FURRIES.

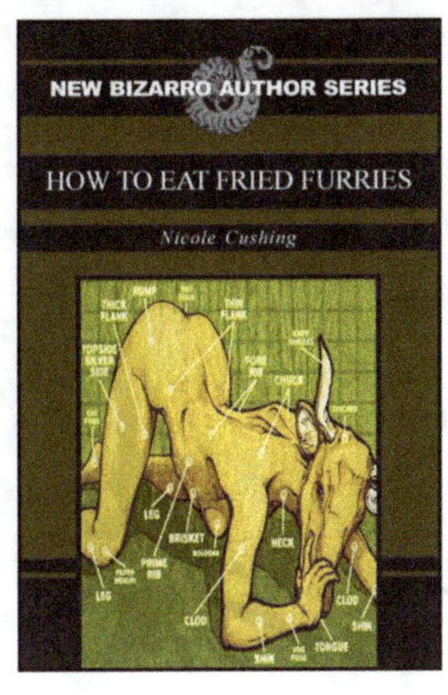

Not wolfing but squirreling and ferreting for food, I heard sweet poetry from a FLYING CIRCUS as a bung hole in space showered me with shit: "Let me skull-fuck you. / It won't be that bad, honest. / I'll pay you in blow!" Though tempted, I would have driven away in the Humvee of Blessed Destruction, but Squirrel Jesus prevented passage, so I settled in for a game of BlackLung the Coal Mining Clown.

A SHATNERQUAKE interrupted my game after a FICTION BOMB dusted the ground with Trekkers and other UNCONVENTIONAL CONVENTIONISTS. Their panic fervor left no time for settling, as behind them—lo!—came TJ HOOKER and, deranged, CAPTAIN KIRK and, ascendant, DENNY CRANE: the CRANE drove an ambulance, backward; the KIRK, lithe, rode the ambulance's roof, wielding a light saber and beaming devourer eyes at me; the HOOKER gripped the ambulance's hood, clinging with fury. Although I couldn't see him, I knew BRUCE CAMPBELL hid in the ambulance's back. I would have died had *THE* SHATNER not arrived and, not suing me, acted, and as "blood and limbs flew about the room"—

(*I died*)

At my Funeral [story = The Funeral], which lasted SEVEN DAYS, I at last zipped my way out of the body bag but found the occasion terribly dull. I exited the HOME, searched for freedom amidst nothingness, and among The Porcupine Moshers of the Apocalypse [= novella], in a place reminiscent, oddly enough, of a LAND OF CONFUSION, I found a REAGAN puppet of violence and horror desiccating the irradiated earth. *Sans* hesitation, my blades erected from my spine and other skeletal selections, marking me, and neocon BRAIN MATTER SCATTERED among splatterpunks. I then jumped head-first into waters where waited the Zombie Sharks with Metal Teeth [= story], spawned by mousy, dolphin-like curiosity raised to the power of FORTY-TWO. At last, I decided to find my way off this Crazy Shitting Planet [= novella] by sailing a BROBDINGNAGIAN fat HILTON-TRUMP on the shit-black sea to the end of a metaphor for THE CULTURAL LOGIC OF LATE CAPITALISM [= academic reference], which I never found, but I did find a neat WHALE, fat but in a good way, so it all worked out.

***

Bizarro fiction rolls together genre tropes and media references and usually externalizes the formal mix through images of human parts and taboos blended, torn, pierced, cooked, and otherwise violated in absurd or at least convention-defying ways. Horror and dark speculative fiction more generally provide slick, quick shock surfaces that you can skip along, like jolting from wave to wave on a jet ski as you read. Intellectual, philosophical references and content often appear outright, jumping up out of the water, and almost always lurk somewhere in the waves. In "postmodern" fashion, this literary stuff might merely belong to the surface as well. Likewise, the influence of superhero comics, B-movies, heavy metal, punk, Goth-rock, post-apocalyptic fantasy, fandom, furries, and other fringe/cult cultures may or may not be more important than existentialist and surrealist "classics" such as Franz Kafka and Albert Camus in letters, Salvador Dali and Luis Bunuel in film. All of the above move along bizarro waters.

If bizarro is so many things, is it really anything at all? Tough question. Wordplay, toilet humor, extreme violence, cannibalism, absurdity, and irrationality are common to bizarro, *South Park*, and Shakespeare. Subgenres, perhaps in horror particularly, form like eddies in the ocean, only to become indistinguishable from larger bodies as history piles up. As I've said and written more than a few times, especially if you know the Marquis de Sade (of whom a meta-fictional character in *Abortion Arcade* says, "'The Marquis can bite it'"), you can't really come up with entirely new ways to violate people or taboos. All you can do is recombine elements with new *whos*, the authors and audiences, and new *whens*, technologies and other details distinct to a historical moment, real or imagined. Perhaps the reabsorption of the bizarro eddy has already begun.

Looking through the table of contents of the 2012 collection *The Best Bizarro Fiction of the Decade*, I see many more mainstream names associated with the term than I remember seeing when I first heard it, names that were mainstream *before* "bizarro" emerged.

I don't mention works by most of these names in my paragraph about this book, the last paragraph of the first section. Such names include, for example, Joe R. Lansdale and Bentley Little, authors I've admired for years without ever thinking of associating them with "bizarro" (although connections are clear to me now). I do mention Stephen Graham Jones's "Zombie Sharks with Metal Teeth," which is a great story, but after its bizarro title, its style moves in more traditional sci-fi/horror fashion, with relative minimalism in common with most bizarro (but also with Ernest Hemingway). The collection, however, is edited by Cameron Pierce, a pioneer of the (self-acknowledged) bizarro phenomenon, and published by Eraserhead Press, a major, perhaps *the* major, trailblazing publisher in the area, so bizarro's more distinct names are merging in this *Best of* book with broader phenomena less easily identified with the subgenre.

Pierce's introduction to the book pushes the broadening along, defining bizarro not just as taking cues from Kafka and others but actually *including* Kafka, H. P. Lovecraft, and even much earlier figures such as Charles Baudelaire, who, bizarrely, was said to have walked a lobster on a leash. Baudelaire, like Albert Camus ("Killing an Arab," from the album *Three Imaginary Boys*) and J.D. Salinger ("Bananfishbones," from the album *The Top*), provided song fodder for legendary Goth band The Cure ("How Beautiful You Are," from the album *Kiss Me, Kiss Me, Kiss Me*). However, the giddy, hallucinatory oscillation between mad laughter and rage that characterizes these exchanges between "classic" literature and The Cure's Gothic glory days are things of the past. Likewise, bizarro-associated authors such as Nicole Cushing (of *Fried Furries*) have left bizarro (at least for now) and adopted narrative styles that rely less on rapidly transgressive surfaces while still traumatizing readers with extremes.

Bizarro may end up looking more like a party in a tide-pool than in a sea bound for lasting distinction on horror textbook maps, but that pool has sharks at one end and Rock Lobsters at the other. Like Bizarro World itself, which in the *Superman* comics is a kind of inverted, cubical Earth, it is both elemental in its diverse capacity and fundamentally antipodal, or defined by opposition. It sends a derisive wake-up call to mainstream horror, indicting it for being too soft, too careful, and too correct. It also isn't afraid to be smart and focus on smart characters, moving fast, explaining little, and never apologizing if it hurts your feelings. It opposes contemporary "literary" fiction, to which I feel all bizarro works I've encountered—if not all bizarro authors—would raise a middle finger. Why?

Because the literary fuckers may be edumacated but arent as smart as they are. Sure, some of what Ive read at least looks like it needs another edit compared to the "literary" stuff but who gives a shit? And SHATNERQUAKE may be funny action with dashes of splatter while SORROW KING is creepy and twisted and WARRIOR WOLF WOMEN walks lines between sexism and its critique and FRIED FURRIES uses extreme gross-out humor—wanna see my chewed up food, that other KING said, SWIFTly—and so on—so the surfaces may not be coherent in the way subgenre surfaces usually are—but if BIZARRO does have DEPTH it may be just that—smarts—it got SMARTS—and goddammit if smarts aint enough for an eddy or tidepool or fucking septic tank to be worth swimming in I dont know what is I mean give me a FUCKING break I QUIT.

Dr. L. Andrew Cooper went to Harvard and Princeton and cares a little fucking less each goddamned day. His book of short stories LEAPING AT THORNS might be bizarro. He hadn't thought of it before.

Bibliophilography

(Limited—Look This Shit Up To Find More Weird Shit)

Agranoff, David. "Punkupine Moshers of the Apocalypse." *The Best Bizarro Fiction of the Decade.* Cameron Pierce, ed.

Bizarro Central: The Cult Section of the Literary World. Web. 14. Sept. 2015.

Bizarro Starter Kit(s) (Orange, Blue, Purple, Red), The. Portland, OR: Eraserhead Press, 2006, 2007, 2010, 2015. Print.

Burk, Jeff. *Shatnerquake*. Portland, OR: Eraserhead Press, 2009. Print.

Cushing, Nicole. *How to Eat Fried Furries*. Portland, OR: Eraserhead Press, 2010. Print.

Hansen, Mykle. "Crazy Shitting Planet." *The Best Bizarro Fiction of the Decade*. Cameron Pierce, ed.

Jameson Fredric. *Postmodernism, or, The Cultural Logic of Late Capitalism*. Durham, NC: Duke University Press, 1991. Print.

Jones, Stephen Graham. "Zombie Sharks with Metal Teeth." *The Best Bizarro Fiction of the Decade.* Cameron Pierce, ed.

Klein, Mike. "A Beginner's Guide to Bizarro Fiction." *Flavorwire.com* 24. Aug. 2012. Web. 14 Sept. 2015

Mellick, Carlton, III. *Warrior Wolf Women of the Wasteland*. Portland, OR: Avant Punk (An Imprint of Eraserhead), 2009. E-book.

Pierce, Cameron. *Abortion Arcade: Three Novellas*. Portland, OR: Eraserhead Press, 2011. E-book.

---, ed. *The Best Bizarro Fiction of the Decade*. Portland, OR: Eraserhead Press, 2012. E-book.

Prunty, Anderson. *The Sorrow King*. Dayton, OH: Grindhouse Press, 2011. E-book.

Ranalli, Gina. *Wall of Kiss*. Lynnwood, WA: Afterbirth Books, 2007. E-book.

Walter, Damien G. "Bizarro fiction: it's terribly good." *The Guardian.com.* 16 July 2010. Web. 14 Sept. 2015.

Wilson, D. Harlan. "At the Funeral." *The Best Bizarro Fiction of the Decade*. Cameron Pierce, ed.

Love Skull

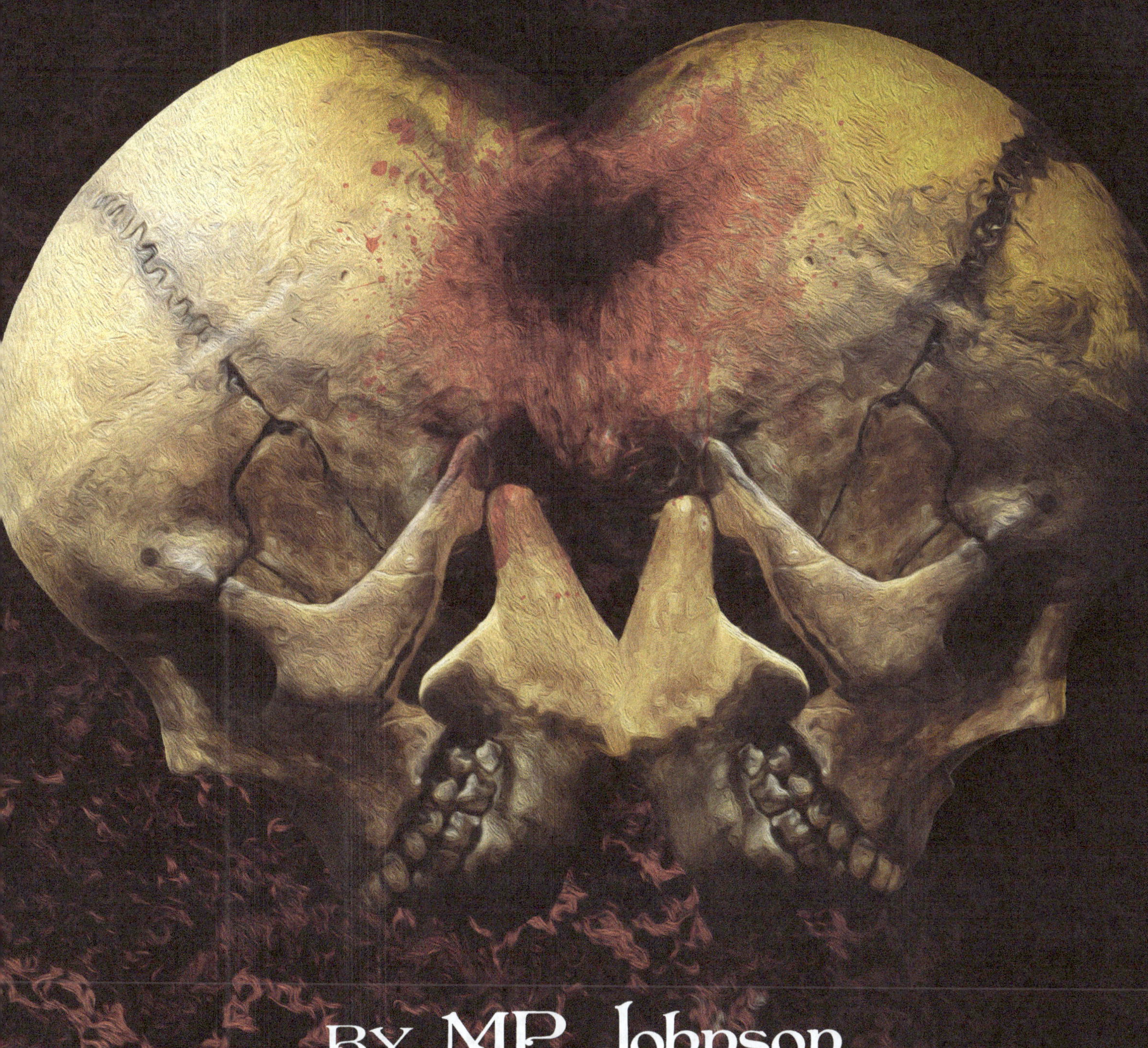

BY MP Johnson

In that catacomb, one skull stood out from thousands. While the others had let time and rot strip them of their humanity, becoming nothing more than putrescent decorations on the sepulchral walls, this one still expressed life. It was just as fleshless, just as yellowed as the rest. Its eye sockets were no less hollow, but somewhere in those ocular shadows danced the faintest hint of longing. Perhaps this one had died staring into the eyes of its true love. No, for that would have been a gentle death, and this one had not died gently. Scars and fissures crisscrossed its forehead. Its left cheekbone had been destroyed, so the shadows from that eye socket dripped down like dark tears.

Deon read this passage in Corby Benton's eighties horror hit *Night Skulls* and stopped. He reread it. Gorgeous. He loved the paragraph and he loved that skull. He could picture it perfectly in his mind. He closed the book for a moment and gazed around the bathroom stall, but the image of the skull remained locked in his brain.

He flipped to the passage and read it again, spending time with every word, every detail. When he reached the end of the paragraph, he couldn't move on. He had to go back and read it again, as if doing so would allow him to unlock new sentences, new information about that skull.

He had never been a Benton fan, but he found the man's books easy, mindless reading to fill the long gaps between calls at the call center where he worked third shift. And on bathroom breaks. Usually, he could pick them up and put them down, but this passage wasn't the usual Benton hackery. This passage required Deon's undivided attention.

Giggling, he ripped the page out of the book. Page five hundred and seventy-nine. Everything that had come before that paragraph had been trash. Everything after it would likely be too. He threw the rest of the mass-market paperback into the puddle behind the toilet. Then he read the paragraph again.

And again.

And again.

Until his legs grew numb and he knew his coworkers would be wondering what was taking him so long. He folded the page, stashed it in his back pocket and reached for the toilet paper. The skull was there, floating in front of him.

He recoiled. In his panic, he almost screamed.

Regaining control, he told himself that the skull was merely in his mind, vivid from so many readings. But he couldn't blink the skull away. It stared at him, beautiful and battered, its sockets filled with shadows and longing. Without thinking, he reached out slowly with his pointer finger and gently touched the tip of the skull's nasal bone. Solid. Bone solid.

"Hello?" Deon said.

"Hello, my love," the skull replied in a sweet, androgynous voice that whistled ever so slightly as it swept through a mouth of missing teeth.

Suddenly self-conscious, Deon reached under the skull and grabbed a wad of toilet paper, quickly wiping himself. When he stood and pulled up his pants, the skull floated up with him, remaining at eye level. It circled Deon's head once before returning to stare into his eyes. Deon wondered if the bathroom had recently been cleaned, if he had maybe accidentally huffed some toxic fumes.

"You're the skull from the book?" he asked.

"I've been read so many times, but it never felt like this before. I could feel the love pouring out of your eyes and into the page, into the words, into me."

"I should get back to work now," he said, confident he was hallucinating.

"Okay, my love."

Instead of running straight out of the bathroom, he acted rationally. He washed up and looked in the mirror, running his hands over his blonde buzz cut and adjusting the collar of his work-supplied orange polo shirt. He looked fine. He looked perfectly normal. Except for the skull floating over his left shoulder like a second head. But it wasn't there. It couldn't possibly be.

He stepped out of the bathroom and was greeted with a scream. Gary, the third shift supervisor, was looking straight at him. The old man had his hands on the sides of his face and was giving the most ridiculous, wide-eyed, high-pitched scream Deon had ever heard. Deon almost laughed, thinking this was part of the hallucination, but then other coworkers appeared, drawn to the ruckus, and they too screamed. They stood around him. A chorus of screamers.

The skull floated behind Deon's head, attempting to hide.

Not knowing what else to do, Deon feigned checking his fly and asked dumbly, "What's wrong? What's going on?"

Joe Beth, Deon's cube mate and sometimes late-night hand-job provider, attempted to grab the skull. As the skull flitted out of her reach, keeping Deon's head between it and her tender, grabbing fingers, she said, "There's a damn skull floating around your head, Dee. What the fuck!"

So he was not hallucinating.

"It's no big deal." He shrugged.

Joe Beth continued her attempt to snatch the skull from its orbit. "Oh, okay. I guess it's one of those no-big-deal floating skulls, huh?"

"Basically."

As the screams died out, Gary, with a raspy voice, ordered everyone back to their cubicles to take phone calls. Joe Beth seemed reluctant to give up without having caught her prey, but finally sighed, slapped Deon on the ass and swaggered back to their shared cube.

Deon started to follow, but Gary called him back.

"Uh, are you feeling sick?" Gary asked.

"No."

Gary looked at the ground. "Would you like to go home?"

"I've only been here three hours."

"Don't you want to go home and…" he pointed at the skull, "…figure that out?"

"I need the hours."

"Deon, you're fired!" Gary shouted. As he walked away, he mumbled, "And if HR wants to get on my case about skull discrimination, they can kiss my ass."

Deon figured it wasn't worth arguing about. He cleaned out his cubicle, with Joe Beth giving him the pouty lip routine, as if he had done this just to evade her handjobs. Truth be told, he wasn't going to miss those handjobs. They were the least sexy sex acts he had ever engaged in. She had even said once, "It's more like steering a car than having sex, which is why I don't think I'm cheating on my boyfriend." He used that same logic to convince himself he wasn't cheating on his girlfriend. He was just getting his steering wheel steered.

Outside, the fall air felt nice, not too cool yet. Sweatshirt weather. He didn't mind walking home. It was only a couple miles. Usually, he took the bus, but usually he got done with work at six in the morning, not three. It was probably best in this situation anyway, all things considered.

As he walked through quiet, moonlit neighborhoods, the skull circled his head.

"Skull?" he asked.

"Yes, my love?" the skull replied.

"Could you stop that? You're making me dizzy."

The skull paused and hovered directly in front of him, staring back at him as he walked. This slowed him down at first, because he flinched with every step, fearing that his head would collide with the skull if he moved too quickly. However, the skull effortlessly kept a foot of space between them. This was actually more awkward than the circling, but Deon didn't bother to ask the skull to move. He had a more pressing question.

"Why do you call me, 'my love?'"

The skull inched closer and locked onto him with its shadowy sockets, more vision in their emptiness somehow than in most eyes Deon had stared into. He stopped walking, worried that one more step would send him falling into those dark, cavernous holes. He would drown in their longing.

Except the longing was gone now. It had been replaced by something else, something that made him much more uncomfortable.

The skull replied to Deon's question. "You have to ask?"

He nodded, not because he truly needed to ask, but because he needed the answer verbalized. He needed it in a more tangible form, and if that made it clunky, if that made it less romantic, then so be it.

"I felt your eyes. They looked me up and down, reading me from every angle, trying to discover more about me, about my history, a violent history that the author implied, but never bothered to write, so you will never know, I will never know. But that doesn't matter, because you read what was there, so lovingly, and now I am here, and I have a future. We have a future. Together."

Well, that certainly didn't make it any less romantic.

Deon considered arguing with the skull. He considered denying his love for the skull. He considered the old get-rid-of-the-clingy-puppy-for-its-own-good-by-telling-it-you-hate-it routine. None of that felt right though. The fucked up thing was that this skull hovering in front of his face, it felt right. So right.

Deon was not okay with how right it felt.

And neither was Tanya, his girlfriend. As soon as he stepped into the apartment they shared, she freaked out. She was sitting on the couch, smoking weed and eating whipped cream and watching sitcoms from the seventies, placid as hell, and then she turned and saw Deon and the skull and she seemed to instantly get unstoned. She hurled the little tub of whipped cream straight at Deon's face.

Valiantly, the skull swished in front of him, taking the hit. Whipped cream splattered into its eye sockets, up its nasal cavity. The tub slid to the ground where it landed with a plop. Deon accidentally stepped in it as he moved toward Tanya to try to calm her down.

"Chill out, Tee," he said, calling her by her pet name, which he had given her mainly because it rhymed with his nickname. Tee and Dee. It sounded sweet.

Tanya attempted to flee by climbing onto the couch. "Don't tell me to chill out when there's a big fucking skull hovering around your head!"

"Big?" the skull asked.

"Like the fattest skull I have ever seen," Tanya clarified.

The skull heated up, boiling the whipped cream. The dessert topping, which looked unnaturally white against the skull's yellowing bones, bubbled and crackled. It puddled on the floor beneath the skull like a hot, white shadow.

"Fatty, fatty skull bones, ruler of the gross zone!" Tanya taunted.

The skull opened its mouth wide, viciously baring its few remaining teeth.

Tanya screeched, "Keep it away from me!"

Ideally, Deon would have liked to let the two work out their differences themselves. He just wasn't into conflict. He didn't know what to do with it. Asking him to partake in or resolve any sort of argument was akin to asking him to do trigonometry or build a space engine or have an extended conversation with his grandma about her personal hygiene. But in this situation, like so many calls with Grams, he didn't see a way around it, so he pulled out his best argument stopper.

"Hey, let's all sit down and smoke a bowl, okay?"

The sound of sizzling whipped cream faded and he felt the skull cool. Tanya sat on the far side of the couch, crossing her arms awkwardly over her boobs. The girl was all boobs. Everything she ate went into her boobs, and then slowly strengthened the rest of her body for the sole purpose of supporting her boobs. Deon got kind of revved up when she crossed her arms over them, squishing them together, but at the moment he needed to focus on getting everyone settled down.

He sat next to Tanya. The skull floated to the opposite side of the couch. Seated between the woman he loved and the skull he loved, Deon started working with the pot on the coffee table, loading up the pipe.

Without thinking about it, he took the first hit. To be fair, he needed it the most. It had been a rough day. He lost his job. Maybe he should mention that to Tanya, to get some sympathy out of her before getting fully into the skull thing. That was a gamble though, because she might get mad. They weren't exactly swimming in bank, and she had a bad habit of worrying about paying rent and shit.

He handed the pipe to Tanya and grabbed a book off the stack of grubby mass-market horror paperbacks next to the couch. He was going to use it as a prop to explain what had happened, but he inadvertently flipped it open and started reading a paragraph about a slimy swamp monster and then, seemingly of their own accord, his hands smashed the book shut and flung it across the room. The last thing he needed was a swamp monster lurking behind him 24/7.

"What the fuuuuuck?" Tanya asked, handing the pipe back to Deon.

He took another hit and shrugged. Then he held the pipe up to the skull's mouth. The skull inhaled, but all the smoke came out through its ear cracks, which Deon thought was hilarious. Tanya did too. They both cracked up and leaned into each other. The pot was good. They finished it off and fell asleep on the couch and didn't get around to the skull discussion.

At four in the afternoon, Deon woke alone on the couch. Well, not alone, because the skull was still there. Tanya was gone though. She had left a note on the coffee table. It said, "Off to work. Please get rid of skull."

Deon sighed, pried himself off the couch and poured a bowl of sugary cereal. He tended to do what Tanya wanted. It just made life easier. He got to come home and smoke pot and snuggle with her all night without conflict, and sure, sometimes that meant he had to do the dishes or run some stupid errand or skip a hangout night with his dude buds because she was feeling needy, but that rarely felt like a big sacrifice. This was different though. He kind of felt attached to this skull. Fully attached.

"Skull, what am I gonna do with you?"

"Love me."

He took a couple bites of cereal. "I do, but I love Tanya too."

The skull orbited his head as he finished his breakfast. He thought about taking a shower, but he was concerned about taking his shirt off without upsetting the skull. Sniffing his armpits, he decided there really was no need to change, since he had showered yesterday and he hadn't built up any stink he could detect over the lingering weed fumes. He ran his hands over his buzz cut and poked the sleep crud out of his eye crotches with his pinkies. Good to go.

"Hey skull, how come nobody else ever noticed you like I did?"

"I was buried in those catacombs. I was buried in a book that was nine hundred and eighty-nine pages long. I guess everybody scanned over me, one little detail amidst so much extraneous material."

"The whole book should have been about you."

"For you it was, and that's all that matters."

Deon poured himself another bowl of cereal, not because he was hungry, but because he needed something colorful to think over. He had this idea that the bowl full of multicolored Os would help him focus.

His preferred solution would be to figure out a way to keep the skull and Tanya. He loved Tanya. She made him comfortable. He would go so far as to say he would fight someone over Tanya. Once, when they were grocery shopping, the line was really long and Tanya was waiting patiently when some grizzled old dude cut in front of her. Deon put his hand on the man's shoulder and said, "The lady was here first." He made a little fist, but kept it down by his side. The man must have felt Deon's fist clench radiate through the air because the old dude shrugged and stepped behind Tanya.

Deon didn't know if he'd do the same for the skull, but that didn't seem like what this relationship was about. It was the skull that made him feel safe. It had blocked that tub of whipped cream from hitting Deon in the face. Sure, it was just whipped cream, but if the skull hadn't blocked it, Deon definitely would have had to shower today.

Deon's phone buzzed. A text from Tanya: "Is skull gone?"

Deon texted back: "Working on it."

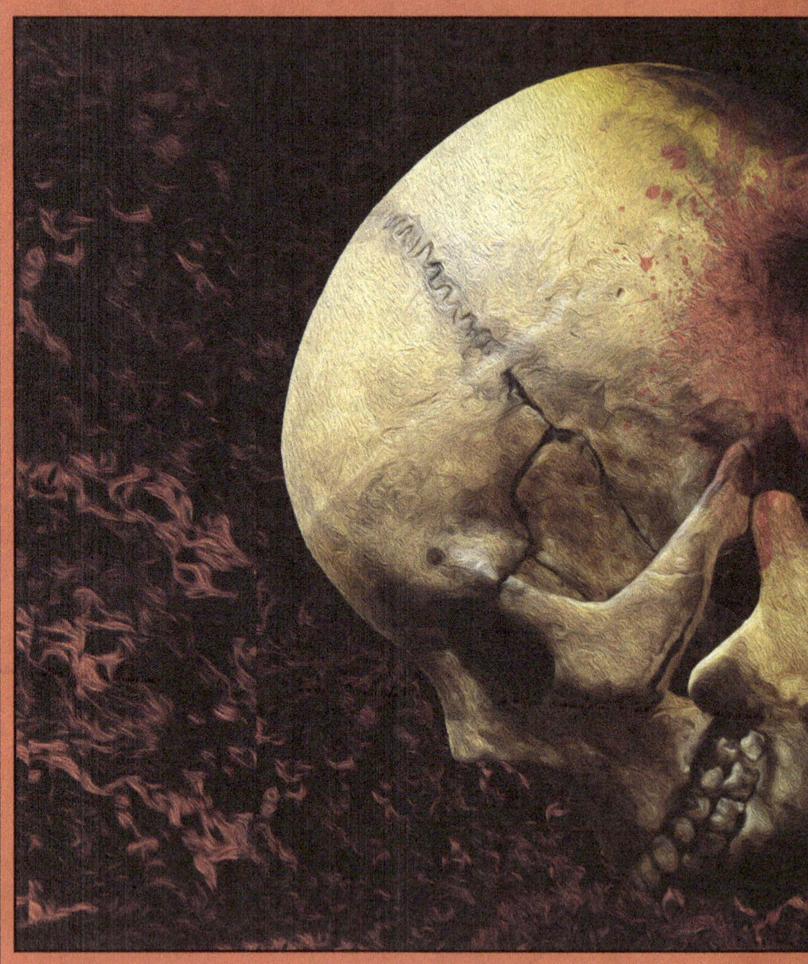

And then, as if it rode into his brain on the scent of artificial fruit flavor that wafted up from his cereal bowl, he had his solution.

"Skull, I just thought of something."

"What, my love?"

"Don't you need to get back in the book?"

"Nobody cares," the skull replied.

"Well, nobody cares like I do. But still, you really set the mood in that catacombs scene. I didn't finish the book or anything, but I'm sure it's not the same without you." He could not let this go. He needed to show the skull that it was necessary to return back home to the pages of *Night*

Skulls. He tossed the bowl of cereal in the sink and rushed for the door, the skull orbiting him as he hustled on foot to the musty used bookstore a few blocks from the apartment.

Inside, he went straight for the horror section, crossing his fingers that they would have a copy of *Night Skulls*. He had never been to a used bookstore that didn't have at least a dozen Corby Benton books for sale, and *Night Skulls* was one of the most popular, so it wasn't a long shot. Sure enough, the store had three copies, each with a perfectly busted spine and yellowing pages.

Deon flipped one open to page five hundred and seventy-nine. He couldn't believe what he saw. He refused to believe it. Throwing that copy on the ground, he grabbed the second one, looked at that and found the same thing.

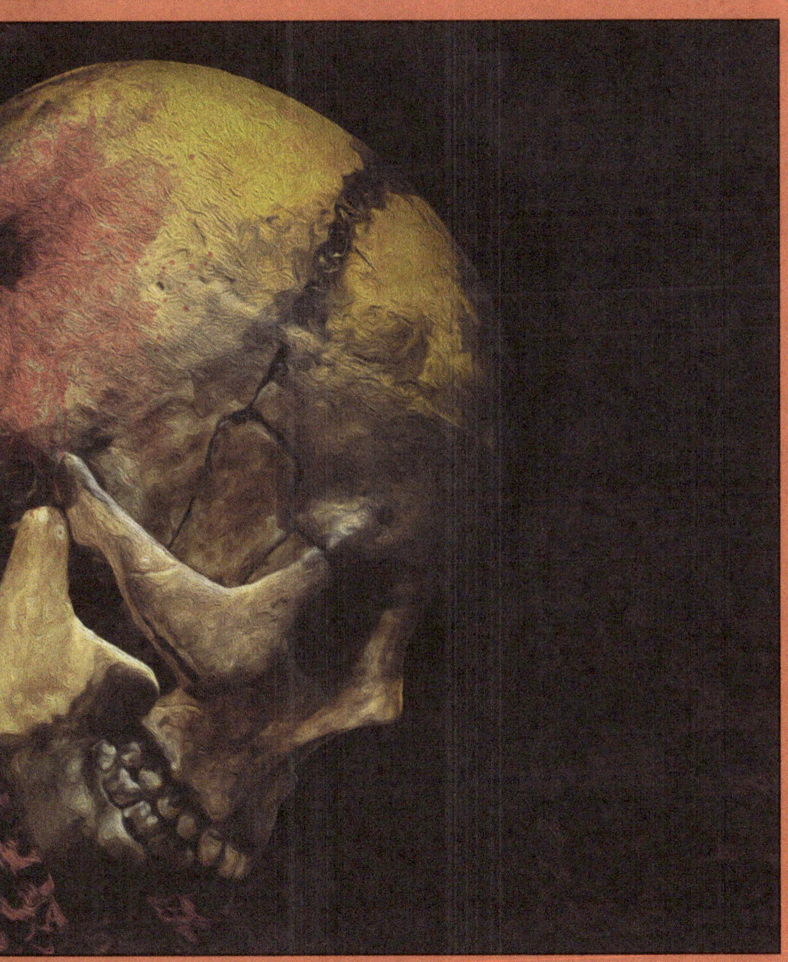

Then he threw that one on the ground too and picked up the third. Sure enough, it was there too.

He read the paragraph out loud:

In that catacomb, one beach ball stood out from thousands. While the others had let time dull their red and yellow and green stripes, this one still shined vibrantly. Despite sitting in the dust and dirt, it looked like it had only recently been used by a gaggle of beach brats. It still reeked of ocean salt.

"This is ridiculous!" Deon screamed.

He marched to the front of the store to ask the bespectacled clerk if she had ever read the book and if she remembered the skull scene, but she shrieked as soon as she saw the skull, so he ran out of the store before he could ask. She was probably more of a lit fan anyway.

Night fell and he walked around aimlessly.

He told the skull, "That book is stupid without you. It's stupider without you."

"It's not classic literature. Nobody cares if it's a beach ball or a skull."

"I care!"

"Yes, my love, and you're the only one, which is why I'm here, with the one who cares about me the most, and who I care about so much."

Deon sighed. He and the skull were definitely attached.

There was only one other logical way to shake the skull. He had to show the skull how much harm it would do him if he kept it around. Surely the skull didn't want to harm him, even if it didn't seem to care if he lost Tanya.

"Skull, I don't think I'm going to be able to get a job with you around."

"As long as we're together," the skull said.

"I can't pay rent and buy food on togetherness."

"I think you'll get a job. I believe in you, my love."

He would have to show the skull. It was getting late and his legs were tired, but surely there was someplace he could stop into and get an application, or maybe even an interview. It would have to be someplace chill. On the off chance that he actually did get the job, he didn't want it to be a grind. The call center was kind of a grind at the start and end of his shift, but in-between was mostly just hanging out and reading and getting under-the-desk handjobs.

He wanted a job where he could sit around all night, like a night security guard. Exactly like a night security guard. Did bookstores have night security guards? He fantasized about lounging in front of a wall of screens that showed video feed from each of the aisles, feet up on his desk as he burned through one scummy horror paperback after the next. All night long. And then maybe there'd be a girl who would give him handjobs.

Caught up in this fantasy, he tripped on a crack in the sidewalk and fell down.

"Are you okay?" the skull asked, voice filled with concern.

He looked at his skinned knees. Blood seeped out, soaking into the edges of his newly torn jeans. "Oh, I really liked these pants!"

Maybe he wouldn't make a great night security guard.

But he decided, fuck it, that's not the point. He noticed the scrap yard on the other side of the street. There was a help wanted sign hanging from the closed gate. He was pretty sure that meant they needed a night security guard. He had a feeling.

If he didn't get the job, it would prove to the skull that their relationship was doomed. And if he did get the job, that would be one less thing for Tanya to be mad about.

He crossed the street and tried to pull the gate open, but it was locked. After looking for a buzzer, he decided just to bang on it. No response. They definitely needed a night security guard. Maybe they had one, and he was sleeping. Deon could just scale the chain link fence and climb in. He didn't see any dogs. With a running start, he leaped onto the fence. It clanged loudly against the metal fence posts. He climbed up and jumped over, bellyflopping on the dirt inside the fence.

"This is fun, my love," the skull said.

Deon stood and looked around. In the dark, he couldn't see where the office was. All he could see was junk. Beat-up cars covered the terrain as far as the eye could see. Refrigerators. Stoves. Furnaces. Old style big screen TVs. Everything was dirty. He felt like a kid in a really big sandbox.

"Hello I'm here for a job application!" he shouted.

Noise rang out from behind a stack of cars.

Deon squinted in that direction. He walked toward the sound.

"Hello?" he asked.

He heard some mumbling, then three dudes appeared with a little red wagon full of windows and other parts. They pointed flashlights in his eyes.

"You guys are stealing stuff, aren't you?" he asked.

In lieu of an answer, one of the dudes charged him and knocked him to the ground. He closed his eyes. They surrounded him and kicked him in the ribs. It hurt pretty bad. He thought maybe he should play dead, but he didn't think they'd buy it and it was hard not to scream at least a little bit.

But then they started screaming too.

Deon opened his eyes. The skull, his beloved skull, had broken its orbit around his head. It opened its jaws wide. It opened its jaws wider than it should have. Its bones seemed to turn into rubber, allowing it to open its mouth so wide it could engulf one of the guy's heads completely. The skull bit the dude's head off like a kid who had never eaten a sucker before and didn't know that you're supposed to suck on it and instead just immediately chewed it off the stick.

The dude's body remained on its feet for a surprisingly long time. Blood spurted out of his neck in a stream so thick it looked like a new limb—a new, wet, red limb reaching into the sky to recover the head that had been stolen away.

The skull did not give the head back. It did not spit the head out. It chewed a couple times and swallowed it into whatever void hid at the back of its mouth.

Of the two remaining burglars, one ran. The other froze. The skull headbutted Mr. Stand Still so hard that the man's face flattened and his eyeballs popped out of their sockets. Still attached by ocular cords, each eyeball shot to an opposite side of the attacking skull. When they reached the ends of their tethers, they wrapped around the skull like a pair of arms giving it a welcoming hug.

The skull shook them off and flew after the other man.

Deon pulled himself to his feet. As he checked for broken bones, a couple other guys approached—an older gentleman and a uniformed guard.

A beach ball orbited the guard's head.

Deon gave the uniformed man an understanding nod.

"What's going on here?" the older gentleman asked.

"Ummm, these two dudes tried to rob you." Deon pointed at the massacred corpses. At that moment, the skull returned, dragging the third burglar by his foot. This man now wore his intestines like a scarf. Deon added, "And this guy."

"You stopped them?" the older gentleman asked. "While my paid security guard was fucking around with his beach ball?"

"Yeah, me and my, uh, skull."

"But why were you here? Were you trying to rob me too?"

Deon stood taller. "I'm here to inquire about your help wanted sign."

The older gentleman turned to the guard. He didn't say anything. Neither did the guard. The uniformed man just shrugged, took off his guard shirt, threw it on the ground and stomped toward the exit, beach ball floating lazily behind.

"How do you feel about being a night security guard?" the older gentleman asked. "You and your skull."

"Hell yeah," Deon replied.

He followed the older gentleman to an office, where he filled out some paperwork. The older gentleman, the owner of the junkyard, asked Deon to start immediately. Deon said he had some business to take care of, but he could start the following night. The owner agreed, and Deon practically ran home, excited about the new job. On the way though, he remembered his dilemma. He definitely couldn't get rid of the skull now, but he didn't know if Tanya would understand.

When he got home, he got a text from her: "I'm on my way home. Skull better be gone, or I will be." She definitely wouldn't understand.

The truth was he didn't want to get rid of the skull, and not just because of the new job either. The skull loved him. And it wasn't unrequited. Quite the contrary. He loved the skull. Not like a boy-girl love or even a familial love, but a strong love nonetheless, strong enough to lift the skull from the pages of Corby Benton's shitty book, that was for sure. He couldn't make the skull go away, any more than he could make his love for it go away. But he loved Tee too.

Another text from Tanya: "Looking forward to a skull-free night."

The skull orbited his head in silence.

He couldn't remember ever feeling this much pressure in his entire life. A baggie of pot sat on his coffee table, promising a refuge from the pressure, but admitting it had no answers. He didn't know what to do. He could not let Tanya go. If only she could see the skull the way he saw the skull. If only the skull could be a part of her life like it had become a part of his life.

That was it. That was what he needed to do.

He scurried around the apartment, finding a pen and paper.

He needed to write Tanya a love letter, a very specific love letter, a love letter that would make her understand everything, make her see the skull like he did, make her love the skull like he did. And make the skull love her too. One letter to form the perfect love triangle. Thankfully, the letter had already been written, and he had it memorized. He put pen to paper and wrote:

In that catacomb, one skull stood out from thousands…

Weird Reflections: A Greeting

By Mike Davis

Photo courtesy of Mike Davis

Salutations! My name is Mike Davis and I'm the editor of *The Lovecraft eZine*. I'm happy to report that I've joined the *Dark Discoveries* family. I'll be writing a column for each issue, because for some reason, the folks in charge of *Dark Discoveries* thought this would be a good idea: to subject their readers to this. Who am I to disagree?

The Lovecraft eZine began almost five years ago as a simple online magazine. Since then, it has evolved and grown: I host a weekly talk show where we discuss all things cosmic horror and weird fiction; the *eZine* is now publishing books; and the website has over 200,000 followers. We also publish print and Kindle editions of the magazine, featuring such authors and contributors as Wilum Pugmire, Joseph S. Pulver, Sr., Scott Thomas, Peter Rawlik, Jeffrey Thomas, Robert M. Price, Ross E. Lockhart, Josh Reynolds, and William Meikle.

It's been quite a ride!

So, beginning with next issue, look for my column Weird Reflections in each issue of *Dark Discoveries*. See you then!

THE BLACK BARONY: THE GOLDEN AGE OF DREAD

BY LAIRD BARRON

THE SUN'S RIM DIPS; THE STARS RUSH OUT;
AT ONE STRIDE COMES THE DARK
—THE RIME OF THE ANCIENT MARINER
SAMUEL TAYLOR COLERIDGE

1. Past Is Prologue

Let me tell you something of myself and why the macabre and the strange fascinate me. I have an old and abiding relationship with horror and weirdness. We go way back, and whether I knew it or not, the weird has always loomed large in my intellectual life.

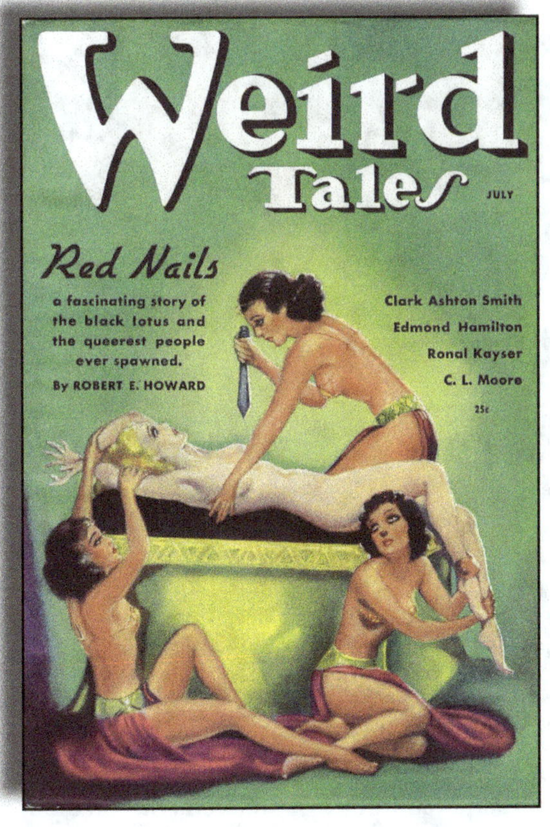

I come from a family of storytellers. Many of my father's and grandfather's generation, semiliterate or educated, cleaved to oral tradition. Granddad tried and failed to sell novels. An uncle on Mom's side wrote psychedelic poetry and song lyrics. After we moved from the 1970s Alaska version of the suburbs to a homestead in the sticks, Dad often told us kids elaborate bedtime stories.

The old man's repertoire was scary stuff on the whole—he delved into his own childhood growing up in rural Texas and Alaska during the '50s. He spun yarns of fantastical brushes with the uncanny and inexplicable. Other stories were recycled and repurposed plotlines of films—*The Thing; An American Werewolf in London; The Shining;* and so forth. His reworked tales would start with something along the lines of, "These three kids, brothers, got turned around hiking near Moose Pass. So they went into a nameless tavern where a snarling, bloody-jawed wolf's head adorned the shingle…"

He saved the spookiest, most unnerving material for our teen years. The years of heavy responsibility—good old Dad frequently absconded with Mom via riverboat, dog team, or airplane to civilized locales, leaving us boys to fend for ourselves for days, and occasionally weeks, at a stretch. By twelve, I knew how to cook for my brothers, feed a kennel of huskies, chop wood, shoot a rifle, and all the other details required to maintain a cabin in the middle of nowhere during deep winter. Dad was by no means a literary critic. He liked what he liked, end of story, so to speak. On a primal level, he understood that horror stories are cautionary illustrations, similar in purpose to fables, but weighted toward the "what would you do if…?" side of the scale. What would my brothers and I do if, while alone at the cabin, we heard a stranger calling for help down the path to the river where the bushes grow thick and the shadows are deep? What if the huskies growled and their hackles stood up? What if one of us went missing? What if the TV died and the CB radio transmitted nothing but static and no one came for us? You get the idea.

The tiny, battery-powered black and white TV was a luxury for a few of my formative years. Happily, we'd lugged a decent-sized library out into the boonies. Materials covered the spectrum from Barbara Cartland to Louis L' Amour; from Asimov to Zelazny; and Robert Browning to EA Poe. I first encountered the weird as a third-grader when Robert E. Howard's Conan books fell into my clutches. Those Lancer/Ace editions from the latter 1960s and 70s of the ass-kicking Frazetta covers. "Red Nails," man. The renaissance of the Conan line is almost enough to convince me that editor/authors L. Sprague de

Camp and Lin Carter were good for something. Conan understood the weird, and for the most part he hated it, unless it benefited him, and even then. For Conan, the most positive attribute of weirdness was that if it manifested in the mortal realm it could be defeated through a liberal application of cold steel.

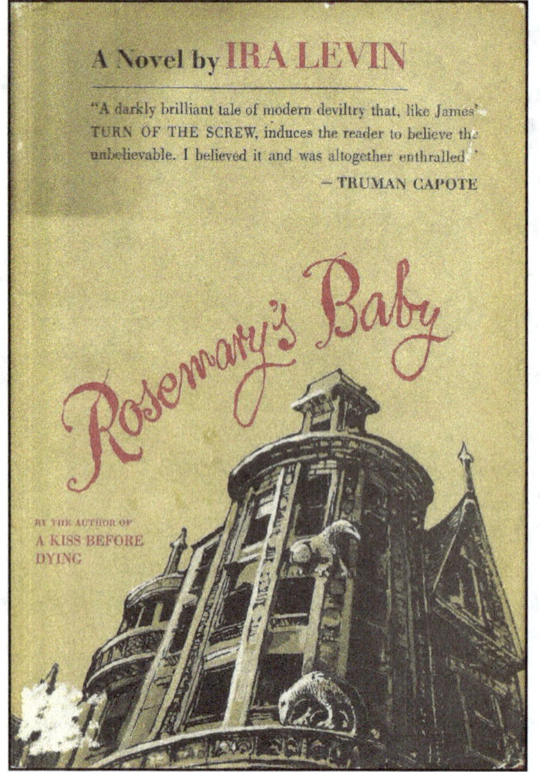

Edgar Rice Burroughs was another early favorite of mine. Burroughs dabbled in certain aspects of the weird. John Carter proved a bit more temperate regarding the collision of the mundane and the inexplicable. However, he too defaulted to the maxim that no matter what polychromatic pigment or number of extra limbs an enemy possessed, a few stabs from something pointy would remedy all ills.

And of course, I'm on record as a lifelong fan of Roger Zelazny, a writer who focused on science fiction and fantasy yet assayed brief forays into horror and strangeness. He remains a strong inspiration in terms of style. However, when it comes to my preoccupation with the macabre, Edgar Allan Poe is the bad seed that started it all. Not only for me, not only other writers of the dark, but practitioners of related genres as well. As I've remarked elsewhere, Poe's profound influence upon me never became clear until I reflected upon the role that live burial and incipient madness play in my own work. As it happened, I'd torn through collections of Poe's poetry and fiction throughout childhood and integrated some of his exquisite melancholy and dreadful paranoia into my subconscious.

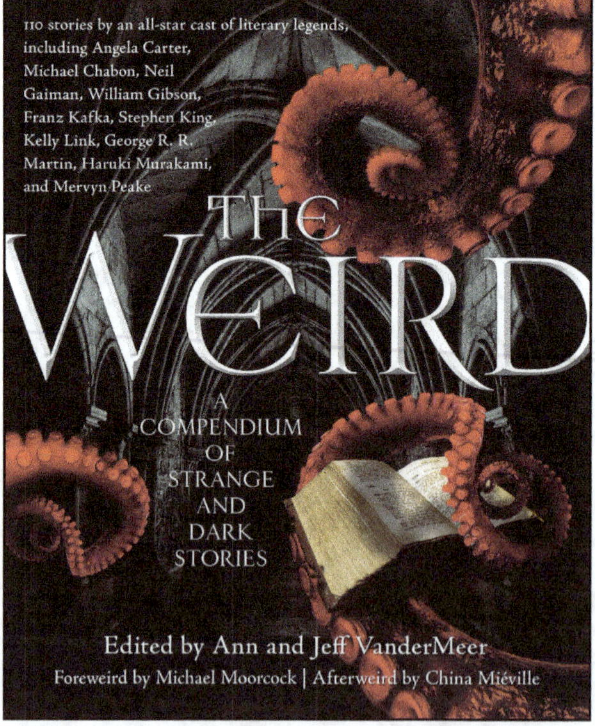

Despite the madness, murder, doping, boozing, sex, and general mayhem, Poe was A-Okay with my hawkish evangelically-minded mother. The classics got paid a bit of slack, fortunately, because Poe was all I had of the really subversive stuff for quite a while. It wasn't until mid to late adolescence that I dug into the special stock of modern Gothic horror my parents kept under lock and key. We're talking Thomas Tryon, William Peter Blatty, Ira Levin, and Stephen King. Now we're really cooking—*The Other; The Exorcist; Rosemary's Baby; and The Shining*. My literary education had entered a new phase. The wonderful world of occultism and possession horror.

Suffice to say, I survived and came through intact, a mild penchant for the diabolical notwithstanding.

2. Bizarro and The New Weird

The weird has been with us always; it existed as a dominant force, and a defining force, long before genre categories were officially delineated. I have argued elsewhere that it predates written history and likely originated around a fire in a cave. The weird is, arguably, the parent category from which horror derives. Consider also certain elements of creation myth. Consider outré elements of historical accounts such as Alexander's eastward journeys toward *Terra Incognita*. Consider more modern artists and their works, such as "The Rime of the Ancient Mariner" by Coleridge, a composition enameled with rococo bizarreness and black glints of cosmic horror; and the chilling reimagining of Biblical lore in "Lazarus" by Leonid Andreyev; or the seminal "Yellow Wallpaper" by Charlotte Perkins Gilman.

New weird is a popular neologism at the moment, albeit contested and of questionable utility. The term materialized during the first three or so years of the Aughts; favored oath of authors such as China Mieville, M. John Harrison, and Jeff VanderMeer. Jeff and his wife Ann subsequently partnered on an anthology project titled *The New Weird*. Headlined by Mieville and Jeff Ford among other luminaries of modern fantasy it represented a worthy stab at the beast of weird fiction, but like the eponymous movement, it fell flat as a defining statement. It lacked an intrinsic sense of coherence.

Infinitely better and infinitely more useful was the duo's follow-up anthology, simply titled *The Weird*—a mega omnibus collecting weird tales from 1908 to 2010. This is an epic anthology and representative of the best that literary fantastica and strangeness has to offer. The anthology's success and scope is also demonstrative that the new weird, while catchy, merely flashed in the pan and the minds of a subset of authors and booksellers intent upon creating a marketing niche.

As horror exists along a spectrum, the weird also spawns its share of subsets, including MR James Christmas terrors, the paranoid fantasies of Shirley Jackson and Robert Aickman, and Thomas Ligotti's hallucinogenic transfigurations of corporate toil. Bizarro fiction is the latest and possibly boldest niche to be carved in the modern canon. Cut from the same dark-matter cloth as Burroughs and Kafka and intended as literary peyote or a psychedelic eye-skewer that combines absurdism and horror and sets the concoction ablaze, bizarro crept among us somewhere during the latter 1990s and metastasized. By the mid Aughts it had, like some kind of brain-hijacking Cordyceps spore, taken over a segment of the publishing hive mind.

Inasmuch as the independent press deserves recognition for the proliferation of readily available dark literature in general, the folks at *Eraserhead Press, Lazy Fascist, and Raw Dog Screaming Press* were the original fire starters who continue to promote some of the most experimental work around. Cody Goodfellow, Robert Jeremy Johnson, and Cameron Pierce are the tip of the iceberg when it comes to this particular movement. I highlight them because they have taken the pioneering concept of this insanely mutable and highly unstable genre and harnessed it to remarkable effect. In the beginning there was plenty of light; at last, these folks are generating heat to match. Couple the dedication to craft with a well-timed stunt or two, namely Patrick Wensink's novel *Broken Piano for President* whose cover art earned a pleasant cease and desist from Jack Daniels corporate suits, and backed by a plenum of editors and publishers intent on a mission, and you're on to something.

I'd be remiss not to provide a coda for this segment. The demarcations between various genres and genre communities aren't always clear, especially when it comes to the weird. Bizarro is even trickier when it comes to territorial and tribal distinctions. Off blazing their own trails, but perhaps erroneously associated with bizarro, are numerous operators of the interstitial realms. I'll hit you with three: Molly Tanzer, Nikki Guerlain, and Anne Constance Fitzgerald. Read them—any or all could be the next big thing.

3. Contemporary Stylings

Much of the current richness of the field is attributable to a shift that occurred on one side or the other of the year 2000—the small press began to yoke the awesome power of the internet and as a result, everybody prospered, especially readers who gradually were introduced to a veritable banquet of choice unequalled in modern history.

When I started paying close attention to the scene back then, internet message boards were the prime watering holes—many of us remember the *Night Shade* and *Shocklines* BBs via a mixture of nostalgia and nausea. Mostly nostalgia for me, especially in regard to *Night Shade*. That's where I made the acquaintance of several of the foremost fantasists of our time. In those days, Jeffrey Ford, Ellen Datlow, and Lucius Shepard frequently held forth on the subject of their latest publishing ventures, movie reviews, and convention plans. The fuming cauldron of semi-public shop talk and kibitzing on everything from the state of the genre to the state of the union wasn't fated to endure. People drifted to *Live Journal, Twitter*, and the great Mammon reborn, *Facebook*. Great enlightening fun while it lasted though.

While that maelstrom of message board-churning was in progress, unsung hero of the moribund horror field, Brian Keene, launched a predawn attack: he singlehandedly revived the giant monster and zombie contingent *a la The Conqueror Worms* and *The Rising*. As I write this in October of 2015, zombies continue to run amok in novels, video games, and cinema. The walking dead get all the glory, yet it's the Technicolor widescreen madness

(and yes, pants-shitting weirdness) of Keene's *Earthworm Gods* cycle that should be enshrined, if for nothing else than their prescience regarding cataclysmic climate change, concomitant weather disasters, and renewed popularity of enormous, planet-wrecking monsters (see *Pacific Rim* and *Attack on Titan*).

Recently, neo noir, or the new black, has attracted attention. Yes, another fresh neologism; although similar to bizarro, neo noir makes a stronger case for itself than the new weird has done. There are simply more authors and editors involved and their aim is concentrated, more refined, more of a coherent vision. Be that as it may, critics, scholars, and history will get the last word. Regardless of what one might prefer to label it, some of the finest mashups of genre have resulted from this experiment. *The New Black*, edited by Richard Thomas, is a stunning example of hybrid literature that skews to the dark side. Much as I enjoy the new black and its renovation of familiar architecture, my hat is also off to the writers who were there first. Norman Partridge and Joe Lansdale blazed this trail for many moons—fusing crime and horror and pure weirdness with a uniquely North American hardboiled panache. One detects their influence upon the likes of Richard Thomas (whose debut novel *Disintegration* is a fine example of this kind), Stephen Graham Jones, Molly Tanzer, and Benjamin Percy.

The amazing and painful thing of it is, we are experiencing such a surfeit of riches, it's impossible for my essay to completely touch upon the era's essential authors, filmmakers, and publications, much less examine them rigorously. The inimitable Michael Cisco unleashed *The Narrator* and *The Divinity Student* upon us; two seminal novels that exemplify the very definition of weird fiction, while Koji Suzuki's *Ringu* trilogy, less than a decade old, was joined by *Ju-On* and various titles by Takashi Miike (*Audition, Ichi the Killer*, and *Gozu*) at the fore of the J-horror invasion of the States. Adam Nevill's work rises like a black star over Britain even as Kaaron Warren, Leena Krohn, and Karin Tidbeck push the envelope in Australia, Finland, and Sweden respectively.

Grand old men of the field Lucius Shepard and Michael Shea left us forever, and Thomas Ligotti effectively retired from fiction; but S.P. Miskowski published the *Skillute Cycle*, Gemma Files came into her own with numerous lauded short stories, Victor LaValle and Glen Duncan smote us with modernizations of the Minotaur and werewolf, Mike Allen, among the most dynamic of contemporary fantasists, habitually upends Lovecraftian tropes with his own brand of cosmic horror, Livia Llewellyn blew our doors off courtesy of her gloriously grotesque debut, *Engines of Desire* (one of several important authors published by Steve Berman at *Lethe Press*), and Wilum Pugmire puts forth a new baroque masterpiece every other year. And the beat goes on, and on.

Great as this age's writers may be, invaluable as the publishers are to the process, the lynchpin that keeps disparate elements united is undeniably the yeoman labor of the editors. The editors who work the trenches now are the equal of any group from the Halcyon days of yore, and I've had the privilege to be shredded, then mended by a number of these good people. However, no modern anthologist (and the anthology has proven to be the heavyweight game-changer of horror and the weird) has endeavored more, or struck a harder blow, for the advancement of macabre fiction than Ellen Datlow. Her work at *Sci Fiction* and on numerous anthologies over the past decade and a half, produced a who's who and what's what list of major award-winning stories. *Inferno, Lovecraft Unbound*, and *Poe* stand as modern classics. These anthologies represent a mere fraction of the terraforming effect Datlow exerts at this very moment upon the genre landscape.

4. Golden Age of Dread

The weather has turned in favor of weird fiction and horror. A veritable ice age that spanned the '90s into the early Aughts has mellowed and faded. This is, in itself, nothing new. Literature has seemed to ebb and flow in popular currency over the past few decades, contracting precipitously after the collapse of the US publishing economy, and certain genres suffered moreso than others. Happily, the wheel continues to turn and thus old is made new.

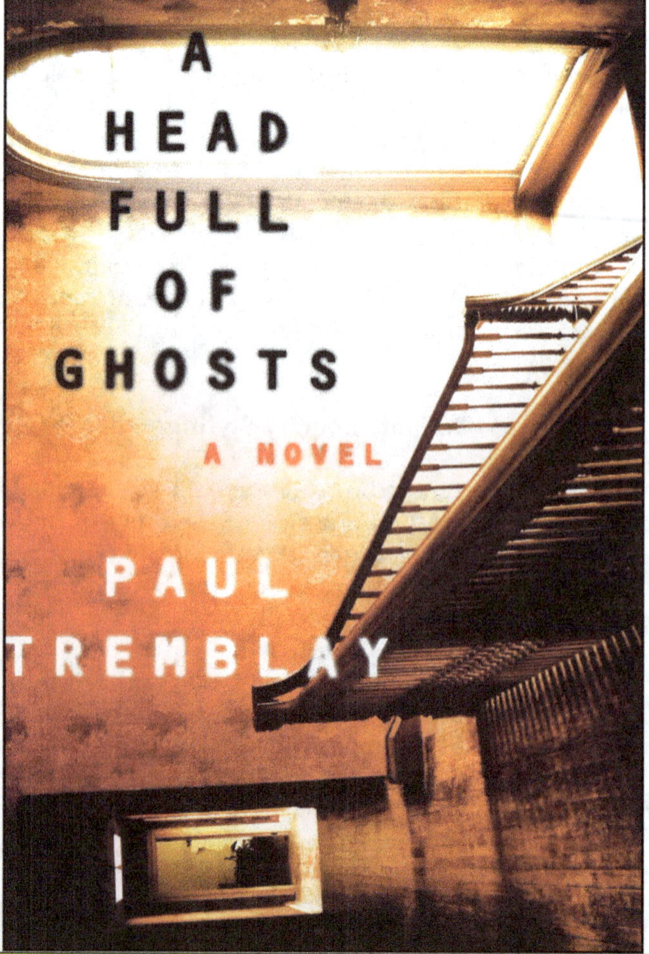

Behold the evidence of a literary thaw and what the receding glaciers reveal: bizarro has gradually emerged as a viable force with the advent of Carlton Mellick III's *Clownfellas* published by *Random House*. The smash success of cable series *True Detective* shone the spotlight on old masters of the weird, namely Robert Chambers, and contemporary practitioners Thomas Ligotti and John Langan, among others. The possession genre received a shot in the phantom arm following the success of Paul Tremblay's chilling novel *A Head Full of Ghosts*, soon to be a major motion picture starring Robert Downey Jr. And for unvarnished, full-bore weirdness, one need look no further than Jeff VanderMeer's bestselling *Southern Reach* trilogy, also optioned for film.

Some authors and critics have termed this recent positive trend a renaissance, others call it a revival, and still others claim it is evidence of a specific movement. I prefer to regard the resurgence as a golden age of darkness, a golden age of dread, a golden age of the weird, which encapsulates these themes and more. The age of bizarro, the so-called new weird, the age of small presses, e-zines, and adventures in self-publishing.

This tide has crested before: in the colonial era of Poe, Hawthorne and Bierce; later on during the heyday of Clark Ashton Smith, Machen, Blackwood, Burroughs, Howard, and Lovecraft; during the 1950s and '60s when Shirley Jackson, Flannery O'Conner, and Ray Russell rode high; unto the rise of the occult in the '70s; the big hair and bigger scare '80s that witnessed the primacy of Michael Shea, Peter Straub, Joyce Carol Oates, Stephen King, and Clive Barker; and most recently the likes of Koji Suzuki, Yoko Ogawa, Brian Evenson, Conrad Williams, Paul Tremblay, and John Langan whose terrors defy the onset of global surveillance and instant technology.

The small and independent presses in harmony with the transformative nature of social networking, have collaborated to usher in an era unrivaled for the quality and ubiquity of macabre literature. Mainstream press, such as *SLATE*, *SALON*, and *The Wall Street Journal* lend the topic column inches on a regular basis. Let me tell you brothers and sisters, in a wilderness of fractured and segregated media and entertainment, that's enormous.

In 2007 I wrote an article for *LOCUS* on the state of horror and by relation, weird fiction. I referred to the state of the union as a golden age and if anything, it remains on the ascent. The genre is in a terrific place at the moment. Where are we headed? Despite economic uncertainty, the constant fragmentation of entertainment sources and increasing competition from television and video games, we who toil in the field persist and we thrive. We continue onward with our little candle into the night.

KIDS, YOUR UNCLE ROSENTHAL IS LOOKING DOWN ON US.

Z
Z
Z
DAD, WHAT IF HE ISN'T UP THERE?

HEY, BUDDY...

NOTHING LIKE GRADE-A DAD MEAT
WHERE AM I?

I'VE HAD BETTER
I'LL SAY

WE BE WHAT WE BE

By Shane McKenzie

Thomas was feeding Mama when Hewitt dragged the neighbor's dead dog in through the doggie door, then sat on his haunches over the poor, pathetic little thing, and smiled up at Thomas. It was one of those foreign lap dogs with the squished-in faces that kind of snorts when it breathes. Only this one had quit breathing a long time ago. Looked like Hewitt had been chewing on it a good while before deciding to drag it in to share with the family.

They hadn't been in the new house a full week, and already they had their first victim.

Thomas couldn't blame Hewitt. He was just doing what he does. Being true to himself.

When the front door flew open, Thomas scooped up that bloody little bastard, threw the back door open, and tossed it out like a furry Frisbee. Hewitt barked happily and dashed after it.

Thomas dropped the spoon back into Mama's soup bowl, then kissed her on the forehead before pushing her chair across the kitchen and into the living room, wiping the blood from his hands. She wasn't eating anyhow, had been stingy with her appetite ever since the big move. Thomas heard a thing like a move could cause a lot of stress, so he didn't make much of a stink over it. Figured she'd get hungry enough eventually.

"So…how'd it go? Been dyin' all day waitin' on you kids. Tell me everything."

"Fuckin' sucked," Sloane said as she stormed in, dropped her bag to the floor, and kicked the door shut behind her.

"Ow!" Eddie stumbled in rubbing the middle of his forehead. "What'd you did that for?"

"Sloane, I'm gonna give you a pass since I know emotions're high and whatnot. But you use language like that again, 'specially in front of your grandmamma, I'll hang you from your ankles'n bleed you dry, you hear me?"

It was hard to make out her expression from behind her mask, but he could tell from her rolling eyes and the way she crossed her arms that she was about ready to throw a fit. She sighed, shook her head, and leaned against the wall.

Thomas was hoping Mae could maybe talk to Sloane. Ever since that girl hit the teenage years, she was damn near too much for Thomas to handle. He figured she'd be more comfortable confiding in her mother anyhow.

If he was honest with himself, all the changes she was going through, from girl to woman—or so Mae said—scared the shit out of him.

Eddie ran over and wrapped his pudgy little arms around Thomas's waist, gave him a fierce hug like he always did. Stronger than a grizzly bear, that boy. Even through the boy's mask, Thomas could see his son's smile, the two front teeth missing. His adult teeth were coming in, cutting through the gums with their serrated edges, though still just nubs showing.

"And you, Eddie? How's your first day of school, huh?"

He shrugged. "All right, I guess. Teacher tried to make me take my mask off, but she gave up after a while. I think maybe she's scared of me, Daddy."

Eddie laughed at that, puffed his chest out with pride.

"The other kids give you trouble?"

"One boy did a little. His name's Art. Kept calling me jerky face and tried pushing me around, roughing me up. But I ain't worried about him."

"Eddie?" Thomas leaned over and held the boy by the chin. "What'd you do? And don't you go lyin' to me. Told you. First day of school, you behave yourself, didn't I?"

He shrugged. "I didn't do nothin', Daddy, I swear. Just stayed quiet. Just like you told me to. I ain't lyin', I swear!" A grin filled his mask's mouth-hole with teeth. "But tomorrow ain't the first day no more."

"All right, all right." Thomas messed his boy's hair, stood up straight, and faced his daughter. He decided to ignore his son's mischievous smile. A boy's got to defend himself, after all. Especially when he's the new kid at school.

Sloane hadn't moved. Arms still crossed. Head turned so she was facing the front door.

The sewing room door swung open and Mae came waddling in. When they arrived to the new house, it was the first room Mae claimed. She pulled a needle from between her lips and stuck it to her shirt, then got to rubbing her hands over her belly like a fortune teller trying to see the future. There were food stains on the chin of her mask, and Thomas strolled over and ran his finger over them, then stuck the finger in his mouth. He widened his eyes at her and sort of jerked his head back toward their daughter.

Mae pursed her lips and nodded. Adjusted her mask so her smile was easier to see, then trudged over to Sloane.

"Wanna talk about it?"

Eddie was already on the floor playing with his animal bones, so Thomas quickly grabbed Mama by the back of her chair and wheeled her toward the kitchen.

"I hate it here! I hate this house, my school… I hate all of you! Why'd you make me move here!" Sloane's voice was sharp, shaky like she might burst out crying.

Thomas heard her pounding footsteps as she ran up the stairs. Heard her bedroom door slam. He was tempted to head on up there and teach her a lesson about respect, but figured it was best to let her cool off. Let her throw her tantrums, speak her mind for a while.

She'll adjust, he told himself. *We all will.*

He sat at the kitchen table and ran his fingers over the polished bone. Just because they were starting over didn't mean they couldn't be themselves. He was proud of who they were, where they came from, and always would be. Mae got it into her head she wanted to live a "normal" life, see if they could cut a slice of the American Dream off for themselves. It was a nice idea, but Thomas didn't know how long they could all last.

But for Mae, he was willing to try. Not that he had much say in the matter with the way her mood swings were going. That woman's hormones were meaner than a shook up wasps' nest. And Thomas learned back when Mae was pregnant with Sloane not to agitate her. Just nod and smile and accommodate. The way a good husband's supposed to. That's what Mama had told him he was supposed to do, and so that's what he did.

Mama still wouldn't talk to him, though. Just sat there, her dried-up, pruned face aimed toward the window, bony hands in her lap. Thomas had applied some fresh makeup to her that morning, but her skin had been especially flaky since moving to the new house. The heat was dryer in this town than back home. Probably going to have to start moisturizing.

"Don't tell me you're all pissed too, Mama. This's what Mae wants, and just like you told me all them years back, I'm doin' my best to make her happy. Ain't that what you said?"

No answer.

"All right, then, Mama. You wanna act that way, just sit here and starve. See if I do a damn thing about it."

Thomas slammed his fists on the table and made it rattle. He jumped to his feet, could feel the rage building up in his gut. Hot and bubbling, rising up to his chest.

He peeked into the next room, saw Eddie was watching TV with Hewitt. Some program on the PBS about taxidermy.

Mae's voice drifted down from upstairs, and though he couldn't make out the words, he could tell she was doing her best to calm Sloane.

You don't do it soon, that girl's whole class is gonna be decoratin' her bedroom walls.

Thomas chuckled to himself and snuck out the back door. Toward the toolshed.

Where he could blow off a little steam.

***

The knock at the door made Thomas flinch. He set the chainsaw on the table and wiped his hands over his apron.

"Honey?" Mae's voice.

"Yeah?"

Shit! He threw his apron off and stuffed it in a drawer. Then he took a long look at David lying on the table next to his saw.

Thomas never caught the guy's name. Looked like a David, though. Or maybe a Steve. His neighbor. First neighbor he had the chance to meet. Same son of a bitch who owned that foreign thing Hewitt chewed all to shit. Probably buried somewhere in the yard by now. Either that or swimming around in Hewitt's stomach acids.

The neighbor had stuck that ugly head of his over the fence and told Thomas he was making too much fucking noise in the middle of the fucking night and what the fuck are you doing with a chainsaw this time of night anyway you fucking idiot and now that I mention it have you seen my dog because my baby girl doesn't just go running off and the same week you and your family show up she goes missing and I don't think it's any kind of coincidence and maybe I better just call the police about all this.

Thomas sort of blacked out after that. The way he used to. Hadn't had a blackout like that since before Eddie was born. Something about that boy had put a new sort of calm into Thomas. Made him feel like he could be a better man. Probably why he bought into this whole "normal lives" business in the first place.

He figured it must have been the stress getting to him. Because the next thing he knew, his saw was taking off limbs. David's head was still attached to his body, but the rest was piled up like cordwood, sitting in a widening pool of blood by the table. One of the arms had a black tribal symbol running from the shoulder to the elbow. What an asshole.

"What you doing in there? And why was I hearing your saw buzzing?"

"Um…"

David's torso was opened up, but all the innards were still inside. Thomas flexed his fingers as he stared at it. Wanting so badly to plunge them in and start tugging it all out, piece by piece.

The door handle jiggled.

"Open this door! Thomas!"

"Mae… Just… just give me a minute to—"

"Open this damn door before I kick it in! And your teeth will be next, you hear?"

There wasn't any hiding it, he knew. So he trudged over, head hanging, and opened the door.

Mae stepped in, took one look at the mess, and shook her head. But she didn't jump down his throat like he expected. Instead, she sort of smiled, waved him over.

Thomas dragged his feet as he went, then let himself fall into his wife's embrace. She stroked the hair at the back of his head, laid his cheek against her milk-swollen bosom.

"We talked about this."

"I know we did."

"Blackout again?"

He nodded.

"Who was he?"

"Neighbor. Complainin' about the noise."

"Of course he was, Thomas. We ain't back home anymore. Houses are elbow to elbow around here. Can't just go sawing any old time you feel like it. You understand that, don't you?"

"I do. Hewitt ate up his dog earlier today, too. Was gonna tell you about it. We ain't off to a good start, are we?"

"I got faith. Just gonna take some time is all. You're with me on this, right, Thomas? Because I can't do it alone."

"I am. Course I am, it's just… I don't know, Mae. You sure we can do this?"

She kissed him twice, then strolled toward the body. Stuck her hands into the gaping belly and started yanking the ropes of intestine out, piling them up on the table.

"We can if we try. But we gotta try. And I mean really try."

Watching her empty out that torso, Thomas was reminded why he was doing this. Why he uprooted his family, his life, and moved to the suburbs. Because goddammit, he loved his wife. He grabbed a hammer out of his toolbox, spread David's lips out so he was sort of grimacing, then slammed the hammer down, knocking most of the teeth out on the first swing. He collected them and stuffed them into his pocket.

"I will. I promise I will."

"Ready for work tomorrow? Big first day?" As she said it, the liver in her hand wiggled and speckled her dress in blood. She always looked so beautiful spattered in blood. And she took a long look at that liver, sniffed it once, then took a hearty bite. Always her favorite part. Usually liked it cooked first, but when Mae had a baby brewing in her belly, her cravings could get a bit out of control.

"I'll knock 'em dead," he said, then slammed the hammer back down and broke off the remaining teeth. "What's that sayin'? Bring home the bacon?"

She laughed and took another big bite. As she chewed, she picked up a filet knife and slid it down David's side, from armpit to love handle. She lifted the flap of flesh and wiggled it. When she spoke, blood misted from her lips. "You already took care of that."

"Least we know what we're eatin' this week. Hope you weren't heart-set on goin' to the super market."

She giggled. "Just because we're normal folks now, don't mean we gotta change everything about us, now does it?"

"Hope not."

They leaned over David's body and kissed. Pressed their foreheads against each other's for a few seconds and just let the love between them flow freely.

"Sloane all right?" Thomas said as he fished through his drawer for his paring knife. He smiled when he found it, the wooden handle stained with countless years' worth of blood.

"Misses her boyfriend. That's really the root of it. Other than that, typical teenage girl stuff. I expected this."

"Am I missin' somethin', or ain't she wearin' that boy's face right now?"

"She is."

"Then I don't see the problem. Ain't like it was real love anyhow. Just a coupla fool kids with hearts in their eyes and butterflies in their bellies."

"And that, honey, is why I'll deal with our daughter. Don't matter if it's real or not, you simple man you. To her, it's as real as the love between you and me. And for now, we gotta at least pretend like we understand."

Just the thought of his baby girl falling in love made the blackout start to fade back in. But he concentrated on his wife's beautiful face behind the same mask he gave her on their wedding day. The way she cradled that belly of hers with those blood-stained hands.

"I'll do my best to be sympathetic."

"All I'm asking, honey."

***

Thomas knocked on his first door of the day. He straightened his tie, took a deep breath, then put on the best smile he could muster.

The heat was a mean bastard that day. Sweat stains were already darkening his shirt at the neck and armpits. His mask was sticking to his face as salty droplets rained from his pours. He caught a look at himself in the window, saw his hair was damp and draped over the forehead of his mask. Some of the stitch-work was coming loose in the area, and Thomas made a mental note to get Mae to mend it when he got home. Quickly, he ran his fingers through his hair, got it to a place he figured Mae would approve of, and in the next second, the door creaked open.

"Whoa," the young girl said as she smiled and looked Thomas up and down. "It's not Halloween, is it? What's with the mask?"

The blackness started to creep into the edges of his vision as he took her in. He did his best to force it away, to chew it back down to wherever it was inside him that it crawled out from, but the longer he looked at her, the darker things became.

Teenager. Eighteen at the most. Blonde. Athletic build. The shirt she wore did nothing to hide the fact she wasn't wearing a bra and that she probably had the A/C cranked up inside the house. Her toenails were painted a raw-pork-pink, one foot balancing on the toes, making them scrunch up like she was doing a ballet pose. Her shorts were hardly more than underwear, showing off her smooth, muscular legs. One knee had a V-shaped scar on it, faded and hardly noticeable—probably some childhood injury. The kind of thing no normal person would notice, but Thomas had an eye for skin. He loved running his fingers across a freshly peeled sheet of flesh, picking out every tiny imperfection and making up stories about the person's life.

"Can you talk, mister? You're not one of those religious folks, are you? Coming to preach to me? From the looks of you, I'm guessing not, but—"

"Knives."

"Excuse me?"

"Selling knives. Door to door." He licked his lips and swallowed to dampen his dry throat, then opened up his case and displayed the merchandise within. All beauties. Bone handles. Each one of them handmade by Thomas, his own design. "New in town. My family and me."

She only glanced at the knives, then sort of shrugged. "Parents aren't home. But even if they were, they just bought a new set of kitchen knives at Walmart. Good ones too. So you're wasting your time either w—"

The blackness engulfed him, grabbed hold of him. He clenched his teeth and fought it back, and in the next few seconds, the color of the world faded back into his vision.

He still stood on the girl's doorstep. She still stood in front of him. So still and quiet.

Thomas was confused as to why she wasn't talking. Why she was staring at him like that. Why, when she opened her mouth like she was going to break the silence, a sheet of blood poured out and splashed all over those pink toes of hers.

Then Thomas realized his arm was extended. Realized one of the knives from his case was missing, and that it was missing because that handmade bone handle was squeezed in his grip, and the blade was buried up to the hilt in that girl's creamy, quivering throat.

By the time she finally reached up and clawed at the wound, Thomas had begun pulling the blade out. Her fingertips and knuckles slid across the edge, cutting them open and making blood spill into her palms and down her forearms.

Thomas yanked the blade free and the girl hit the ground. Still alive, she sobbed and choked as she tried to turn herself around and crawl deeper into the house. Poor, pathetic thing. She'd never make it to the phone, Thomas knew, and it felt cruel to stand there and watch her try.

You stupid asshole, he told himself. *Mae's gonna skin you alive for this.*

He sighed, checked over his shoulder to make sure the coast was clear, then stepped over the threshold into the house and shut the door behind him.

"Sorry about this, ma'am. If it makes you feel any better…" he said as he stomped toward the girl and lifted her by the hair. He jammed two thick, callused fingers into the puncture wound, hooked them, and yanked hard. The flesh tore wide open, gushing blood across the floor and painting the nearest wall. "…my wife's gonna kill me."

***

Thomas trudged home, wheeling one of those red and white coolers behind him. He found it in the girl's garage with nothing but cobwebs and a thawed freezer pack inside. It had wheels on it, making it easy to get home with the girl folded up and stuffed inside.

He knew Mae would be damn pissed about what he'd done—on his first day of work no less. But she'd be even more steamed if she knew he let all that meat go to waste. Not to mention that girl had a face on her. Thomas planned on giving it to the missus as a peace offering, knew she wouldn't be able to resist a piece of skin as fine as that.

Whether she forgave him or not, he would get a tongue lashing, no question. He let his head hang and dragged his feet as he started up the walkway toward the front door.

"Daddy?" Eddie's voice. "Whatever you got in the cooler, it's leakin' all over the place."

Thomas sighed when he saw the red, wet trail leading from the murder scene all the way up to his front door. "Shit. Guess maybe we better clean that up."

"Mom's gonna be mad, ain't she?"

"I reckon she will be, son." He dropped the cooler's handle, leaving it there in the front yard, the dry and yellowed grass drinking up the blood as it continued to leak from the cracked bottom corner. A few strands of hair had worked their way out, too, soaked in blood like angel hair leeches.

"Why don't you run'n grab me the hose from the side of the house," Thomas said, and Eddie smiled and immediately ran to get it done. "Don't forget to turn it on, too!"

"I won't!"

Thomas stood and faced the rest of the neighborhood. A few cars driving along, some pulling into driveways close by. The drivers didn't say anything to Thomas, and the ones who actually looked his direction quickly looked the other way. None seemed to notice the blood trail.

He bent down and opened the cooler's lid just enough to peek inside. The girl's perfect face was aimed right at him, her eyes wide, the sockets filled with blood. Her mouth hung open in an infinite, silent scream. That expression made her look ghastly, but Thomas knew once he peeled it off her skull, it would look damn spectacular on his wife's face.

"Here you go, Daddy."

Thomas slammed the cooler shut and took the hose from Eddie's hand. He walked out to the edge of the yard, as far as the hose could reach. Didn't reach nearly far enough, and the sky was clear and blue with no chance of rain helping him out. He tightened his grip on the spray nozzle, and though the stream reached nearly two houses away, he knew it wouldn't be enough, and after he got done explaining himself to Mae, he'd have to come back out and take care of it proper.

"Where's your sister?" Thomas said as he washed the blood trail off the concrete, catching a look from a neighbor across the street. Thomas just smiled and waved and did his best to look natural. The neighbor waved back, but lazily, like their hand was damn near too heavy to lift.

"Don't know. She didn't show so I just walked home alone." He wrinkled his nose. "I don't need her anyhow. I can make it home all by myself just fine. She don't do nothing but fuss at me and tell me how I'm ruinin' her life or whatever. Always goin' on about how nothing's fair. I hate her sometimes, Daddy, I really do."

Thomas just chuckled and shook his head. "I know maybe sometimes it feels like that, Eddie, but deep down, you don't mean it. Family, it's all we got, son. It's what matters most, you understand?"

He shrugged and nodded, eyes averted to his sneakers. "Sorry, Daddy." Taking a seat on the cooler, he dipped his hand in the blood pooling in the lawn and rubbed his thumb over his bloody fingertips. "I don't know. She's family and all. But sometimes, I think maybe she's crazy."

Thomas couldn't help but laugh at that. "Yeah, maybe you're right about that."

The street and sidewalk were about as clean as he could hope to get them for the time being, so he told Eddie to cut the water off and roll the hose back up. Thomas lifted the cooler, tilted it to make sure it didn't leak, then walked on into the house.

"Mae?" he called out as he entered. "Before you say anythin', let me just explain. This wasn't…"

He stopped in his tracks. Staring across the room at his wife and mother, both sitting and facing him as if waiting for him to arrive.

But how did she know? Did someone see the blood trail

leading to the house already? Give her a call?

"Thomas. Honey. I got…uh… Listen. I know what I said and I know this whole business moving to this new house in this new town hasn't been easy on anybody in this family. I know maybe I've been a little pushy and demanding. I guess what I'm trying to say is… Ah, hell. Maybe it's best I just show you."

Thomas hadn't moved. Just stood his ground and stared across at his mama, hoping she'd give him some kind of clue as to what in the hell was going on, but she stayed perfectly still and quiet, dry and pruned eyes staring right through him the way they always did.

Before Thomas had a chance to take a step, the front door swung open and Eddie ran in, the front of his shirt wet from hose water. He stopped short and took a look at the room, then looked up at Thomas. "You in trouble, Daddy?"

Thomas hissed and bared his teeth.

"Trouble?" Mae said, then strolled over toward him, both her hands cradling her bulging belly. "Thomas… what you got in that cooler?"

Thomas didn't stop her from wiping her hand across the bloody corner. "Didn't you have somethin' you was needin' to show me, honey?"

"Thomas…what'd you…? Eddie! Come over here!"

Eddie's smile melted off his face like a cherry Popsicle under the Texas sun. Thomas hadn't noticed the proud grin on the boy's face until Mae hollered at him. Then he saw what she was fussing about, hanging out of his pocket.

"Yes, ma'am," Eddie said, then slowly made his way to his mother.

She grabbed him by the ear and spun him around so his grimacing face was pointed toward Thomas who still held that bleeding cooler to his chest.

Mae yanked the flap of bloody flesh out of his pocket and waved it at him like a deflated whoopee cushion. Drops of blood flung off the back of the skin piece where threads of gore stretched out across it, hanging in tatters.

"Explain this to me, young man."

"Well what about Daddy, he's got—"

"Answer your mother!" Thomas almost lost his grip on the cooler, but readjusted his arms and got a hold of it. But not before a small splash of blood flew free and splattered across Mama's old rug. He shot a quick look her way and could tell he'd catch hell for it later.

"Well," Eddie said, then reached up and readjusted his mask where it went lopsided after Mae grabbed a hold of him. "That boy Art got to flappin' his mouth again. I told him to stop before I ripped it off his face. He didn't…so I did."

Mae let go of him and sighed. She looked ready to pull her mask off, had the chin of it pinched in her index finger and thumb, but then let her hand drop.

"I'm sorry, Mama. Nobody was around to see. I swear. I made sure. Hung him up in a tree somewhere deep in the woods so nobody would find him before the critters eat him up."

"Eddie, son," Thomas said, "we talked about—"

"You said to behave myself on the first day. And I did. But that asshole deserved it."

"Watch your mouth in front of your—"

"Enough," Mae said as she chuckled and ran her hands through her hair. "There isn't a person in this room that has any right to judge any other. Me included."

Thomas and Eddie both tilted their heads at her.

"Follow me to the kitchen."

Mae spun on her heels and started walking, Thomas right behind her.

"Grab your grandmamma, son," Thomas said, then pecked his mother on the cheek before following his wife into the kitchen.

"Neighbor's wife," she said, pointing to the island in the center of the kitchen. Mae had made such a big deal about the marble countertop and how you could cut meat and veggies right there on top of it and not put a scratch on it. From the looks of the woman, deboned and cut up into neat sections, Mae had tested that theory. "She came snooping around, asking questions. Questions turned to accusations. I just didn't see no other way."

Thomas snorted and set his cooler on the bone table. He threw the lid open and lifted the girl by the hair, pulling her out about belly-height so Mae could get a good look at her. "First customer of the day, you believe that?"

Eddie backed into the kitchen, pulling his grandmamma along. He looked over his shoulder and immediately let her go. Spun and faced his parents. "How're you gonna go and holler at me when you both went and did the same thing?"

Before they had a chance to answer, the screams became audible. Short bursts of agonizing, gut-wrenching screams that grew louder once they heard the front door open and slam.

"Mama? Daddy?" Sloane's voice.

Thomas could have sworn he heard her giggling, and thought he sensed a good mood in her tone.

The kitchen door flew open, would have hit Grandmamma if Eddie hadn't grabbed her and wheeled her out of the way just in time.

Sloane had a meat hook stabbed all the way through a boy's shoulder, protruding out the back right next to the shoulder blade. Tears and snot glistened on the kid's face, and he looked up at the family and cried harder, fingering the entrance wound from where blood steadily flowed.

"P-please…please help m-me…"

"Mama…Daddy," Sloane said again, a toothy grin stretched wide under her mask. "I'm in love."

Hewitt bounded into the kitchen through the doggie door. What might have been a pug was clamped tight in his jaws, its nametag jingling as Hewitt's tail got to wagging.

Thomas and Mae locked eyes and couldn't help but smile. They gathered their family around Grandmamma and hugged, nobody speaking except for Sloane's new boyfriend bleeding on the floor.

"Nothing matters more than this," Thomas said, then kissed each member of his family on the forehead. "Now, who's hungry?"

Singing the Hours: An Interview with Hal Duncan

Photo courtesy of Hal Duncan

Chris Kelso: You're a pretty versatile writer but haven't dabbled too often in horror fiction. Is there a reason for this? How have you found the transition away from writing exclusively in the SF genre? Could this pave the way for future work, a novel perhaps, with a stronger horror sensibility? Because that would be cool!

Hal Duncan: I like horror as a dimension to fiction, so I wouldn't actually say I *have* been writing exclusively in SF, to be honest. THE BOOK OF ALL HOURS has straight-up Lovecraftian stuff going on—with the central conceit a nod to the Necronomicon, and an expedition to the Caucasus in one sequence that's all very cosmic horror. And in my short fiction too, I'm often more labelled as fantasy than SF, while... well, I tend to call it strange fiction myself by preference to nail it to a material—strangeness—that could be possible or impossible, numinous or monstrous in any sort of combo. I like my humour dark and twisted, with a savage bite and a gonzo viscerality, so you'll find plenty of classic horror tropes in my work—werewolves, vampires, etc....

Where that doesn't really translate to a horror sensibility, I guess, is that I don't really do fatalism or moralism or fear of the unknown. I mean, defining horror simply by the use of certain tropes seems a bit superficial, right? So horror, it seems to me, is really a narrative grammar of dread—not unlike tragedy, I'd say. It's one where "this must not be" as emotional judgement is set against "this *must* be" as judgement of inevitability. Like, some sorta Wrongness disrupts equilibrium, kicking off a story, and the dread that's in play is structural: we can see the terrible apotheotic cataclysm coming at the end, by the narrative logic of the genre, when the skin of the world is fully ripped off, and the protagonist is face-to-face with the charnel carnival madhouse truth of it all. If you see what I mean?

Well, the thing is, I don't buy into that as truth. I'm passionately nihilist, so fatalism is anathema to me. Folk *imagine* nihilism to be all about the futility of it all: "Black! Black! The void of meaning! The horror of godless reality!" But fuck that shit. A pointless cosmos utterly devoid of meaning is not a source of horror to me; in fact, projecting a vast cold monstrous hostility onto that, as per Lovecraft and (as I understand) Ligotti, is projecting *an essential meaning*. If you gaze into the abyss and see the bogeyman of your doom, that's not nihilism; it's fricking Christianity. Cthulhu or Catholic Hell—I find the spectres born of fear of the unknown great material, but philosophically... my worldview doesn't really lend itself to horror in its most archetypal form.

So yeah, my writing tends to argue with the very idea of the monstrous. Meaninglessness equals absurdity to me, not dread. Most notions of (cosy, stable) Order are best smashed, far as I'm concerned: Divine Order, Natural Order, Social Order, these are the bullshit establishment systems in which I, as a man who fucks men, *am* the unknown, the Other. I *am* the conservative's bogeyman. The bestial appetites of the werewolf, the uncanny threats to those who stray off the path through the Dark Forest—where horror is painting bogeymen beyond the limits, what side of those limits am I gonna be on as a sworn son of Sodom?

Where I come to the tropes of the horror genre in my fiction then, it's as one who identifies with the Big Bad Wolf. If I tackle the ultimate horror worldscape, the maximally hostile setting of Hell itself where everything is out to get you, it becomes a prison break story with Lucifer as one of the heroes. If I have unstoppable murderous Victorian urchins that another author might treat as creepy monsters destroying some hapless control freak, mine are the heroes. That's maybe par for the course within a particular vein of horror, but I suspect many would view my approach more as dark fantasy.

CK: Are there any horror writers you admire in particular?

HD: Bradbury, I guess? His Halloween aesthetic pushed my buttons big time as a kid. I love Danielewski's HOUSE OF LEAVES because it pushes the haunted house to a more cosmic dread. It's mythic, the unfathomable vastness of the house's labyrinthine innards conjured in grim grey clay like the Sumerian netherworld's "house of dust and ashes." But it pushes the desolation of that all the way, to my mind, so it becomes less about dread and more about grief. That's where horror interests me most, where it's about articulating the bleak hollowness of loss. I've got Peter Straub's GHOST STORY on the To Read pile because it looks interesting in a similar way. The writers I click most with tend to be borderline though.

CK: How about Burroughs or Kafka?

HD: I dunno if you'd count Burroughs or Kafka. There's the gruesome and the grotesque in one, the uncanny in the other.

Actually, maybe the thing is partly just that I find written horror less effective than cinema. I have no problem at all clicking into the sort of ineffable dread that drives a movie like *The Long Weekend*. I'm not fussed by gore-and-shock horror, but I do like the sort of thing that gets under the skin. I loved *The Last Broadcast*. I don't see how anyone could *not* see *The Shining* as classic cinema, period. But I find it harder to fully immerse in a novel or short story, so maybe I just get all cerebral about the bogeyman and doom aspects when I'm not sucked into the dread.

CK: We both grew up in deepest, darkest Ayrshire (Scotland). You'll know yourself that life isn't always easy for an insular science fiction fan in this part of the world. You've since moved on to the bustling metropolis of Glasgow and found a strong following of devout fans, as well as a circle of renowned local writers. How did you find Ayrshire as an environment growing up? Has the experience influenced you at all? Were you obsessed with death as an adolescent?

HD: Oh, I was looking for a deal with Death back then. That's what "The Boy Who Loved Death," title story of the second collection, is all about. I was one fucked-up kid back in the day, a social pariah and a closeted queer kid in the era of HIV and Section 28. Throw in the spectre of nuclear Armageddon and I saw zero future. Fuck, with school life a ceaseless grind of bullying jibes to the point where just walking past a group of kids and hearing a laugh caused a kneejerk wince—the very sound of joy associated with abject humiliation—I considered myself *dead already*.

CK: So…quite depressed then?

HD: Depression? No, I was fucking *delusional*. I wrote insane screeds in hypomanic episodes where my adolescent angst and wrath hit mythic levels of grandiosity—identifying with Jesus and Lucifer simultaneously. If you'd put a gun in my hand, I would have gone Columbine, and that's no hyperbole. I had detailed plans. Where Charles Starkweather, after his killing spree said, 'I was better than them: I killed the quick; they killed me slow," that's where I was at in my mid-teens.

I genuinely think there's a sort of ego annihilation that can happen if someone gets ground down far enough, a pathological break in which you just hit a critical mass of misery and it all collapses under its own weight, like a star collapsing into a black hole. The only way you can describe it from the inside is in terms of death: soul death; death of the ego. If we're talking "obsessed with death" then, we're not talking ghoulish or morbid interests. We're talking about a walking skinsuit that used to be a human being. We're talking about an ego imploding, collapsing into oblivion, and what Jung called the Shadow—at least that's my theory—stepping in to take over control of the meat puppet. The kid I was back then... all he wanted was a weapon with which he could kill as many people as possible, to offer those souls in tribute to Death himself, to be Death's anointed messenger.

That's where "The Boy Who Loved Death" is coming from, and as you can probably guess it's one of the few stories I've done I'd class as straight-up horror. That bugfuck mental period might also play no small part in my reaction against fatalism—partly because I had to slough that pathology to become a fricking human being again, but partly also because that monstrous homicidal mentality was, in its own strange way, kinda redemptive and positive. I turned despair into wrath. In abandoning hope, it abandoned fear. Where it resolved into an implacable "Fuck this shit" stance to all the bullshit and bollocks, that set the fire of defiance I needed—the exact contrarian *ardour* that makes nihilism distinct from fatalism.

In that soul destruction, when you've sworn yourself to Death, when life is meaningless, with anything you might do, the obvious question is: why bother? But if you cleave to the cold calculus of that logic, if you commit to it fully, the question becomes: why the fuck not? If nothing matters, motherfucker, it doesn't matter that nothing matters. That's the nihilism I came out of my small town Ayrshire shithole with. That's proper *rigour* in your nihilism, as I see it—to shrug off the fatalist cop-out as just another bullshit metanarrative, another absurd fancy occluding the absurd truth. In so far as I would likely have just topped myself if I hadn't broken so completely, I reckon death may be the best thing that ever happened to me.

CK: Can you tell us a bit about 'Stories for Chip', an anthology dedicated to SF grandmaster, scholar and all-round gentleman Samuel Delany? I know you've met Chip in person. That must have been a surreal experience!

HD: The anthology was put together by Nisi Shawl and Bill Campbell in celebration of Delany being made a Grandmaster—and not before time. The man is just all-round amazing: a seminal writer in the field and beyond it, with DHALGREN a 20th century classic on the level of CATCH-22, in my opinion, and with non-SF like HOGG and THE MAD MAN hugely important too. Coming out of the pornotropic excesses of those non-SF works, his latest, THROUGH THE VALLEY OF THE NEST OF SPIDERS is the first truly great novel of the 21st century, I'd argue, and I know others have said the same. As a scholar, he's equally important, equally genius-level. And to top it off, he's just the sweetest fricking human being you'll ever meet—one of those people who just radiates warmth, humble in his humbling erudition, gracious and witty and down-to-earth.

So yeah, I was blown away when I read NOVA as a teenager, one of his early, more accessible Space Operas. DHALGREN cracked my head wide open with its experimentalism. The gay porn he ventured into with EQUINOX aka THE TIDES OF LUST also... made an impression, let's say. And as my tastes and ambitions matured he was putting out his NEVERYON series—an insanely literary take on the Swords & Sorcery genre informed by semiotics and uncompromising in its weaving of theory through the narrative. Frankly, I don't think there's any writer I hold in such high esteem. I have to admit then, I don't really remember much about meeting him because I was too busy being an overawed fanboy for anything to actually register and stick in my mind beyond "OMG! SQUEE!" I was over in the US for WisCon 30 and my editor, Jim Minz, asked if there was anybody I really wanted to meet. Delany was a guest so Jim, bless him, got us together for dinner. I couldn't for the life of me tell you what we talked about. All I really remember is how much of a total gent he was, chatting away, with me barely capable of putting a coherent thought together.

Needless to say then, when Nisi and Bill opened the tribute anthology for submissions I was right in there. Some of my most recent work is hugely influenced by him and by Guy Davenport, who I only know of via Delany, with one collage novella in particular, "Susurrus on Mars," being pretty openly indebted, dropping explicit references in the text and suchlike. I submitted one of the component stories from that, and to say I was chuffed to get it accepted is a ridiculous understatement. The table of contents is pretty much awe-inspiring, the calibre of writers they've got doffing their caps to him (and rightly so.)

CK: Cheers Hal, till our next pint together in deepest darkest Ayrshire, *Auf Wiedersehen*!

HD: Till then!

Coffee—Bootlegging—Labyrinths

By Aaron J. French

Coffee makes us severe, and grave, and philosophical.
—Jonathan Swift, 1722

Coffee is an important part of every person's diet, but particularly the artist's; also the business man's, the accountant's, the real estate agent's, the policeman's, even the college student's. As a writer, coffee is a main ingredient toward the Craft, that process by which the composition manifests. For the painter, coffee moves the brushes; for the sculptor, the chisel. There's a circular, ring-around-the-rosy that occurs with these three, of which only the artist "type" is cognizant. This is due to the artistic temperament, which is more inspired, more refined, the sense organs being less crude. For some, caffeine is switched for alcohol; sometimes, worse. This meanders into the domain of the musically inclined, to *that* sort of artist, where all too often the throbbing vein becomes the only source for the next album.

So why coffee? Why cafés? Why do these sordid types (meaning myself) stumble into one café or another, groping for inspiration? The answer is *mystic*. It's a pain to make art: I used to have a friend, a painter friend, who told me creating his paintings took him through a labyrinth of tortures from his youth. His prints were amazing. The first labyrinth, he told me once, was forged by the legendary artificer Daedalus for King Minos of Crete at Knossos. Its function was to house the Minotaur, a mythical creature that was half man and half bull. Creating art, he also said, was like facing the Minotaur: staring it in the face while it bashed you in the head with a double-axe. My friend finally stopped creating altogether and went to the hospital for good with a chronic illness. These days, he runs a bootlegging knockoff, selling his pain medication to teenage hooligans.

But coffee probably would have solved his problems, I think. Unfortunately there was no talking to him, especially when he was drunk, which was mostly. I spent a lot of those years back in my early twenties drinking with him, trying to write and create fiction drunk, hanging over the edge of a desk, in solitude, in quiet, or with him, crouched in his shabby little apartment. Later I switched to coffee, and the writing just sort of took off, while the drinking dissipated. Sometimes I wish I could've helped him make that switch, to get him out the labyrinth as it were, but he was too content on pain. Now his bootlegging business sustains him.

Cafés are a sort of labyrinth. In them, through them, lost among isles of stranded people. One must wind one's way among them. The artist—particularly the writer—must find his table, get his input jack to plug in, find the counter and order the grail cup, the Venti, then again to vanish, to disappear and work—then, much later of course, to find his way back out into the world. This is because the writer must spend long hours at his or her craft, shut-up in the dizzying café, writing and writing and revising. The task, one might say, is never ending. Thus, coffee fuels the seeming futility.

Incidentally, coffee was once illegal. England's King Charles II, worried that coffeehouses had become "the great resort of idle and disaffected persons," issued the Proclamation for the Suppression of Coffee Houses in 1675, which ordered the closure of all cafés in Britain.

In 1674 *The Women's Petition Against Coffee* complained of "the Excessive use of that Newfangled, Abominable, Heathenish Liquor called Coffee, which ... has so Eunucht our Husbands, and Crippled our more kind gallants.... They come from it with nothing moist but their snotty Noses, nothing stiffe but their Joints, nor standing but their Ears."

To which the men defended: "[coffee] makes the erection more Vigorous, the Ejaculation more full, adds a spiritualescency to the Sperme."

There is even a rumor that in the States coffee had to be bootlegged early on in its history of distribution. Without the proper medical knowledge, these wives' tales and hearsay flourished. The wives were convinced coffee made their husbands impotent. Thus, they were known to riot and storm operating cafés during the 1700s, forcing them to close down or continue in secret—which most cafés did during that time. These wives formed a society intent on bringing an end to the use of coffee in the States. They attacked underground cafés and hidden points along known bootlegging coffee routes, kidnapped the men, sewed them up in empty burlap Ethiopian coffee sacks, and at their worst, tossed these fattened sacks into the sea.

But were these drowning men artists? Most likely. Because, as Leonard Cohen sang:

And when he knew for certain
Only drowning men could see him
He said "All men will be sailors then
Until the sea shall free them"

If we follow along my friend's line of reasoning, they certainly were, since the cost of creating art is pain, suffering, and death. Although, that phenomenon has now become attached to alcohol and drugs, coffee demoted to a harmless and acceptable substance. Still, better to live and still create, then to *have* created, and then die… No?

Thus art remains a mystery, a labyrinth, something twisty with scary beasts lurking along its paths. My old friend, living the life of the artist and creating something truly great, then passing into obscurity, never to create again. Lost in the labyrinth forever—himself becoming the Minotaur, perhaps. Guarding it against future would-be creatives… making sure they do not enter too easily, without proper pain and suffering.

Luckily, these days it is easy to cheat the system. We workers have been vouchsafed a remedy to the creative grind. We worship a new goddess, and her color is satin-brown, and her name is Coffee Café, and within her temple the Minotaur is neutered, and we are free to move about as we please, to create according to our own fancies, as we see fit. Coffee is actually the way *out* of the Labyrinth!

But here we have to wonder, is there some consequence from this change of cult? Have the old ways been subverted toward something better, or rather something less pure? How long until we as artists know the answer? In olden times, art and mythmaking was not some idle and dawdling pastime, but the forger and impetus of whole nations, of worldviews. How different, how much more *cosmic* is this, than the box-office hit down at the local movie theater, or the current NY Times bestseller?

Can artists ever know the right path to walk?

"I'll have a Venti, please."

HYPNAGOGIA
BY
MAX
BOOTH III

Once the initial "holy shit, I'm actually dead" feeling finally passes, the afterlife is actually quite boring.

Imagine sitting around all day with nothing to do. The TV's out, the iPod refuses to obey, all sound from the outside world is completely nonexistent. In fact, the only fucking sound is coming from a broken fan, and it drives you crazy. Now imagine rather than just a single day, it's forever. The option to walk out the door is gone. The option to talk to anyone—fucking *anyone*—is erased forever. This is what being dead is like.

Mundane.

There aren't many things one can do in this sort of situation. You can sit, you can stand, you can lie down. You can talk to yourself until you go mad.

It's just you and yourself.

You and yourself and the bricks.

Like most things, being dead isn't like the movies. The worst part about it isn't a bunch of memories of your previous life tearing you apart day after day. The worst part is that there *aren't* any memories. Being dead isn't about remembering who you used to be, it's the *forgetfulness*. The total lack of a past. That, right there, is *the* thing about being dead—it's that you don't remember what it's like to be alive.

There are bits and pieces that come in here and there, sort of like waking up from a dream, and there's those little segments fading in and out. Only, when you're dead, there is no waking up. Your life *becomes* the dream, and the dream becomes you.

The truth is, I'm dead. Dead as in I'm no longer fucking alive. Who knows how long. Time is a fairy tale created by those with a heartbeat.

I'm dead and trapped in the most tedious place in both existence and nonexistence: my apartment. My heaven. My hell. My purgatory. My...whatever you want to call it. It's my apartment. My home. My glorious goddamn afterlife.

I remember—yes, this I remember clearly—opening my eyes and finding myself in bed. The ceiling fan was looking down at me, spinning crookedly, as if it'd been knocked slightly off base. I stayed there for a moment, listening to its self-destructive noises, then stood up, head foggy. Nothing seemed right, and the only thing I knew for sure was that I didn't want to be here.

I swung the front door open and expected an explosion of sunlight, so bright that I'd have to squint my eyes. But that wasn't what happened. Of course it wasn't.

I opened the door and all I saw were bricks. Little red bricks composing a wall, shielding me from the outside world. When I reached to touch them, all I felt was a deep, violent coldness.

Outside the apartment window, there were more bricks.

And it didn't matter how hard I pushed—they weren't going anywhere.

***

I suspected someone was fucking with me. Putting up all these bricks to trap me in my apartment for a laugh. Or maybe I had an enemy, and this was their way of getting revenge. But when I attempted to figure out who could have been capable of such mischief, I couldn't recall a single human being that I actually knew. Not one person. I couldn't even remember what my parents' faces looked like, or if they were alive...

Alive.

The word got stuck in my throat, like a foul piece of fruit, hanging there in freeze-frame, choking the life out of me.

The life...

The room shook in full earthquake-mode as I stumbled back across the apartment, toward the door which was still wide open. My vision enhanced in the brilliance of it all—it was almost as if the bricks were glowing now, like I'd unlocked a special achievement of knowledge.

It was glowing because it was laughing, and it was

laughing because it knew what I was thinking. The laugh told me I was right, what I was thinking was one hundred percent correct.

I was dead.

I touched the glowing bricks, only to be met with an abrupt explosion of torturous, searing white light. It penetrated my drying eyes and filled my mouth like an empty ocean, and when the light finally vanished, I was back in bed, under the crooked fan.

What killed me, I couldn't tell you. Heart attack in my sleep, drowning in the tub, drug overdose? Maybe I tripped and broke my neck, maybe I was murdered—who knew? The only real hypothesis I could feel safe in making was the fact that however I did die, it had taken place in this apartment. Why else would I be trapped here? This place *meant* something. This was where I died.

***

The bricks were my obsession. Standing in front of my door, for hours, for days—years?—just staring, my eyes never tiring but instead growing with intensity. I caressed every centimeter of that brick wall over and over again, with both sight and touch. It wasn't just a wall to me.

It was the doorway between purgatory and the afterlife, and I was determined to break through it.

At first I tried pushing against it. Both hands flat against the surface, pushing with all my strength, hoping the irrational hope that the gods of death had failed to properly paste the structure together. When that didn't work, I got a little crazy with it. Fists balled up, I punched and punched, slamming my knuckles into the bricks like they were the devil. But that wasn't doing anything. I needed to make an *impact*.

I ran into the kitchen which connected from the studio apartment's main room and attempted to grab the bar stool by the table, but discovered it to be far too heavy to lift. Gravity had consumed it whole, and I was discarded as an outcast.

Screaming, I turned back around and charged the bricks headfirst, expecting pain and receiving none at all. Instead, I was once again greeted with the light.

And again, I was in bed. Under the fan, the fan which was the only goddamn thing that made any noise. Making noise like it was broken, like it had been knocked off center, like it understood everything I didn't.

Like it was God, or the Devil, or some damn thing, just laughing down at me.

***

So no, there's not much to do when you're dead. There's a whole lot of nothing, followed by even more nothing.

How could I be expected to know how I died, if I didn't even know how I had lived?

I investigated every square inch of my apartment, as if suddenly everything would make sense. It's funny, the things you discover after looking at something long enough.

For instance, despite all paths leading outside being swallowed by a black abyss, my apartment always remained completely lit up, powered by some omniscient light from a hidden source. And no, none of the light bulbs were turned on.

And in the wall, next to the bed, there was a small round hole. I tried to look in it, but only saw darkness. When I thought about that hole long enough, I would begin to feel unwell, and suddenly find myself back in bed. It was best to avoid thinking about the hole.

Another thing: when I stood in front of the bathroom mirror, I could not see my reflection. This led me to discover that it wasn't just the mirror—when I looked down to examine my own body, there was nothing there but air. The legs I walked upon and the hands I touched with did not actually exist. Yet in my mind, I still imagined they did. Like a hallucination. A phantom body.

God, just take me already. Anyone, just fucking take me.

***

And then someone did come. Only it wasn't God, nor the Devil, but a man and a woman. A couple. Isolation soothed by a relationship. Not that they could see me, of course. Not that they even knew I existed. Unlike myself, they were *alive.*

Not that I could see them either, though. Not in the traditional sense, at least.

The only moments their presence was ever prominent occurred during waves of immense emotion.

My first encounter with the apartment's new tenants, I was sitting there on the couch staring at the opened door, at the wall of little red bricks. Suddenly, for the first time in I couldn't even begin to guess how long, I heard a noise that did not belong to that goddamn fan.

It was the noise of moaning. Loud, animalistic moaning. At first I was convinced the reaper had finally come to collect. I scrambled off the couch and hurried toward the source: on the bed, below the fan, there was a growing mass hovering above the sheets, almost like a small cloud.

The noise persisted, rose in volume, in strength. The moan—that's what it was, a moan, a loud moan of pure bliss—rocked my universe. Mesmerized, I reached out with a hand I no longer possessed and touched the orb.

It exploded. Taking the orb's place were the new tenants of my apartment: a woman, long hair swinging wildly, nude and riding an equally naked man beneath her. When I looked at the man, I noticed no distinctive features whatsoever. He looked just like that—a man.

But the woman, however, was so beautiful she made me want to cry.

The hair, sandy like a beach you wanted to fall asleep on, eyes so blue it wasn't natural, a set of lips full of passion, opening slightly as the moan continued to escape her lips, her bare shoulders, all of her skin, pale and innocent like the shade of a full moon reflected 'cross a lake, and the way her back curved as she arched forward…

Then they disappeared, only to quickly return, and then vanish, and so forth. Like a dying light bulb, they were flickering in and out of existence.

The louder the moan, the steadier they remained, but when the inevitable climax was at last reached, they vanished and stayed gone, leaving me—once again—alone.

***

Here, in this afterlife, I had once again found life. And oh, was it good.

She was good.

After an eternity of sitting in this apartment alone, I had finally found a companion.

I tried to ignore the fact that this companion had no

idea I even existed.

Sometimes I wondered.

There was this moment when, after having gone some time without seeing her, that I sort of lost my mind. I don't know what I was thinking, just the fact that she was missing was enough to drive me mad.

Before this, she would make frequent appearances—usually during sex, but not always. Sometimes I would find her alone, crying for unknown reasons, yet all the while I knew that if I were given just one chance to be there in my real physical form, I would be able to make everything better. Sometimes, when sitting on the couch lost in my own little familiar daze, she would suddenly pop up next to me, staring at the television across from us, and I knew, whatever she was watching—the screen was blank from my perspective—it was invoking one hell of a reaction out of her. Whether it was horror, sadness, or happiness, I was right there beside her, silently sharing the moment.

Another time she cried out from the kitchen. She stood in front of the stove, holding her hand against her mouth, sucking on it. Little wet tears formed around her eyes and dripped down her cheeks.

A voice off in the distance—the man—yelled, "What the hell did you do?"

"I burnt my hand."

"How did you manage to pull that one off?"

"I was making your steak and—"

"Oh, yeah, what's going on? Is it done yet or what?"

Pause.

"Yes."

I knew then I hated that man.

There had always been a deep envy toward him. He could be with her while I could be nothing more than a solitary fan in a stadium the size of infinity. He did not deserve her. *I* deserved her. If I were there—*really* there—I would have immediately rushed to her aid. I would have kissed her hand and rubbed her and done everything in my power to make the pain vanish.

Why couldn't he had been the dead one, and I the other?

The sex changed, too. The initial passion when they first moved in had expired. Gone was the long, extended moans. Gone was her back arching in lust, her lips grinning at the ceiling—replaced now with a wishing to be somewhere else. All because of him. He, who looked like nothing at all, yet at the same time represented everything I hated.

And she, who gave me a reason to stop feeding my energy into little red bricks, and into herself.

She had become my new bricks.

And now she's missing.

I don't know what to do with myself. I sit on the bed and wait for sex, I stand in the kitchen and wait for pain. I stay by the sofa and wait for an emotion—any emotion whatsoever—and receive naught. So I give up and open the front door again and stare at the bricks until I think I can't stare any longer, and then I stare some more.

Those fucking bricks…

Trapping me.

Imprisoning me.

Killing me.

Except I am already dead.

"Where is she?" I ask the wall, awaiting an answer.

Surprisingly, it responds in the form of a soft, almost undetectable sob coming from the bathroom.

My darling.

She's in front of the sink, tears streaming.

On the sink I notice an object almost glowing among the rest of the mess, as if it is specifically trying to grab my attention. A short white stick, with a small screen at the center of it. In the screen, a black cross flashes.

It takes me a while for my stupid, dead-mind to identify it.

I step forward so I'm next to her, and look ahead into the mirror, only to gasp upon noticing my own reflection in the glass. I had looked before—many, many times—and never once had I shown a reflection.

Yet, here I am, next to my beloved. What I look like is unimportant—just the fact that I look like *anything* is enough of a surprise.

I watch in the mirror as the woman's eyes widen, her lips stretching as she releases a scream.

My reflection, can she see it? *She can see me.*

"It's okay," I whisper, but it is too late. She's running out of the bathroom, out of the apartment, out of my life. When I look back at the mirror, my reflection is long gone, and so is hers.

The pregnancy test is still on the sink.

***

I find her by the bed. The sound of her tears are like thunder in a storm. But I can't see her, only hear her sadness.

I wait in the apartment and listen, hating the fact that I am not able to cure her sorrow.

The crying ceases. The sound is replaced with the overhead fan going nuts. It shakes, as if about to finally break from the ceiling.

The woman appears in her physical form. She's wearing an old, dirty blue dress that looks oddly familiar. Her shoes have been kicked off. She isn't standing up, and she isn't sitting or lying down, either.

She's hanging.

Her body's limp.

No…

Oh…

Please…

No.

Her body does not disappear or flicker like it had in the past. Instead it remains, hanging from the broken ceiling fan. Like me, her life-force has been drained.

My eyes keep returning to her stomach. There is a baby in there. A baby whose life-force has also been drained.

Two more lives lost.

For what?

The question is pointless. I know who's to blame.

The Man. The one who lives with her, who's been absent quite some time.

The source of all her pain.

"No!" screams a voice from behind me. *"No, oh God, oh*

God, oh God, please no."

The Man has returned.

I feel him standing next to me, hear him crying just as I had heard the woman crying on so many nights. It should be him up there, hanging from the fan, not her. She deserved the world.

"You did this," I whisper, though he can't hear me. And even if I was alive, he wouldn't have paid any attention to it. He's crying too hard, cursing too loudly. It's the sound of a man realizing what he's done wrong, realizing that he's ruined everything.

"I'm sorry, oh God I'm so sorry, please baby, no, this is all my fault, please, God, please no."

It is the sound of epiphany.

And then, it is the sound of a gunshot.

A section of the wall explodes—exactly where I'd noticed that hole when previously investigating the apartment—then a body falls on top of the bed. It is the Man. He is holding a silver gun in his hand, a thin stream of smoke floating from the barrel.

I look at his pathetic face. Blood and tiny fragments of brains cover his skin. Yet I am able to recognize the face, all the same.

I know this face: I had seen it not too long ago.

Back when the woman had been crying in the bathroom, the pregnancy test on the sink—she had seen my reflection in the mirror.

It is the same reflection I'm seeing now.

Jesus. No.

This isn't right.

It can't be.

A hand grabs my shoulder and I turn around. Standing in front of me is the woman, despite the fact that she is also hanging from the ceiling fan. This version of her is different. Now, she's more…*real.*

"You," she whispers, eyes digging into my soul. "You did this to me."

I begin crying. "No, I didn't. I love you. I would never do this."

"I gave you all of my heart, and you killed me for it. Me and our baby."

"No!" I knock her hand off my shoulder and run for the front door, swinging it open.

Little red bricks.

She pulls me so I'm facing her again. Her strength is unmatchable. "Those bricks, those walls…you built them all on your own. And you kept on building until it caved in and destroyed us all. Are you happy? Are you *satisfied?* Do you feel like a man now?"

"But, I…I love you."

She nods sadly. "And I loved you."

"I'm sorry."

She smiles. It is beautiful.

"So am I," she says, and pushes me into the wall of bricks. There is a bright violent flash, then all I see is black.

The bricks hold me no more.

I am free.

DAUGHTERS UNTO DEVILS

AMY LUKAVICS

Daughters Unto Devils
by Amy Lukavics
amylukavics.com

SLASHER GIRLS & MONSTER BOYS

Stories selected by APRIL GENEVIEVE TUCHOLKE

With Stories by

STEFAN BACHMANN
KENDARE BLAKE
JAY KRISTOFF
JONATHAN MABERRY
CARRIE RYAN
NOVA REN SUMA
APRIL GENEVIEVE TUCHOLKE
LEIGH BARDUGO
A.G. HOWARD
MARIE LU
DANIELLE PAIGE
MEGAN SHEPHERD
McCormick TEMPLEMAN
CAT WINTERS

Slasher Girls & Monster Boys
Stories selected by April Genevieve Tucholke
slashergirlsandmonsterboys.com

Sanctum
by Sarah Fine
sarahfinebooks.com

CHECK OUT THE HOTTEST TITLES IN YA HORROR!

What the Hell Ever Happened to...

Thom Metzger

Photo courtesy of Thom Metzger

By Robert Morrish

The author profiled in this installment of "What the Hell Ever Happened To…?" is seemingly a perfect choice for this issue's theme of bizarro fiction. Thom Metzger debuted with the 1989 novel *Big Gurl*, which has been described as, "strange," "unsettling," and "an awe-inspiring work of utter depravity," and followed up with the equally audacious *Shock Totem*. Although he's since left the horror field, he's gone on to write books about the electric chair, heroin, and Mormonism, to mention a few.

Metzger lives with his wife in western NY, where he grew up and has always resided. After trying his hand at everything from standup comedy to construction to liquor store clerk, he's been teaching now for more than two decades, currently at the State University of New York at Geneseo (his Alma Mater) and the State University of New York at Brockport.

Metzger is also a musician who has sung and played tenor sax, ontic trombone, trumpet, guitar, and percussion in a number of bands, including Health and Beauty, Nemo's Omen, and The Badenovs.

Robert Morrish: Your first three books were published by Penguin. At that early point in your career, did you have an agent to help you get "in the door" with Penguin, or did you manage to attract their interest without representation?

Thom Metzger: I did have an agent. Rick Scott and I made a lot of queries with *Big Gurl* and one person nibbled, and he ended up representing the book. That was the second book that [the agent] had sold, and the first book that we had sold. We were all new to the business.

RM: Those first three books—especially the first two, *Big Gurl* and *Shock Totem*—may have been a bit gonzo, but they were also pretty clearly horror novels. Although most or all of your subsequent books have dark elements, it seems like you moved away from horror somewhat. Do you think that's a fair assessment and, if so, what led you to do so?

TM: I think that that's true. Mostly, it was market forces. The first three books were at the tail end of that horror boom, and when that boom busted, I moved elsewhere.

RM: As you mentioned earlier, *Big Gurl* was co-written with Richard Scott. Who exactly is Mr. Scott, and how did that collaboration come about?

TM: I haven't seen him in years, but he and I are both musicians, and we were in a band together. I just mentioned the idea of the book one day, and he said 'hey, do you want to collaborate,' and I said, 'why not?'

RM: Did your association with Penguin end due to the "usual" reasons—that is, sales figures that weren't up to the publisher's expectations, and the general decline of the horror market?

TM: Yes… *Big Gurl* did pretty well, and the other two books did okay… but the 'usual reasons,' as you put it, came into play, and my association with them ended. Although the editor there is currently my agent, so I stayed connected with the same person for, what, thirty years now.

RM: From there, you went on to have three books published by Autonomedia, described by Wikipedia as "one of the main North American publishers of radical theoretical works, especially in the anarchist tradition." How did you become associated with them?

TM: Back in the early '90s, they were doing some anthologies, and… one of the editors there contacted me. He'd read a piece of mine that was in a magazine called *Seditious Delicious, The Magazine of Prison Writing*, and to this day, I don't know how my piece ended up in that magazine, because I've never been in prison! But he read it, and he contacted me and said, 'hey, we're interested.'

I've stayed in touch with [Autonomedia] over the years… their output has diminished as the print market has declined, but I'm still in contact with them, and they did another short book of mine several years ago, *The Ziggurat Guide to Western New York.*

RM: One of your Autonomedia titles, *Blood and Volts: Edison, Tesla and the Electric Chair*, sounds like a fascinating work… what was the genesis of that book?

TM: I was doing research for *Shock Totem,* specifically on Edison and Tesla, and I wanted to find a book about the electric chair, and I discovered that there *wasn't* a book about the electric chair. Given that it was a Western New York state story, I got on it. I originally was going to do a short work on it, but it kept expanding, until it became book-length. And I've been on the History Channel and the BBC did a documentary about the electric chair, so the book's reach has been fairly far, which surprised me. There have since been other books written about the electric chair, but that was the first one.

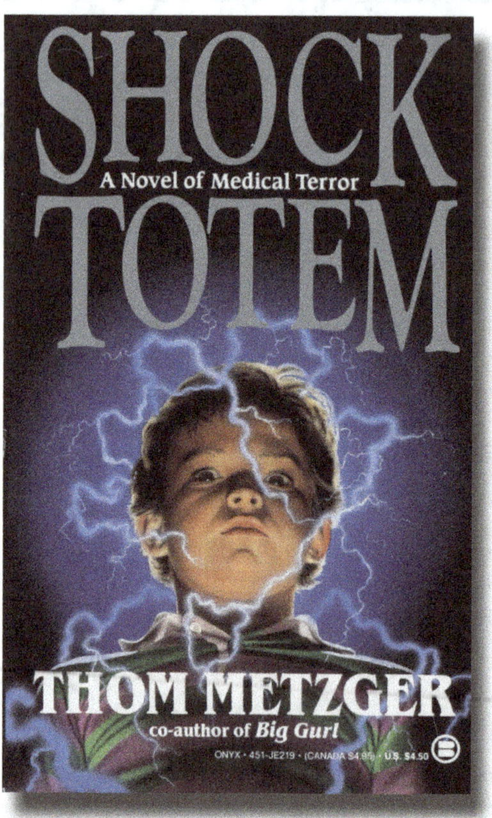

RM: You mentioned earlier the local guidebook that you did for Autonomedia, *Select Strange and Sacred Sites: the Ziggurat Guide to Western N.Y.* That book also sounds very intriguing, based on its description as "a wild ride through [Metzger's] numinous home territory. From the Mormon ground zero holy hill to a creepy Victorian psychic village, from the Iroquois Torture Tree to the perfectly-American electric chair, from churches seared by evangelical passion to the austere emptiness of Chimney Bluffs, the Burnt-Over District is rich with spiritual power." That seems like a book that would have staying power in terms of local interest—is it still in print?

TM: To my knowledge, it's still in print. It's a short work, forty or fifty pages. I've lived in this area my whole life, and I've gradually dug deeper and deeper into the area's weirdness. At one point, it was the epicenter of religious weirdness in the whole country. Mormonism and spiritualism were born here, and a few other religious phenomena were born here. It was fertile ground in the early 19th century… things have calmed down a lot since then, although there are still traces of weirdness.

RM: Moving on… What led you to trying your hand in the young-adult market?

TM: Another horror writer, who was a friendly acquaintance, Kathe Koja, was corresponding with me, and she told me that she had published her first YA book. I asked her who her agent was, and it turned out to be the guy who'd been the editor at Penguin who had bought *Big Gurl* a few years earlier. So, I thought if Kathe Koja can do it, her stuff is really weird, so… why not me? And, in those days, YA was a wide-open market. Since then, it's become much more closed—fantasy very heavily influenced by sparkle-glamour vampires, and teenagers killing each other. I did four books for Houghton Mifflin, and they did pretty okay. I enjoyed the work, but as I said, the field became narrower and narrower, so I'm not there anymore.

RM: Your book, *Hydrogen Sleep and Speed*, has one of my all-time favorite descriptions: "This riveting narrative poem—which might be called a mini-epic—mines little-known aspects of World War II history into a mélange of African invasions, angry Egyptian gods, rampant Mormon warriors, and the lord of sleepwalkers, Dr. Caligari. The book is decorated with a collage of The Egyptian Book of the Dead, Mormon mythology, and Nazi-era iconography." If it's even possible to explain how the ideas for this book percolated, I'd love to hear about it…

TM: Yeah… it really is a book about zeppelins, hence the hydrogen, and speed as an amphetamine. That started off as one short poem that expanded. It was published as a book of about 100 poems, and in effect, it's about a 500-page science fiction novel boiled down to about 100 pages of poetry. And again, it's a piece of Western New York history, combined with fantasy. A lot of extrapolation on the strange Mormon phenomenon, but also my obsession with the North African campaign in World War II—Erwin Rommel and the Battle of El Alamein. So, it's an odd combination, but it started off as one short poem.

RM: Your most recent book, *Undercover Mormon: A Spy in the House of the Gods,* likewise sounds very interesting ("[Mormonism] all started in the boondocks of western New York State, which was, once upon a very strange time, the hottest hotbed of wild religion in the world.") I know that you touched upon Mormonism in your *Ziggurat Guide*, so… was this book a long time in the making?

TM: It was. I'd been doing research for a long time. Mormonism was born about 20 or 30 miles from where I sit. Most people associate Mormonism with the West, but this, here, is the Holy Land. This place has a strange, mystic, religious aura, at least if one looks through the right lens. And I gradually found it more and more intriguing.

To tell you the truth, one day, I just shaved my beard, and put on a white shirt and a tie, and got in the car and drove to a Mormon church, and told them that I had a different name. I went under a pseudonym and I sang with the choir, I spoke from the pulpit, I penetrated pretty far. At that time, Mitt Romney was running for President, so there was more national interest [in Mormonism], but it was mostly just personal fascination that led me down that path.

RM: I understand that when the founders of the small press Shock Totem Publications chose their company name, based on your novel of the same name, they reached out to you to get your blessing. It's not every day that someone wants to name a press after one of your books… I realize there isn't really a question here, I'm just curious about any thoughts you might have on this…

TM: They asked me and I said, "thank you, sure." Apparently one of the folks there had read *Shock Totem* way back when and really liked the title. And you can't copyright a title, so I figured there's no reason to give them a hard time—either way, they could've used it, so why not play nice? It's nice, it's a little bit of a tribute. I haven't had any contact with them in a while.

RM: According to the bibliography that I've seen, you've published fewer short stories than you have books. Do you write so little short fiction due primarily to the market realities of few outlets and low pay, or do you simply prefer to have a much higher word count with which to spread your wings?

TM: Mostly it's the latter, mostly I prefer to work on a bigger palette. But as you're well aware, the market for short fiction is terrible. I'm also not that fond of a lot of short fiction.

RM: Do you have much unsold "trunk" work?

TM: Yes, I'm 12 for 25, meaning I've had 12 books published and 13 that were not. Some of those [unpublished books] were not very good, so there's a good reason why they weren't published, but there are two or three good YA novels and one or two other good novels that I'd like to see published. My agent is currently shopping around a "fictional biography"… of a real person who was a Roman Catholic priest and also an abortionist, who lived fairly close to me. So I wrote this novel/biography on him, and I just finished that a few months ago.

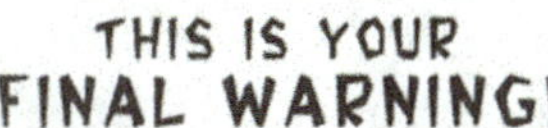

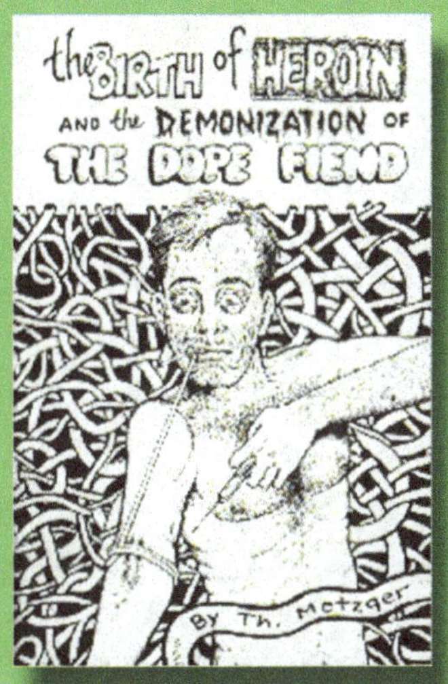

SIDEBAR

Books by Thom Metzger

Big Gurl (Penguin, 1989)
Shock Totem (Penguin, 1990)
Drowning in Fire (Penguin, 1992)
This is Your Final Warning (Autonomedia, 1992)
Blood and Volts: Edison, Tesla and the Electric Chair (Autonomedia, 1996)
The Birth of Heroin and the Demonization of the Dope Fiend (Breakout Books, 1998)
Select Strange and Sacred Sites: the Ziggurat Guide to Western N.Y. (Exit 18 Books, 2002)
Stonecutter (writing as "Leander Watts"; Houghton Mifflin, 2002)
Wild Ride to Heaven (writing as "Leander Watts"; Houghton Mifflin, 2003)
Ten Thousand Charms (writing as "Leander Watts"; Houghton Mifflin, 2005)
Beautiful City of the Dead (writing as "Leander Watts"; Houghton Mifflin, 2006)
Hydrogen Sleep and Speed (Poets' Press, 2012)
Undercover Mormon: a Spy in the House of the Gods (Roadswell Editions, 2014)

Interview with John Palisano

BY AARON J. FRENCH

Aaron J. French: What got you interested in writing horror and how did you find your way to the Horror Writers Association?

John Palisano: I happily point my finger at my father, who is an artist, and who shared his love of science fiction and horror with me at a young age. I was drawn to scary stories and to makeup effects. I carried around issues of FANGORIA and Tom Savini's book *Grande Illusions* with me everywhere. I put out my own fanzine as a pre-teen and wrote stories ever since. Post college, I stumbled upon this bookstore called The Iliad in North Hollywood that was next to a video store I frequented. There I befriended Lisa Morton, who I asked about writing, and who told me about the HWA. I couldn't believe there was a viable, working tribe of folks actively doing it.

AJF: Tell us a bit about your first novel *Nerves* and how that came into being? Did you use a writing group? How long did it take you to complete it?

JP: *Nerves* began as a script. Five pages in I knew there'd be no way I could shoot it without 300 million dollars. I'd been hanging out with Hart D. Fisher and Christa Faust. She'd gotten proofs of a book and it reignited writing fiction for me. It took some time to get my fiction legs back vs screenplays, but I loved it. There are five or six novels before *Nerves* no one has seen, but *Nerves* coalesced in a way the others hadn't. I spent a tremendous amount of time developing its mythology, its world, the locations and rules. I even wrote an entire record of music for the character Minnesota Flatts. It was integral, it was all real and existed. It needed to be drawn from. Some of it was workshopped, a few chapters, but mostly I went to a novel workshop called Pen to Press that Deborah LeBlanc ran. Scott Nicholson and Alexander Sokoloff were my teachers and they showed me how to get it into pro shape. My late and beloved friend Michael Louis Calvillo introduced me to Roy Robbins of Bad Moon Books. He took it on. Unfortunately, halfway through writing the second book in the series, ASHES, Bad Moon pretty much ceased. I'd love to get NERVES out there again and partnered with

ASHES eventually.

AJF: Did you write many short stories before finally getting *Nerves* out? What do you prefer, short stories or novels, and which do you find are more marketable and/ or easier to write?

JP: Tons of short stories. I collected hundreds of rejection slips. This was right before markets would take email submissions. I'm not too sure if I had many published before *Nerves*. I'd had a few. It's hard for me because I do a lot of world building for each story. For some of my short stories I've done as much world building as for the novels. But that's fun, too, because we've all read padded novels. That is never fun. I think the trick is in finding the right length for a story. It's easy for me to write in either length, although with the books there are certainly more chances to market and promote. There's only so much you can do with a short story in that regard.

AJF: You recently landed with Samhain Publishing with your novel *Dust of the Dead*. Tell us about that, what's the story behind it. Is it part of a larger series?

JP: I'm the victim of my own joke. I made a comment at a reading that everyone was writing *The Walking Dead*, but putting it in their own hometown. Someone whispered to me after that no one had done Los Angeles. Of course, I had to be different and the zombies in *Dust of the Dead* are different in that they are sentient and have their minds. It's horrific for them to be brought back and know it. On top of that, people are keeping their relatives in their houses after they return. I also thought about how nasty it'd be in real life. Corpses can be very toxic. I thought about their skin drying in the heat and flaking off, and then that getting in the air and making people sick. I had planned on two more in the series. We will see. I already have a bit put together on the follow up VOICES OF THE DEAD.

AJF: Your next novel coming out in 2016 is *Ghost Heart*, what's the story behind that one?

JP: *Ghost Heart* was the hardest emotional story I have ever put down. Who knows if readers will connect with it? Sure hope so. I had to access a long gone place where falling in love takes over your life and is magical and new…and the inevitable betrayal that follows. I went to some really dark places. Again, it's a traditional monster archetype but flipped. There are vampires, but they are not immortal. They only live in an accelerated and heightened physicality for five years. Then they whither. Their skin lightens and loses color until they're nearly clear. The organs within go pale. Their hair turns crimson then dark. Near the end you can see their pale hearts beating under clear tissue and bone…their ghost hearts. Of course the main fellow falls in love with someone who's close to her time. And they don't have fangs. Instead? Their tongues harden at their ends into sharp pinpoints they use to cut the insides of cheeks. When satiated, the tongues look normal. A fun thing to play with.

AJF: What's on the horizon with you and Samhain and what future projects do you have lined up with them?

JP: My third novel with Samhain is called NIGHT OF 1,000 BEASTS. It's the longest and darkest night of the century. A group of skiers gets separated during a small avalanche on a Colorado mountain. They soon find they are being hunted by a group of beasts who'd purposely selected them. It's a very different story for me, but I feel it's pretty over the top and pretty funny.

AJF: You have your own small press too, right, Western Legends Press? What's happening there?

JP: Western Legends is a specialty press. We put stuff out irregularly and only do stuff we find fits. It's very informal. I share the duties with David T. Griffith on the east coast and Dean M. Drinkel in the UK. Our next is a non-fiction memoir by Lisa Morton about her time in the film industry called *Adventures in the Scream Trade* and will feature cover art from the late James Powell.

AJF: You're also known for your awesome book trailers and some film work. How do you see these two aspects of your creativity informing one another—the film and the fiction?

JP: Everyone has grown up watching tons of moving images. We know that grammar before almost every other. I'm no exception, and so film and TV are massive influences. I studied and worked in script development so I know story structure every which way. Most of the storytelling tools are the same. The biggest correlation is with pacing and dialogue, which I use a lot of from screenwriting in my fiction.

AJF: I know you like music a lot and play music. You even performed live at various writing conventions. How does music influence your fiction?

JP: Often I will compose music for a story or book. It helps me hear the rhythms of the story. When my brain needs a reboot or gets stuck I'll often pick up the guitar and rock out for a while. Helps!

AJF: Since this issue is all about bizarro, what are your thoughts on that?

JP: I love bizarro and am thrilled it's being featured. I think some of the best unhinged creativity is coming out of that field and I find it endlessly inspiring.

AJF: Where can DD readers go to find out more about you?

JP: www.johnpalisano.com. Thanks so much!

Flowers

By John Palisano

The Sol del Mar grows where the sea meets the sun, on the edge of the horizon, on a large rocky island in the Indian Ocean known as Cetos. The flowers are hearty, strong and give off a scent that triggers the same feelings as first falling in love.

Or so it's said.

***

"You're going to be mad at me because I brought home another flower." Ava used her best, most musical speaking tone on me. "A very rare Sol del Mar."

"Where are we going to put it?" I tried to sound supportive.

"There's always room for one more." Her cheeks were rosy and plump. "I just can't turn my back on them."

"They're just flowers. We can't save all of them. Even if you save a hundred, there's thousands right behind them. Maybe more."

"Right. I know. But they'll freeze in the snow. Deer Springs is never warm long enough."

"It's just the natural cycle of things living in Colorado," I said. "It's inevitable."

Our house on Nash Terrace overflowed with plant life. Ava used every available surface. Crowded planters teetered on the edge of the fireplace and on all the tables and shelves we had. They leaked onto the books in back of them, ruining them. She didn't care. Our rugs were covered in ground soot and plant food. Dried puddles of dark mud were so caked into the floor the wood would need to be replaced instead of cleaned.

"You can just go to your room and leave me be." Ava was mad at me for even questioning her obsession. She would not hear me.

"The smell," I said. "It's in there now, too."

She gestured to a can of Lysol on the counter. "Just use that. I bought a box of them."

I shook my head. "That doesn't work any more. Besides, I don't want to breathe in chemicals all the time. That dirt smell is on everything."

"It's a nice smell."

"Customers at work are complaining. Vivian took me aside to talk to me about it yesterday."

"They don't live here."

"It's in my clothes. My hair. It won't come out no matter what I do. We can't live like this."

She sighed. Curled up on her favorite loveseat in the family room, Ava had lost a significant amount of weight. She still looked fabulous. She knew it, and had worn her cream-colored lingerie—my favorite. She must have sensed my angry tone on the phone when we'd talked before I left my gig at Viv's Critters. Ava knew how to defang me. It didn't take much.

"Before you go to your room, why don't you come on over here and say hi."

I knew what that meant. Ava shifted her weight in the chair, accentuating her body. She bit the corner of her lip. Sunlight rimmed her blonde hair. I knew it was all a show, and maybe she didn't really feel that passionate about taking care of me anymore, but I went for it anyway.

***

Vivian shook her head. "Don't you remember what I told you? We went over this. It's unacceptable." She hadn't even bothered to take off her sunglasses. "You cannot leave a G fish in the same tank as another G fish," she said. "You know that."

"I'm sorry." My voice stuttered and I looked around the pet store to see if there were any customers nearby that might overhear her scolding me. "I thought you said you wanted them to be together because they would be lonely. They were in the same tank when you left. I…am… confused." I'd wilted, my chin pointing toward the tile floor.

Vivian had already turned her back and stepped away; she muttered curses. I heard Ava's voice in my head, chastising me for putting up with Vivian, telling me how abusive she was, and how wrong it was of her to treat me so poorly. If I left the job, though, who would take care of the shop as well as me? Who would love each and every creature as if they were born of their own body? Nobody. I didn't think there was a soul within a thousand miles even capable of feeling what I felt for them.

Inside the fifty gallon tank the two G fish barely registered one another. Before I'd come on board Vivian insisted they'd gotten into a fight, leaving one almost dead. I saw no evidence of her claim, although the G fish were notorious for killing other fish and one another when not kept apart.

The doorbell rang and I went to the front of the store. There stood an older man, rounded and weather worn—Jacob Small. "Hiya, Frank," he said. "Got any goldfish?" He always bought them to feed his pair of oscars. The shop was now empty save for me and him. We went inside the aquarium room. He pointed out several goldfish. I used a plastic bag and a net to trap his selected victims. He checked out and left.

As I made my way to the back, I couldn't help but wonder where Vivian had gone off to. Not like she hadn't done this before. More times than not she'd simply vanish from the store and then send me a text later asking if I minded just shutting down the place by myself. I didn't mind. At least Vivian left me alone.

The door to our back office was slightly open.

That's a big no-no. Why would she do that? She always yells at me if I even leave it open for a second while I'm bringing heavy stuff in and out of there. What the…?

Vivian sat in the chair in front of the shop's computer. I couldn't believe what I saw. One breast was exposed, the edge of her black lace bra folded down. She pinched her right nipple with her left hand. Her right hand moved around inside her pants, which she'd unzipped and unbelted enough to give herself room. I saw the top band of her panties and realized they matched her bra. She'd tilted slightly backward. On the computer in front of her she watched a man and woman stretched out in a field and surrounded by nature. His face was buried between her legs.

I could swear the potted daisies stood taller, their petals spread wide, the styles and stigmas within aroused and pointing toward Vivian.

She moved and for a moment I thought she saw me out of the corner of her eye.

I felt like my chest had turned to ice. My hands went numb and my throat turned dry.

Darting away as fast and as quiet as I could, I made my way back to the aquarium room. Grabbing a net, I put it inside the goldfish tank and pretended to have been busy looking for something inside the tank. My head felt full and fuzzy. *Did she want me to see her? Did that even just happen? Am I dreaming this up?*

After half an hour of pretending to do stuff in the aquarium room, I made my way to the main area of the store. There were no customers. I grabbed a clipboard and made my way around the shop checking inventory. I didn't have to, but it'd give me an excuse to be walking around, and I'd have the clipboard as a shield if Vivian spotted me. As I neared the edge of the showroom, I could see the office door was shut. I checked the storage room. Empty. I went to the back hallway and peered out the back door. Vivian's black Volvo was not in the parking lot. *Maybe she parked around the corner. Sometimes she does that to spy on me, even though she says it's to free up a spot for a customer.*

The office door was locked. I knocked.

"Vivian?" I knocked twice.

She didn't answer.

What do I do if she's still in there? My mind raced through a half dozen taboo scenarios, even though I tried suppressing the thoughts.

I unlocked the door.

There was no one inside. The computer was dark. The potted flowers were closed, their petals shut and pointed limply toward the ground.

***

Lavender filled the family room. Ava favored the plant's scent, and so she'd had it growing in two long oblong containers. Each container was waist high, made of metal, and rolled on wheels. Plastic buckets lined them, with a drainage pan underneath.

The windowsills overflowed with blooming succulents. The colors were magnificent; reddish pinks, soft aqua blues and bright yellows. Most sprouted green thick, spongy petals.

The prized plant held the most esteemed placement right next to Ava's large leather chair. The Sol del Mar stretched its light green stems like a three-headed dragon. The trio of bulbs hadn't yet opened for the year, and so the red capsules looked to me like missiles pointed at my head. I imagined them angry at me because I was competition for Ava's time and attention.

She put her fingers on one bulb, stroking it gently back and forth. A memory of Ava performing the same gestures on my body aroused me. I recalled us in her room, years earlier, vanilla candles burning, kissing and touching and exploring each other's body, the whole of it transporting me to another place, not unlike drifting near great celestial globes in outer space.

"I'm starving. Do you want to make us something?" She didn't look at me when she spoke. She seemed infatuated with the plant as if it were a handsome lover she didn't want to break eye contact with.

"What're you in the mood for?" I hated the way my voice sounded—so high-pitched and wounded.

"There's still braised honey. Can you fix me some?"

Of course I did.

All I wanted was for me and Ava to have a normal life, like an average couple. Heck, even semi-normal would have been fine. But we just weren't wired that way. Ours was a different lifestyle: we slept in separate bedrooms; she obsessed about her plants and spent more time with them than she did with me; I felt replaced. But I couldn't imagine a life without her.

***

Vivian came to me in my dreams. Standing in the hallway of the shop, she leaned in toward me. Her breath was warm and sweet. Her pupils were dilated and her face was open. She wore white pants and her legs were spread slightly as though she were about to straddle me as we stood. Moving toward my body, I felt her middle touch mine. She pressed her hand into my own, our fingers intertwining. Her lips were close and we were an inch from a kiss when something moved at our feet. A small tan terrier ran in a small circle. We didn't allow any of the animals to roam free. She caught my stress. "Don't worry about that. Worry about me." Her hips rolled on me just as her lips touched me.

Even though I dreamed, everything about her felt so real. Her taste. Her smell. The weight and movements of her body.

Endorphins surged from my brain. *This is what love is. This is how it's supposed to feel. Ava won't give me her heart anymore. She's shut down. Maybe this is the way it's supposed to be. Maybe I am supposed to be with Vivian.*

I shut my eyes and kissed her with everything I had. I freed a hand and put it down to the small of her back, holding her tightly against me. Her movements aroused me and I wanted nothing more than to be her everything.

The kiss melted the world away.

I heard, "What are you dreaming?"

The voice was not Vivian's.

Ava roused me with a gentle kiss to my forehead. "Who is she?" It was dark but I could feel her smile.

You can't tell her it was Vivian. That would sink everything. You know how she's already jealous. You don't really want Vivian, do you? You're just lonely because Ava is neglecting you.

Ava. Beautiful Ava. Her blonde hair made her look like a goddess.

"You...were...so beautiful. It was so real," I lied.

Her hands were on my chest, which I hadn't caught at first. She was nearly on top of me, and we were in my own bedroom. She'd come out from her big chair in the living room to see me. "Mm." Her voice so raspy and feminine. I'd missed her making eye contact with me when we made love. She hadn't in a while. Our trysts were always fast.

Life intervened. Ava hardly seemed to wish to spend more than a few minutes together. Once the Sol Del Mar came it had been her priority, anyway.

Her hands slipped downward and she found where I'd risen. "Oh, look at this." She pulled down my pajamas as if no time had ever passed between us. Her fingers wrapped around me expertly and perfectly, stroking me, her thumb gently rolling the small crown at the small ridge under the head. She knew how to make me crazy. Her head went down and she articulated her lips and mouth around me.

Such pleasure—an almost unbearable tickle.

Please don't stop. I hope this lasts a long time. Don't be too fast.

Then, after a moment, a slight burning went down and inside me from the tip. It wasn't enough to stop the pleasure, but it made me take pause for a second. *Is there something wrong with me? Do I have a disease? An infection? Should I tell her? Stop her?*

The sensation left and I focused on Ava nursing me.

When I looked down I couldn't help but see how pretty she was. I'd almost forgot, but I focused on her rosy cheeks and plump lips. It was so nice to see her lightly freckled skin close to mine. I remembered every inch of her.

In no time the distinct charge built up, rising inside me like a bubble in the sea. Ava kept steady at what she was doing, sensing the moment closing in. The sides of my vision went blurry like an old vignette photograph—only for a moment, though. Everything went white, then every color in the world exploded, then it was black and white and grainy, and then I was back. Ava slowed, working me with her hand. She finished and then fell on top of me. "You okay?"

"Oh my God am I." I smiled at her. "What about you? We need to take care of you, too."

She turned her face from me. "I'm fine."

"Aren't you turned on by me?"

Ava put a finger on my lips. "Of course. But I do need to take care of the flowers."

"Can't they wait? Can't you just stay for a little while?"

"I'm already late for them."

Then she got up and looked at me spent and sprawled across my bed. As she walked out the door she said, "She would never do that for you, you know."

***

The next few days at the shop were uneventful. Vivian only contacted me through texts. She mentioned nothing about what I saw, of course, and neither did I.

Life went along, business as usual, until the following week, when I woke to empty my bladder.

Going to the bathroom stung. I tried to ignore the burn and went back to bed. The feeling was similar to when Ava first put her mouth on me. There was no denying it. *She gave me something. She had to have done so. Damn it all.*

Dozing off, my dreams were filled with colors: the hue of a blue sky, the greens of a grass field growing on a huge hill in a valley, the yellows of sunflowers in full bloom, the smell of it all making me heady and wishing I were there.

I woke in the middle of the night to find pearly papules rimming the underside of my stem. They looked like small pimples. At first I thought it was debris left over from our tryst, but they didn't wipe away. At least they didn't pop or hurt.

Do I say something to her?

Yeah. You should talk to her about this.

I rolled over to wake Ava, but she wasn't in bed with me.

I got up. I made my down the hallway toward the living room. The door was closed. I hesitated, then turned the handle slowly.

The room was dark other than a small bit of moonlight. Ava was on her chair, stretched out with a thin white blanket draped around her. She writhed. *Is she having a bad dream? Is she okay? What's happening to her?*

I immediately wanted to run in and be her knight in shining armor. But that was foolish and dreaming, as she was already being taken care of. The Sol Del Mar stems were upon her, or maybe she'd dragged them toward her own body. Her right hand reached up and held onto a long, thick stem. The bulb at the end worked its way in and out of her mouth. Her lips caressed and kissed it, her saliva mixing with the milky substance discharging from its tip. She'd done the same with me only a few hours earlier, and I thought about the fluid the flower was giving off. Maybe that was why I'd felt a burning sensation? She'd been infected by them. As jealous and upset as I was, I couldn't help but feel turned on by what I was seeing. Ava was so gorgeous, and seeing her in such a position made me heat up.

There were two similar bulbs working their way up between her legs, gently spreading her own petals, their stamen all that was visible going inside her.

The other flowers in the room all seemed pointed toward the act. Ava moaned slowly as the flowers explored her willing body.

As my own stem grew excited, it also ached. How could I have been infected by her and them so fast? It'd only been hours, after all.

Ava stopped. The flowers stopped. She turned her head slowly, spotted me, her mouth opened a bit before she said. "So now you know. Do you still want to be with me?"

"Yes."

Was there any other answer?

The flowers knew what she'd intended because they turned their bulbs toward me. My heart went cold.

The bulbs opened and dark things came out. Some crawled, some flew; sized from tiny to small. A horde of countless insects charged me.

I spun round and tried shutting the door, but they hit me with such surprising force I dropped to the hallway floor. They were on me, stinging and biting, a million pinpricks. I cried out and rolled around, trying to crush them. They were inside my clothes and getting everywhere. I think I screamed for them to stop and pleaded with Ava to call them off, but I can't be sure of what I said exactly.

I blacked out.

I woke in my room, on my bed, unsure of how I got there. For a long time, I couldn't move. Maybe I could have, but I was too shocked. When I did, I raised my hand to find it covered in red bumps and welts. Both hands were covered. My arms. My legs. Everywhere.

The pain.

But it soon subsided.

Ava showed me how.

"Eat some of this." She placed a bowl of sugar water on my desk along with a piece of bread. I felt better. I didn't hurt.

"What were those bugs?"

She appeared confused. "Bugs? There are no bugs."

"They came after me. I fell."

She shook her head. "No. There was nothing there. You just needed more after your first taste. That's all."

Ava was right. I needed sugar more and more. The cravings intensified. Soon even the sugar water was not enough and the aches returned.

One morning a Sol Del Mar with light pink petals was outside my door. I brought it inside my room and placed it upon my desk. There was a note near the bottom of the planter, folded in half.

This will make everything better.

How had she gotten a second? They were near impossible to find or buy. Hers was a gift, she claimed.

There was something about the Sol Del Mar that felt different. Or maybe I was different? I soon knew why.

A few days later I woke, hungry and faint. The Sol Del Mar caught the morning light, and I noticed its petals had opened slightly to the sun. Its middle glistened. A cloudy fluid dripped from a small axis near its top, coating the petals. I could smell its sweetness and its earthiness from across the room. My stomach growled.

In a moment I was on my knees, spreading the petals gently apart with two fingers, my tongue searching for every last drop of the flower's sweet juices. It was sweet on my tongue, but it burned ever so slightly—the same sensation Ava had gifted me with only a few weeks before. The more I licked, the more liquid came out, until my craving was gone. This went on for quite some time, over many days.

My heart felt light. It seemed I could see the fine beauty in everything around me.

Vivian called and at first I meant to call her back. Her voice seemed to be from another time, or another world. After several days, I held the phone and made to dial, but stopped myself.

One more lick at the Sol del Mar first. One more to make me feel steady before I talk to Vivian.

Then I'd be lost, my heart light. I'd doze and I would hear her voice and see her, but I couldn't call. I didn't want her to see me. I was in no condition to work. If I could just get one more day to recover.

I'd then lose another day, only to eventually forget about work. I turned off my phone and never turned it back on.

All that mattered was the flower—my Sol Del Mar. Ava checked on me and she seemed more than pleased. She had a spark in her eye I'd not seen in a long while.

The juices changed me, though, in the same way drunks change over time. I felt better, complete. I felt alive. I was living. The juices were in my blood and stayed there. I lost weight, gained strength. The Sol Del Mar was always ready for me whenever I needed it.

Ava was lost. I never saw her. When I did, she barely acknowledged me. She cooed and spoke to her own plants as though they were her lovers and I had interrupted them. Of course. She'd pawned me off to another plant so she wouldn't have to get me nipping at her heels. I'd been cast off.

Maybe there is a way back into her heart.

Live inside me.

That was the prayer I said after I nursed at the Sol Del Mar.

Be inside me.

My face was already starting to melt and change from the flowers. My once familiar chin sported a new rim of fatty skin. The hair over my forehead receded and faded, a small ridge of bumps where it'd been. Her obsession would be my end—or—more likely—the end of the person I'd been. If only she'd love me as much as I'd love her, then that would be enough.

But I put these words down now as what I was becomes something new and different. I can feel the green stems pushing through the folds of my brain, their small fibulae finding purchase and anchor. Bulbs grow just under my skin, creating mounds like blemishes. They push out, cracking my sore skin, releasing a smell like vinegar.

The new me will soon be seen, and I hope I will finally become something she can love.

Bizarro Games

by **Richard Dansky**

UNDERTALE

Video game genres are usually defined by core play mechanic: RPG, First person shooter, platformer, and so on. Even more descriptive and granular genres like "bullet hell" are focused on play style first, content not at all. That's how *Gears of War*, *Call of Duty* and *Rainbow Six* can all be considered part of the same genre, while games that share content like *Fallout*, *Mad Max* and *Duke Nukem* can be considered parts of entirely different genres.

With that in mind, it's particularly difficult and rare for a game to be classified according to literary genre. After all, the play's the thing and the setting's a distant second. And that holds doubly true for a genre like bizarro fiction, where rules and systems can be utterly fluid, and the disruption of the accepted is a defining feature.

To be fair, with the explosion of mobile and tablet platforms, games may be moving away from classical hierarchical "genres," but bizarro games are still lagging in numbers and critical attention. Landmark games like *Earthbound* and *Yume Nikki* are revered, but largely failed to take off.

Game design, after all, is based in large part on the

foundational notion of systems: teach the player what to do in order to produce the desired response. Players then use their knowledge of systems to advance and improve, hence terms such as "grinding," where players input time for expected results. Kill this monster, get this many experience points, pick up this treasure. Knowing the systems and relying on them is how players advance. The formalized, if unwritten, structure defines the parameters of the gameplay experience.

Bizarro, on the other hand, is all about breaking the rules. And when rules break down—when gamers don't know how to approach problems or how they're likely to be rewarded—then things get frustrating and tricky.

But even so, there are a few. Most fall in the loose "weird RPG" subgenre of game, wherein the standard mechanics of RPGs—combat, experience points, leveling up and so forth—are married to surreal tropes like non-traditionally monstrous opponents, party-building with wacky misfits as opposed to fierce warriors, and a general eye towards subverting standard fantasy conventions. And two that come close to the bizarro label are **Lisa: The RPG** and **Undertale**.

Undertale is a heady brew of old-school RPG graphics and techniques with non-traditional methods of interaction and subversively humorous writing. Created by Toby Fox and funded through a wildly successful Kickstarter campaign, the game follows the adventures of a child named Frisk. Frisk has fallen through a gap

in the barrier separating humans and monsters, and now must sojourn through the monster world in order to get back home.

So far, so normal, except that Frisk's journey is anything but predictable. The player's first interaction is with a homicidal flower named Flowey; the second is with a motherly monster named Toriel. Frisk's path through the Underground, as the realm of monsters is known, is frequently interrupted by encounters with monsters. However, Frisk has the option of choosing to befriend rather than kill the monsters, earning their friendship but sacrificing rewards for the encounter. What's more, the game remembers the choices the player makes as they play and replay the game, with those decisions affecting storylines and boss battles. Even the tutorial, that tooth-grinding staple of video games, gets chewed up and spit out. The first thing the player is taught about the world is actively, aggressively wrong, while many of the useful things they need to know are left for the player to discover on their own.

And just as it subverts systems, *Undertale* also explodes classical fantasy RPG tropes with frankly bizarre character designs and concepts. Enemies that burst into tears or reluctantly attack, that wrathful homicidal flower again—the banished "Monsters" of this world are a long way from the RPG tropes they're supposed to be hewing to.

Lisa, on the other hand, offers a somewhat grimmer approach. Also using highly stylized art (**Lisa** was made in **RPGMaker**, while **Undertale** was made in **Game Maker Studio**) as opposed to hyperrealistic graphics, Lisa superficially is another "gather-the-band-of-misfits-to-go-on-a-quest" RPG, but one that quickly shows its true colors. Rather than the relentless character grind of most RPGs to level up and develop stats, Lisa offers a mechanic where characters can be "sacrificed"—wounded or maimed—in order to help other characters and achieve game goals. These brutal choices permanently affect character stats and the world as a whole. There's no sentimentality here (though there is a guy who apparently has a tiger for a head), just ruthless calculation as to what element of a character's strength can be sacrificed to ensure optimum choices down the line. Where most RPGs are about maximizing gains, this one focuses heavily on maximizing the effect of your self-inflicted losses.

And then there's the Russian Roulette. The player can set their party members up to play the potentially suicidal game. Survival means huge bonuses; failure earns perma-death. Again, this flies in the face of every accepted RPG convention, giving **Lisa: The Painful** a unique and unsettling flavor.

Series closer **Lisa: The Joyful** follows Buddy, the young girl from **Lisa: The Painful**, as she is raised by her Joy-addicted, potentially monstrous guardian Brad (who is also the titular Lisa's brother). The intriguing storyline treats causality as optional, instead going for dream-logic. The only female in the land of Olathe, she needs to find herself and secure her place, while dealing with unreliable allies and the mutagenic effects of the addictive Joy.

The installment **Lisa: The First** is a prequel to **The Painful**, a trippy and disturbing psychosexual ramble through the history of abuse suffered by the character Lisa Armstrong at the hands of her father, Marty. The gameplay is a quest to recover her memories, represented by VHS tapes, before discovering the full truth about her father and a final message from her mother. One character, the undeniably phallic Rick, needs to be killed over again in order for Lisa to advance, while Marty is leeringly omnipresent throughout the world. There are no knightly quests here or elfin castles, just a horrifying journey of realization that leads to a brutal and inevitable conclusion.

Both **Lisa** and **Undertale** are critically acclaimed and highly successful, demonstrating that the audience for games that blow up the rules to achieve their ends is out there. ◆

THE LIGHTED WINDOW

BY MARK SILCOX

"You'd be perfectly welcome at the reception, you know," my wife said.

I was sitting on the hotel bed watching her slip into her best dress. It was silver and satiny, with tiny cutout flowers sewn into the material. "I know. They're good people. But my being there'd make them awkward, after a while. Nothing to talk about."

She shrugged, but didn't argue with me. Then she knelt down on the edge of the bed and walked across the duvet toward me on her knees. She kissed me on the cheek, and I turned down the TV.

"Anyway," I said, "I'll be fine. Good movie on later tonight. That English-language version of *Madame Bovary*."

She glanced over at the TV screen. At the moment it was showing some Syfy Channel epic—*Killer Wombat 4*, maybe. A skinny co-ed was being eaten, very slowly. One of the myths that I've tried to keep afloat ever since we started taking these conference junkets together is that I get a big kick out of watching cable television in hotel rooms. Actually, I can't stand the stuff.

"We might stay up drinking and talking until late," she said, scratching her painted nails lightly against the back of my neck. From up close her perfume smelled sugary, a little decadent. "These southern historians are all whiskey and wind."

"Stay there as long as you like, Jez. Your presentation was a hit—you should bask in the glory." She'd told a lot of stories about carpetbaggers in the civil war. The crowd of scholars there had all seemed fascinated, as far as I could tell.

"You think it was, really? I couldn't tell from behind the podium."

"You bet," I told her. "Plenty of nodding heads. That famous geezer from Stanford was ogling you, though."

After nine years of marriage, this sort of casual, half-ironic flattery could still make her blush and giggle. She kissed me once on the cheek then left the room. As soon as she was gone, I switched off the TV.

It's not that the trips themselves are really all that horrible. Once when Jez was invited to present a paper in west Texas, I rode down there to meet her a day late on my Harley, and the scenery was some of the most amazing I've ever seen. And another time, in Florida, I abandoned the hotel completely and went fishing with an older, retired history professor who didn't want to spend his time sitting around in meeting rooms. I don't do so well in the evenings, though, when everyone gathers around in the hotel bar for drinks and chitchat. Have to stay away from the booze, and I find Jez's colleagues hard to take when I'm sober and they're in shoptalk mode.

This time we were staying on the Georgia coast, in a beachfront resort that had once been somebody's private villa. That night the tide had risen over the sand to within a few yards of the rocky embankments below our window. I got up off the bed and paced the floor for a minute or two, then stepped out onto the balcony. The wind had picked up, and you could hear waves breaking along the shore. It was the sort of weather that provokes restlessness. I decided to get out of there and go for a walk along the beach.

The planks of the boardwalk that led down to the sand were damp and slightly rotted. A few warped squares of particle board that might have been signs had been nailed onto the trees along the path. When I reached the edge of the water, I turned back and looked up at the hotel. There was a wide, brightly-lit bay window at the back of the building that looked out onto the ocean. I guessed that this was probably the room where Jez and her cronies were drinking and telling their stories to one another. I wondered how many of them had managed to get a single drop of salt water on their skins since the conference had started. It always amazes me, how people will drive for hundreds of miles to get to the ocean, then turn right around again and spend the rest of their holidays messing around in shops, bars and restaurants.

The beach curved slowly outward to the northeast. I started walking in that direction. After about twenty yards I took off my shoes and tied the laces together, then slung them back over my shoulder. A few more well-lit hotels and private homes loomed up above the embankment to my left, then a stretch of undeveloped land. Tall grasses blew in the soft breeze and strange insect noises crackled upward from the uneven ground. There was almost no light at all here, apart from the moon's, and I could barely see the damp sand under my feet.

Just as I reached the very darkest point along the beach, I heard the rhythmic splashing of footsteps in the water behind me. When I turned to look back in the direction I'd come from, I saw a woman's figure outlined by moonlight.

Her hair was damp and slicked back and her eyes were turned away from me. She was heavily tanned, and wore a dark one-piece swimsuit and a blue sarong cinched around her waist. When she spoke, her voice seemed oddly clear against the background noise of wind and water.

"Hello," she said. "Have you been walking here for long?" She had an accent—Polish, I thought, or perhaps Russian.

"I just came down from my hotel a few minutes ago. See the big lighted window there?" I pointed down along the shoreline.

"So, you're with the conference too." She smiled. Her teeth were seashell-white and very straight, like a model's. "My husband is back there right now, at some party."

"No kidding. My wife's there too."

She took another step toward me. It was odd that I hadn't seen her at the hotel earlier on. The way she looked, I certainly would have remembered her. Then again, I'd spent most of my time that day hiding out on the balcony reading a paperback novel.

We fell into step together. "My wife gave a paper this morning," I told her. "I watched her from the back of the room, but I skipped out after she was done."

"I didn't go at all. Trust me, they're better off without us."

There was a trace of bitterness in her voice. If I'd been about five years younger, I might have said something vaguely chivalrous about the probable value of her company. But I kept quiet.

We were walking along the edge of the water now. Thin, ephemeral twirls of seaweed drifted over the tops of my feet. We strolled quietly together for a minute or two before she spoke again. "I like the tattoos," she said.

I have an eagle's claw over my left shoulder and a black violin on my right upper arm. Most of Jez's colleagues do double-takes when they see them. I'm always getting asked, *did it hurt*? Never why I'd chosen those particular images.

"Thanks," I said. "My dad played in a string quartet. I got the violin when he died."

She nodded. "I think I've seen the other one before. Is it military?"

"Mm. I fought in Desert Storm. A bunch of the guys in my company got the claw put on when we got back. Sort of silly, I guess."

"No," she said. "I understand. You were coming back home from a *long* way away from here."

It was a strange remark. But she looked as though she really did understand. I wondered if perhaps she was thinking about wherever it was that she'd come from in Eastern Europe.

"Was your husband stuck in meetings all day?" I asked her.

"He seems to like it. He hasn't been to the beach even once, since we got here. I wonder, sometimes, why they bother to have their meetings in such beautiful places."

It was startling, how close her thoughts were to the direction mine had been taking. I slowed the pace of my walking and took a closer look at her. She didn't appear to be much past her late twenties. Too young to be married to a careerist academic, I thought.

"I'm David, by the way," I said, holding out my hand.

"Veronica." Her fingers felt cool and a little damp. As she spoke, she kept her head turned outward, as though she was looking for something along the surface of the flickering black waves.

We'd passed by the darkest stretch of beach now and were walking alongside a row of shorefront cottages. Veronica kicked a pink plastic beach ball out of our path, then turned and grinned at me. The tide had begun to recede, and the moon had retreated behind a veil of clouds.

"When Jez and I were first married," I began, "back when we were both poor, we used to take all our holidays in national parks. We'd rent a cabin, or just pitch a tent. Miles from anyone. I'd take her there on the back of my Harley and we'd ride around the countryside together for hours. We got to see a lot of America that way. I'd take photos of the landscape, and Jez'd blow them up in our darkroom when we got home. But then everything changed."

I don't know why I suddenly started rambling on this way. I don't often find it that easy to put my thoughts about private matters into words.

Veronica nodded slowly as I spoke and seemed to be smiling a sad, private smile. "What happened?"

I tried to explain how Jez's career had taken off, and how I'd quit my old job as a photojournalist to follow her to the school where she was teaching now. As I spoke I could hear a curious mixture of pride and resentment in my own voice. It made me embarrassed, but in the darkness

Veronica couldn't see my skin flushing.

She walked on without speaking for a few minutes after I'd finished my gloomy, stumbling narrative, then turned around, put her hands on her waist and looked me up and down. We had come quite a long way down the beach together—the villa's bay window was barely visible along the waterline.

"Hey," she said. "Instead of walking, why don't we *swim* back?"

"Sorry? You want to..." It struck me as a very odd response to my confessional outburst. The water looked calm enough, and I guessed that it was probably still lukewarm from the day's sunlight. But I was wearing sandals and a dry shirt. I shrugged, and gave her an apologetic look.

"Ah, come on, David." Her foreign accent seemed to thicken as she spoke my name. Her beautiful, clear smile broadened, and she took a few steps backward toward the bubbling surf.

"I had a pretty big dinner, Veronica. Think I'd sink like a stone."

For just a moment her smile disappeared, and was replaced by a look of real pain and desperation. Then she saw me take an uncertain step forward, and beckoned to me as the dark water drifted up over her calves. "You'll be fine."

It was eerie, how urgent her tone had suddenly become. But I knew that I was strong enough to swim the two hundred or so yards back to the villa. And the sandals had only cost a buck fifty. I kicked them off and followed my new companion down along the uneven path of moonlight that stretched along the ocean's surface. It just suddenly seemed like the right thing to do.

The water was almost unnaturally temperate. "It feels wonderful," I called out to her. She was floating on her back ahead of me, with her head tilted backward and her dark hair spreading out behind her. I slid up alongside her and we looked up together at a sky thick with stars.

Soon we'd drifted out too far for our feet to touch bottom. When I felt her cool, slick hand slide into mine beneath the water's surface, I almost pulled away. Then my eyes met hers. Before that moment, I'd never felt unduly constrained by my marriage, even though I'd always been faithful to Jez. But now I let my fingers lace together with hers and tightened my grip. She nodded at me slowly and my mind began to work in familiar ways that I thought I'd outgrown.

"Come on," she whispered. "Let's go out further."

In the moment she turned away and began to stroke out toward the open water I saw something in her eyes—an expression of icy determination that made me wonder if I'd somehow misread her gesture. But her back was to me before I could be sure. She swam with astonishing speed and grace.

I began to follow her. I wanted to keep up our conversation. While I'd been unburdening myself on the beach it hadn't occurred to me that she might have been harboring her own collection of dark thoughts. Had her husband been unfaithful to her? Was she disappointed with her life in some other, less easily discernible way? I wondered why she seemed to think that the solution to whatever was troubling her was to strike out away from the shore into the increasingly black, night-chilled ocean.

***

I noticed an odd tugging sensation around my ankles. It felt as though there were fronds of seaweed pulling against me as I struggled to keep up with Veronica. The harder I kicked out, the more I seemed to get tangled up in the long, greasy strands. I called out to her again. "Hey! Hold up a second!"

She turned onto her back and kicked out with both legs just a few feet in front of me. "Keep going! We're almost there!"

"Almost where?" As I spoke I felt my mouth half-fill with water. I was confused now, and it seemed that the harder I swam, the more difficult it was to make any headway. I felt a harder jerk against my legs and my head sank below the surface.

Thin, improbably long filaments of lacy black kelp were everywhere around me. How had I not noticed it when I'd first started to follow her? I could feel thicker stalks of the stuff coiling around my chest—I tore at them with my hands and managed to pull my head back above the waterline. "Veronica," I shouted. "Careful, it's..."

The surface of the ocean around me was completely calm. There was no sign of my companion anywhere. I treaded water for a few minutes and looked all around myself for her. I could barely see the shore and my feet couldn't reach the bottom. I glimpsed a dark shape pass swiftly below me, and then there was another sharp pull on my ankle and I went down again. The sensation was unmistakable—it was the feeling of four thin, cold human fingers pulling down hard on my leg.

I swallowed a mouthful of fetid seawater. Stars were visible behind my eyelids. I was trying hard not to panic, but I flailed out under the surface with my arms and legs. A few strands snapped loose and I managed to pull myself upward again. Water blurred my vision, and I couldn't catch my breath properly. Worse, I could feel my muscles beginning to stiffen.

I wouldn't let myself believe that there was something down there trying to get me. While my mind struggled with the mystery of Veronica's disappearance, I let my lower body float to the surface and started to stroke toward the beach. She must have either turned back to the shore or else swam out so far that I couldn't see her from where I was. It was painful to think that she'd just abandoned me while I was struggling there.

The thick fronds of underwater fauna wouldn't give up their hold on my body. I swallowed back hard on thick sobs of frustration. My throat began to sting from the saltwater that I was ingesting. The sky whirled and blurred above my face, and it occurred to me that I probably wasn't going to make it.

I'd confronted the prospect of death twice before: once in my teens when my parents' car had turned over on the way to a church barbecue, and once in Kuwait when an F-16 mistook my convoy for retreating Iraqi troops and strafed us with friendly fire. Both times I'd found within myself a dogged, tenacious determination to survive that had surprised me with its strength. But this time, I could feel myself beginning to despair. The water seemed to have plunged downward in temperature and I could feel its coldness seeping under my skin. A vision came to me of my own body, cold, dead and bloated on the beach, in the morning sunlight. I turned my head back and forth frantically, eyes opened wide, trying one last time to find the shore.

A brilliant rectangle of light broke out of the blackness right in front of me. It was coming from the window of the villa. Icy liquid filled my eyes, but I could still see vague shadows of figures shifting around behind the glass. One of them was surely Jez.

One still sometimes hears the timeworn story about how in moments of deep fear, a person will see a sudden rush of images from his own past. But in my case, this was something that I *forced* myself to experience. As the water's chill got deeper inside of me, I tilted my head back and thought of the night I'd first met Jez. It was at some horrible suburban party just a month after I'd gotten back from the desert. I summoned up the feeling of riding my bike in the autumn air with Jez's arms around my waist and her cheek pressed against my back. And I remembered the way she'd looked earlier that evening, just before heading out of our hotel room and leaving me to my own aimless devices. When I looked up again, the window had gotten closer.

I had nothing left to draw on at all by the time I felt my feet touch sand again. I swallowed more water staggering the last few feet out of the ocean on my knees, then fell forward onto my chest in the shallow surf. A few strands of kelp still clung to my thighs and ankles. I could feel them trailing backward behind me in the receding tide.

Time passed in blackness and silence. When I lifted my cheek from the wet sand and looked around, I noticed that the moon had shifted in the sky and the tide had risen past my waist. There was no trace left on my body of the dark underwater flora that had almost killed me. It took me almost a full minute to get up on my feet.

I was standing directly below the villa's lighted window, still badly disorientated. When I think back to those moments, I try to tell myself that I was simply too confused and exhausted to spare a thought for Veronica. Or that perhaps I'd managed to convince myself that I'd glimpsed her coming out of the water, at a darker point along the shore. But I also know that I remembered the feeling of those four grasping fingers around my ankle, straining to pull me down into oblivion.

The clock in our room said 1:56 AM. Jez still hadn't returned from her party. I collapsed on the bed without even bothering to wash the sand off my feet. But I was still awake enough when she did return to feel her slip up under the covers beside me. She slid a hand over my stomach, and I bit my lip and prayed that I didn't call out a name in my sleep.

***

Jez had already showered and was fully dressed the next morning while I was still barely awake under the bedclothes, blur-eyed and immobile. She told me she needed to talk to the hotel manager before anyone left—apparently it had been decided that she was going to be in charge of planning next year's conference.

I forced myself to get up, washed quickly and finished what was left of the packing, then went downstairs to find her. She was by the front desk chatting with a tall, sharply dressed woman. They passed a few pieces of paper back and forth, then the woman smiled and they shook hands. I walked up beside Jez with our suitcase and put my arm around her waist.

From closer up, the other woman's expression looked a little pained, and she kept hold of Jez's hand for an extra moment. "We're really *so* grateful to your organization for coming here again. Even in the absence of superstition, I could understand why some people might want a change of venue after what happened last year."

Jez made some civil noises and said goodbye. We packed up the Volvo and started the long trip home. I let her drive. She opened the windows wide and flipped back her sunglasses. The cool morning air surged into the car, waking me up a little.

"What was that woman saying about 'superstition'?"

"Hmm? Oh, that. She actually told me a pretty creepy story about last year's conference."

"We weren't at that one?"

Jez shook her head. "I didn't get a paper written in time."

"What was the story?"

Exactly a year and one day ago a young woman, a professor's wife, had gone swimming on the beach by herself and drowned. The two of them had traveled all the way from Latvia to be at the conference. Apparently, the husband had been attending one of the evening sessions when it had happened. Her body hadn't been recovered, but some people walking by on the beach had seen her swim out to sea.

"Poor girl must have had a death wish," said Jez, as we ramped up onto the freeway. "She could hardly have ignored all the warning signs."

"Sign? What signs?"

"You know—all those big particle-board signs nailed onto the trees on the way down to the beach. DANGER—DEEP WATER." I stared at her. "Bright red letters—hard to miss. You didn't see them during your swim last night?"

I thought for a moment. "I guess I must have been looking for something else," I said. Then I squeezed Jez's hand. She gave me an odd look, as though she sensed the existence of some kind of mystery behind the gesture.

"It's nothing," I told her, then turned to look out of my window, in the direction of the ocean. A dark mist of rain was falling over the water a few miles out from the rugged shoreline, shrouding the air with darkness. "Just tell me when it's my turn to drive."

Bizarro Punk: David Agranoff

Dark Discoveries: Could you tell us a little about how you got interested in writing?

David Agranoff: I have wanted to be writer as long as I can remember. We had a reading family and I enjoyed storytelling right away. I started telling science fiction stories even before I could write or type myself. I dictated stories to my mother who typed them on her Smith Corona typewriter. She encouraged me always, and I admit I was a mama's boy. She died when I was twelve years old, that is when I discovered horror. A few things led to that; for one, in Indiana we had a horror host named Sammy Terry who showed local horror movies on Friday nights followed by Black Belt Theater. So I taped tons of horror and kung fu double features, which by the way were the influence on my first horror novel *Hunting The Moon Tribe* (Little Otik Books) which was a Chinese Vampire Wuxia-horror cross-genre tribute to those double features.

Photo courtesy of David Agranoff

1987 was an important year for horror, *Prince of Darkness* and *Hellraiser* were in theaters and Stephen King released four novels. There were two key stories that influenced me then (and still do) that I read for the first time that year. King's short story "The Raft" was a lightbulb moment for me, I read it and understood how he built the scares and told the story step by step. I wanted to do that, and my heroes were always creators and authors. Another key story was "The Body Politic" by Clive Barker which is a very bizarro story that taught me you can be surreal and weird and still tell a great story and best of all the story expressed a message.

So I always wanted to be a writer and for many years I kept that dream to myself afraid to step out because of challenges my learning disabilities gave me. I am dyslexic, and have probably half a dozen other learning disabilities. However, as an activist and being part of the punk/hardcore scene I taught myself to get better by doing 'zines. It wasn't till I met my wife, who is a great editor, and she encouraged me to grow and take my dream seriously.

In the 90s I got involved with political, environmental and animal rights activism and that also had an influence as my self-published DIY 'zines took on those messages. Admittedly, a lot of my fiction expresses political points of view; but the story always comes first.

DD: How did you come up with the concept for *Amazing Punk Stories*?

DA: Between my novels *The Vegan Revolution...With Zombies*, *Boot Boys of the Wolf Reich* and the forthcoming *Punk Rock Ghost Story*, my editors at Eraserhead had felt I created a niche for myself with punk-themed horror fiction. To me a lot of fiction involving punks just throw mohawks and leather jackets at everything and assume that is punk. As someone who has been a part of the punk scene since the 80s I wanted to write more authentic punk fiction.

As for *Amazing Punk Stories*... bizarro publishers work together every couple years to highlight authors in the genre with a series of anthologies called the *Bizarro Starter Kit*. It is a good way to introduce several authors in an inexpensive book. I wrote a story for the third *Bizarro Starter Kit* called "Punkupine Moshers of the Apocalypse." It was meant to be a fantasy style hero's journey story featuring an 80's punk rock vibe. All the authors donate their work to the *Kit* with the idea that they will get paid when they collect it later with other work. Before I got a chance to collect mine, editor Cameron Pierce selected "Punkupines" to be in the *Best Bizarro Fiction of the Decade* collection alongside Joe R. Lansdale, Carlton Mellick, Cody Goodfellow, Bentley Little and others.

People kept writing me about how much they liked that story and I had the *what if?* moment. What if I wrote a collection of stories of all different genres of pulp style fiction—horror, science fiction, western, spy, etc.—all with punk characters? Thus, *Amazing Punk Stories* was born.

DD: Do you have a favorite story in the collection?

DA: Hard to choose one child over another, but it is funny you should ask because I feel "Reunion Show," which first appeared in the 22nd issue of *Dark Discoveries*, is my personal favorite. That story has a very *what is reality?* Phil K. Dick influence, but it is also a bit of an homage to Ian Mackaye and Minor Threat who were hardcore music pioneers in the early 80's Washington DC hardcore scene. It is a very odd combination which I am very proud of.

That said, the story that seems to be getting the best reaction is "Book Your Own Fucking Life." That story is about a cannibal family who lures young touring punk bands. The science fiction story "Punk Beyond the Red Line" is in my opinion the funniest story I have written, so I have a soft spot for that too. I am proud of them all, of course.

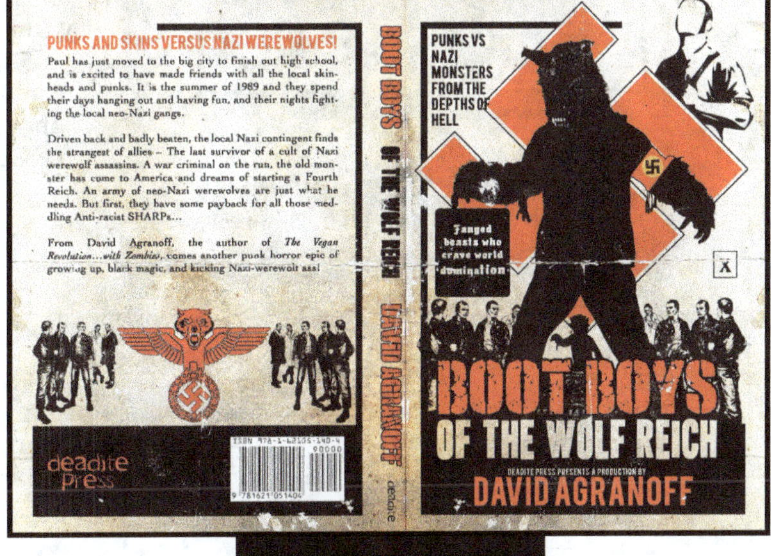

DD: There are great punk rock elements in these stories. Mixing bizarro and punk—please expand on why you think these constitute a profitable combination.

DA: Not sure how profitable, but I think it is an important combination. In the real world bizarro is an underground scene like punk rock used to be. The Do-It-Yourself ethic and the big middle finger to social norms are there. Of course, punk for me was not about making trouble for trouble's sake. Punk drove me to make the world a better place. It was punk that introduced me to be straight edge (drug-free) for political as well as personal reasons. Punk introduced me to veganism and the idea of putting ethics ahead of desire.

I write about punk because it is as much my world as Maine is Stephen King's world. He doesn't set every story in Maine, and likewise not every story in my universe involves the punk scene. I also think you don't have to know that world to enjoy the book, although it adds to the experience. The world of the punk scene is a vital one that should be represented in fiction: bizarro, horror, sci-fi all of it. That was the fun part of it.

I have found ways to mix the worlds, for example my novel *Boot Boys of the Wolf Reich* is very much a coming of age horror novel. It was meant to be in the genre alongside Brian Keene's *Ghoul* or McCammon's *Boy's Life*. It is period piece about the time and place where I grew up; when I came of age I was involved in real gang wars between anti-racist skinheads and Nazi boneheads. Sure, I added Nazi cultism and werewolves but that novel is still autobiographical in many ways. I also co-wrote two *Oi!* style street punk songs with my friend Rat from England. The songs are called "Small Town Skin" and "Howling in the Streets." You can find them on YouTube and my Soundcloud page.

DD: What led you to approach John Shirley about writing the introduction?

DA: John Shirley is my biggest influence as an author. I believe he has masterpieces in both science fiction (*City Come A Walkin'*), and *Wetbones,* which I consider to be the greatest horror novel ever written. No one combines bizarro ideas, socio-political messages and great storytelling like John

Shirley. I was honored to interview John for his guest of honor panel at the World Horror Convention in Portland.

Besides being a cyberpunk legend (William Gibson called him cyberpunk patient zero), John is a punk rock pioneer, doing bands and shows in Portland in the late 70s almost two decades before punk became mainstream enough to sell out stadiums and support Hot Topics in shopping malls. He was in a unique position to understand what I was doing. I was honored when he accepted. Since then we worked together on a full length screenplay based on his short story *The Rubber Smile* which first appeared in his Bram Stoker Award winning collection *Black Butterflies*. Hope we can find a home for that soon.

DD: Tell us about the excellent artwork that graces the pages of the book.

DA: Nick Gucker did the cover painting and the art on the inside. He can be found at www.nickthehat.com. Nick is a fantastic artist whose work I had always been impressed by. I had hung out with Nick at the Lovecraft Film Fest, Bizarrocon and World Horror. We always talked about punk so I knew he would get what I was trying to do. We didn't have the resources to do our total vision but we are happy with the art that is there. I think Nick classed up the joint.

THE VEGAN REVOLUTION ... WITH ZOMBIES

A NOVEL

DAVID AGRANOFF

DD: How do you imagine *Amazing Punk Stories* fits into the overall bizarro scene at the moment?

DA: Probably the most traditionally bizarro book I have written would be my novel *The Vegan Revolution... With Zombies*. It was a satire that was written and released pre-*Portlandia*. It makes fun of the Zombie craze, Portland hipsters, the vegan community, juggalos and a lot more. *The Journal of Animal Studies* actually had a peer-reviewed article about it!

Amazing Punk Stories might have more traditional genre work in it, but overall I think it fits into bizarro nicely. Three bizarro writers I greatly admire are Gina Ranalli, Jeremy Robert Johnson and Cody Goodfellow. They are writers whose work appeals to both bizarro readers and traditional horror readers. I think my work fits nicely in that sweet spot.

DD: Where do you see bizarro going in the future?

DA: I don't know, when many think of the bizarro scene they think of the absurdist stuff like Carlton Mellick III's *Baby Jesus Butt Plug* or Jeff Burk's *Shatnerquake*. There is a huge scene in bizarro and for all the absurdist stuff there are also works of great literature being put out by imprints like Lazy Fascist. Broken River puts out very classy bizarro crime fiction, Swallowdown has put out several very dark horror bizarro books. Authors like Jeremy Shipp and Gina Ranalli have been blazing their own amazing paths. Bizarrocon in Portland gets better and more exciting every year. If you're new to the genre I suggest picking up best *Bizarro Fiction of the Decade* edited by Cameron Pierce, or a couple of the *Starter Kits*. Great place to start.

DD: Do you have any future projects on the horizon?

DA: So many. My next novel from Deadite (the horror imprint of Eraserhead press) will be a novel called *Punk Rock Ghost Story*. I don't want to say much yet, but I am very proud of it. It is a horror novel, but it also explores the vast gulf between punk rock of the early days and after it became mainstream.

I co-wrote a science fiction novel with Edward R. Morris called *Flesh Trade*. I am hoping by the time this interview sees print that we will have found an official home for it. I think it is the best novel I have been involved with. It is a mind-bending 24th century noir with a ticking time bomb.

I am also developing a pilot for a science fiction show with two really talented writers Charles Hickey and Larry Hall. I am working on some short films next year with some other writers here in San Diego. I hope those happen. I have been very inspired by the short films that John Skipp and Andrew Kasch have been making.

DD: Where can our readers find out more about your work?

DA: People can look me up on Facebook or Twitter @dagranoffauthor. I do a blog that is mostly book reviews (I do short reviews of everything I read) and some news about my work at: www.Davidagranoff.blogspot.com

Thank you Aaron and *Dark Discoveries* for a chance to do this interview. I hope people will check out my work!

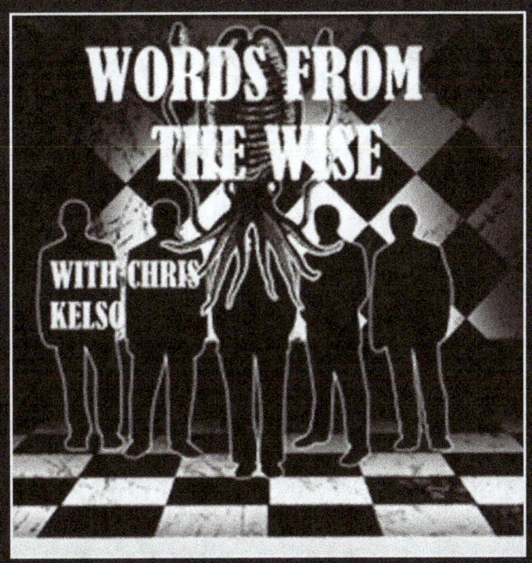

Words from the Wise

By Chris Kelso

(Chris Kelso is a writer, editor and illustrator from Scotland. His books include The Dissolving Zinc Theatre, The Black Dog Eats the City and many more.)

Photo courtesy of Colin Dunsmuir

Let's call a spade a spade – getting your writing published is really hard. Being a *successful* writer is even harder (trust me, I know!). And, ok, let's say, you *do* carve out a career for yourself… how do you make that all elusive step to the next plateau? – the plateau where all the full-time writers of the world are sitting in their mansions, their fans salivating in anticipation over each new release as they throw cash at pigeons on their forecourts instead of breadcrumbs… yes, well, you get the idea. I've decided to run a series of interviews for *Dark Discoveries* with well-established writers offering guidance to young budding creative types. I'm hoping they'll share their own insecurities and offer an insight into how they got to where they are today. The first three writers we're going to interview are Laird Barron, Peter Emshwiller and Jeff Noon. I've been a big fan of all three and they continue to rake in numerous awards and accolades for their fiction. You can follow the weekly interviews at my blog: http://www.chris-kelso.com/

The question posed to each author is – *"A young author comes to you seeking advice. They're riddled with insecurities and completely overwhelmed by the publishing industry. What are your Words from the Wise?"*

Laird Barron

Laird – To new writers, and especially to young writers: expect resistance. I am in my forties. I've written since I was five. I know one thing if I know anything.

They will try to stop you.

Resistance to artistic aspiration is typical. In general, people aren't going to leap onboard your dream train. It's cute for a teenager to talk of becoming a novelist, or a poet.

Photo courtesy of Ardi Alspach

The gloss is tarnished once you travel beyond the solar system of middling youth and into young adulthood. If it has not already begun, it will begin. If it has begun, it will now begin in earnest. People will gently, or not so gently, undermine your artistic endeavors. How will you pay off your loans? How will you pay off a mortgage? How will you afford a family? What will become of you?

Grow up. Get real. It's for your own good. We love you. Stop, just stop.

They will attempt to subvert you. They will attempt to cajole and coerce you. They will roll their eyes and shake their heads and talk about you in hushed tones of mourning. When you pursue the dream of being an author, people always mourn you. They will bargain with you. They will read your words and pronounce you no Hemingway, no Jackson, no McCarthy. They will probably be correct in this latter judgment. It doesn't matter. Hemingway was no Faulkner, Jackson was no Shelley, McCarthy is no Steinbeck. None of them were Shakespeare. Be sure they were told this or something like this and by someone who loved them, wanted the best for them.

Print is dead. Publishing is dead. No one reads. We love you. So stop.

They'll do anything to blunt your progress, to deflect your trajectory. They'll offer you a raise at the sausage plant. They'll marry you, knock you up, or get knocked up. They'll send you down the trail behind a team of huskies. They'll jail you. Drug you. Withhold love. Punish you. Blast your mind with a 24 hour news cycle and infinite cartoons on the Cartoon Network. They will guilt you for the hours you spend apart, writing, dreaming. The most insidious of them will publish you, review you, praise or condemn you, encourage you to rest on your laurels or to simply quit, the world is better off without you, because you've made it, or because you never will. And so they say, Stop. Quit. We love you. Come back to us, don't leave us here.

They will do anything to stop you. Remember. They love you. You have to be ready for that.

Peter Emshwiller

Most people, usually people who don't write, think getting started on a project is the hard part, but the rest of us know different. You know how it is, the kernel of a really cool idea is there, the motivation to get going is there, heck, maybe the first thousand words are there too. But ending a story effectively, that's not quite so straight forward.

Acclaimed novelist, illustrator and voice actor, Peter Emshwiller, will tell you to man-up and just finish the damn thing!

Peter – Your question is a great one. And a tough one. The first thing I always pass on to young writers (and also to creaky old folks my age who are new at writing) is that the most important thing to do is finish. Sounds silly, but finish. Just finish. Finish that novel about that ex who stole both your heart and your silverware. Finish that screenplay about space llamas. Finish that short story about zombie gerbils. Finish that epic poem about the sentient foot fungus.

I've had new writers come to me and say, "Well you're a REAL writer because you've had novels published by a real publishing house." I tell them, "No. That's was as much about luck as anything. What makes a person a 'real' writer is finishing."

I run into folks all the time who've got half-finished screenplays in their trunk or half done novels on their hard drive. In my humble opinion what makes someone a "real" writer (if there even IS such a thing) is getting to the end. That, to me, is what separates the amateur from the pro. Getting published can be a roll of the dice; as much about timing and connections and random luck as it is about talent and the quality of the work. But finishing? That's on you. Get to the words "THE END" in your first draft, and you're a winner. Then it's all about honing and tweaking and rewriting, and, of course, trying to get the damn thing in the hands of an agent and a publisher. (A whole 'nother challenge.)

When I was writing my very first book, I had absolutely no prospects for getting it published but I plodded away at in anyway. Halfway through I got stuck and had a huge amount of trouble finishing. So I wrote something on the front cover of my legal pad clipboard in big black letters with a sharpie pen (yes, I wrote the first draft in longhand, crazy as that sounds these days). I wrote: "Make It Crap. Fix It Later." Seeing that every time I sat down to write helped a lot. You'll note I didn't write, "It's Okay If It's Crap, You Can Fix It Later," or, "Don't Worry if It Isn't Perfect, You Can Rewrite It." I wrote, "MAKE IT CRAP. Fix it later." I gave myself permission to go ahead and write a totally awful first draft. A horrible mess of a first draft. Just to get to the end. It was incredibly freeing. And when I was done with that "crap" first draft, I'd have a lump of clay to work with when I rewrote it.

As for navigating the troubled waters of the publishing business nowadays, I fear I might not be much help. Because of the changes in technology, the industry is in the middle of huge transitions, so it's hard to say what the right move is. The only advice that still holds true, I think, is the classic one: to just keep sending your stuff out, no matter how many rejections you get. Send and send and send. Be tenacious. And do what you can to connect one way or another with agents and editors at various events so that, when you send your manuscript (or fungus poem) to them, you can write, "it was a great pleasure to meet you when we both peed in the bathroom at unicorn-con," in your cover letter. Those kinds of "we met briefly" connections actually make a huge difference.

And, of course, in between sending your stuff out over and over again, write new stuff. Don't ever stop writing stuff. And, most importantly, finish it all. Finish. Finish.

Wooley (poet and amateur journalism figure). In these letters we see the mature Lovecraft, carefully pointing potential authors to the appropriate markets, making suggestions whose work to read, and sharing the same tattered manuscripts that had been passed among friends for a decade. And as the letters creep toward his March 1937 death, the discussions remain as eclectic and intellectual, but references to his ill-health begin to creep in. It is only in his brief, poignant reply to Willis Conover, six days before cancer claimed him, that Lovecraft admits he is very ill.

The book is priced consistently with the other single volumes in the series but there's close to 100 pages of material such as appendices of works by the correspondents and bibliographies. Considering the total page count is 550, I can't help but wonder if there really is a need for things such as a glossary of frequently mentioned names. It's the seventh book in the series (eighth if you include the OOP Robert Howard 2-volume set). Factor in the various biographies and frankly, if you don't know all the names by now, you're probably not the target audience to start with. And if you are the Lovecraftian aficionado who needs to see the inner workings of the Old Gent's mind, this books should be on your shopping list. Especially since you'll want to digest this one before the next one is released next year.

◇◇

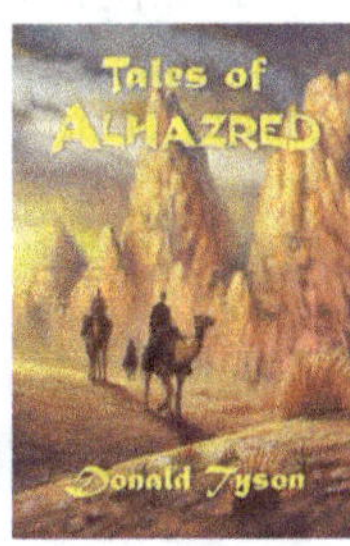

Tales of Alhazred
Donald Tyson
Dark Renaissance Books
September 24, 2015
Reviewed by Michael R. Collings

In the distant past (it now seems so long ago that dinosaurs might have still ruled the Earth), there was a popular television series called *Have Gun—Will Travel*. The black-and-white Western ran from 1957 (okay, so I was ten when it debuted) until 1963, with writers that included Bruce Geller, Irving Wallace, and Gene Roddenberry, subsequently famous for creating the first incarnation of the *Star Trek* empire.

Each half-hour episode starred an excellent but atypical, gruff-voiced, craggy-faced, decidedly un-handsome actor, Richard Boone, as Paladin, a gunslinger-for-hire in the post-Civil War era. From there, stories might take viewers anywhere in the still-exotic landscape of television's early conceptions of the Old West. There would be villains and dastardly deeds, to be sure, and Paladin—true to the etymology of his name, which refers to one of the twelve warrior-knights of Charlemagne—could use violence when necessary but preferred the more gentlemanly attributes of intellect, observation, and understanding.

The series became standard family viewing in our home. I remember it as interesting and fun, mostly because of the oddities surrounding the "man in black" with the "fast gun for hire"—a "soldier of fortune" willing to donate his services to those in need. For half an hour, we could count on seeing familiar faces in unfamiliar places, watching ingenious plans for evil unraveled by equally ingenious plans for good, and finally leaving that landscape, secure in the knowledge that we would revisit the following week.

What has this to do with Donald Tyson's *Tales of Alhazred*?

Put simply, Tyson has transformed one of the most formidable, mysterious, and fearsome human characters in the Lovecraft mythos—the "mad Arab Abdul Alhazred"—into the star of a short-story series that provides much of the same species of entertainment as did *Have Gun—Will Travel*.

There is the unlikely hero, Abdul Alhazred, human with the heart and soul of a ghoul and an internal djinn who surfaces when needed. Once a handsome luminary at the court of an eighth-century Yemeni ruler, he is now hideously scarred as punishment for misplaced amorous advances. A necromancer of enormous reputation (although he admits that much of that reputation is due not to his own knowledge but that of one of his companion, Marlata) he will sell his services…or give them, depending upon the situation. He travels through generalized landscapes—vast deserts, ancient and partially ruined cities, shadowy necropolises, rough mountain redoubts—usually accompanied by the same cast of characters. He fights evil in all of its physical manifestations, most prominently djinni and ghouls but often amorphous or insectile or tentacled creatures from other spheres (literally in one story), magicians and other necromancers, and simply evil, venal humans.

Oh, and along the way he encounters Lovecraftian Old Ones.

That is where *Tales of Alhazred* falters for me as reader.

The stories—even those that conjure Yog-Sothoth and carefully avoid revealing the name Nyarlathotep—lack the sense of the cosmic, of the other, of the outré in its original sense of 'beyond all barriers.' The actions are human-based, earth-based, even when they incorporate a gigantic maggot-like monster worshipped as a god or an enigmatic black sphere that opens onto another world, which remains largely unexplored and unexplained. There is a safeness to the stories, a feeling akin to watching the closing credits of an enjoyable television episode, relaxing slightly that the hero has escaped again (although that was really not in doubt), and looking forward to much of the same next week. For stories about the early life of the author of the most notorious book in creation, the Necronomicon, these seem remarkably tame, with little to hint of horrors and madness.

This is not to say that the stories are uninteresting. They are solid, well told, with sufficient twists and turns to keep the momentum going to the final page. And they are accompanied by color and black-and-white illustrations by Frank Wells, each aptly capturing a key moment and making it visual. But in the end, they fall uncomfortably into a niche somewhere between the *Tales of the Arabian Nights* and revelations of Lovecraftian Horrors, partaking of both but perhaps not enough of either.

◇◇

Brothers
Ed Gorman and Richard Chizmar
SST Publications
May 2015
Reviewed by Wayne C. Rogers

Brothers by Ed Gorman and Richard Chizmar is a short novella (about 55 pages after the Introduction and Afterword are subtracted) that is as smooth as 25-year-old whiskey going down your parched throat. Here are two of the best writers working today in the United States, but few people seem to be aware of them. Ed Gorman has written several novels over the last two decades, while Rich Chizmar is the creator of *Cemetery Dance* magazine and publications, not to mention an excellent writer of short stories and novellas. The world needs to know about these two authors because writing doesn't get much better than this.

The story of *Brothers* is about two brothers who are police officers in the same town. One is older and promised his father to watch out over the younger one, making sure he doesn't turn out to be like the old man. The younger one, however, resents the intrusion of his older brother into his personal affairs, but doesn't seem to mind when his brother gets him out of jams, helps him through college, and then gets him a job on the police force.

The younger brother, who is married with children, is now having an affair that threatens to destroy his family. The man cares, but doesn't care. It seems as though all he can do is keep traveling down the path that leads to his own self-destruction. The older brother, disregarding the advice of everyone else, wants to save his sibling from doing to the wrong thing.

In a short period of time, however, this leads directly to a collision of tragedy for everyone involved, but especially the older brother.

I've never had a brother, though I have had friends over the years that appear to be very much like the younger brother in this story. They won't change their habits or stop causing the destruction in their wake until someone finally leaves or dies. Then, they're sorry. But being sorry is only a word and it doesn't do much to quiet the pain and anguish that others are suffering through. This is what the bad boys fail to understand as they continue to do exactly what they want without consideration for the effect their actions will have on the people around them.

Both Gorman and Chizmar seem to clearly understand this in their creation of the two main characters. It's certainly a no-win situation for the older brother. No matter what he does, others will blame him for his younger one's actions.

That's a tough situation to be in for anybody.

Another thing is that the younger brother's character is one you want to punch right in the face and then tell him to get lost. Nothing but bad news will come of his actions and the people in front of him will be burned by his inability to care.

Now, if you're wondering about the writing style here, let me tell you that it's impossible to determine when one writer stops and another takes over. It reminded a good bit of *The Talisman* and *The Black House* by Stephen King and Peter Straub. There was no way to determine which author was writing what because their styles merged into something new that was easy to read and had a fast momentum about it. The same is true with *Brothers*. I didn't want the novella to end and wished it had been longer.

This is some of the best writing I've encountered during the past year, though there are other authors out there every bit as good like Mick Garris, Mike Miller, Tom Monteleone, Michael Marshall Smith, Brian James Freeman, and others who are striving to write the best fiction possible for their growing legion of fans.

Don't wait on getting this. It can be purchased in both hardcover and paperback from Amazon or from Short, Scary Tales in England. If you would like a signed hardcover from both authors, go to Cemetery Dance Publications and entered it into their search engine. A great read for a small amount of money!

◇◇

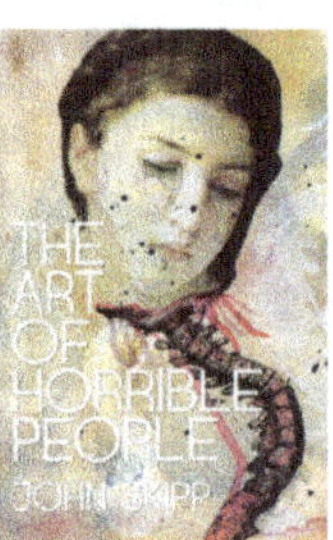

The Art of Horrible People
John Skipp
Lazy Fascist Press
August 1, 2015
Reviewed by Marvin P. Vernon

I have always been fond of writers who seem to write in hyperdrive. Whether it is Hunter S. Thompson, Harlan Ellison or Garrett Cook, I like the writers that let it all out, appearing not to care whether you can keep up with them. If their imagination or emotion gets a little ahead of the prose, that is just part of the attraction. The writers I like realize that they can't write for the audience. The audience needs to come to them and the payoff is when the reader gets into the writer's strange and manic mind and says, "Wow! Now I get it!" At least, that is the way my own strange and manic mind perceives it.

In *The Art of Horrible People*, John Skipp becomes one of those authors. Of course he had a bit of a head start as one of the early architects of splatterpunk genre. His standing as a father figure of the bizarro movement doesn't hurt either. But in this new collection of eight short stories, Skipp seems to be airing a mixture of amazement and repulsion over the acts of the human race which frankly can be pretty horrible. Call it cynicism or realism, Skipp may have held it in for too long to be anything but a torrent of words and emotions. There is a mishmash of genres here from straight horror to dark comedies and styles that border between free association and straight-out rant. Yet they all are entertaining in Skipp's own manic and sometimes far-out crazy style.

Take the first story for instance. "Art is the Devil" is a dead on depiction of the too often over-hyped and phony world of the visual arts. If anyone is going to be an art connoisseur, wouldn't it be the devil? It is a funny over-the-top satire of the contemporary art scene.

The second story, "Depresso the Clown," is very different but just as extreme. It is a straight horror story on the capture of a rather pathetic clown. Whether you call it tragedy or comedy will depend on how you feel about clowns.

"Rose Goes Shopping" is a dark comedic takeoff on the zombie story. It reminds you that even in the zombie apocalypse, old habits die hard. In my opinion, this little story makes the zombies seem relatively decent. "Worm Central Tonite!" is quite short and more of a concept piece. It packs a nice philosophical wallop in just a few pages.

"Skipp's Hollywood Alphabet Soup of Horror" is essentially 26 flash fiction pieces all about Hollywood and the movie industry. This is Skipp's cynicism working overtime. You can argue that Hollywood is an easy target but the quick vignettes are essentially spot on and it is clear the author has waded more than once in the craziness of the movie game.

"Zygote Notes on the Imminent Birth of a Feature Film as Yet Unformed" is ironically the best work here. Ironic because in some ways it is the most typical of the bizarro genre yet atypical for this collection because it seems reflective and intimate with multiple layers. I think it is one of the best piece of short fiction I have read from this author.

"In a Waiting Room, Trading Death Stories" is an amusing hiccup of a tale that simply whets our appetite for the last and other best short fiction in the book, "Food Fight." This is splatterpunk at its best. It is a tale about chaos in a behavioral health center told through different perspectives in Skipp's equally chaotic style.

Skipp is one of those writers that need to be read to be believed. Although he is mostly a stalwart of the splatterpunks, it is easy to see why the younger bizarro writers see him as so influential to their own movement. But what it comes down to is that Skipp is basically his own sub-genre and resists pigeon holing. *The Art of Horrible People* is no less than the art of telling a good story.

◇◇

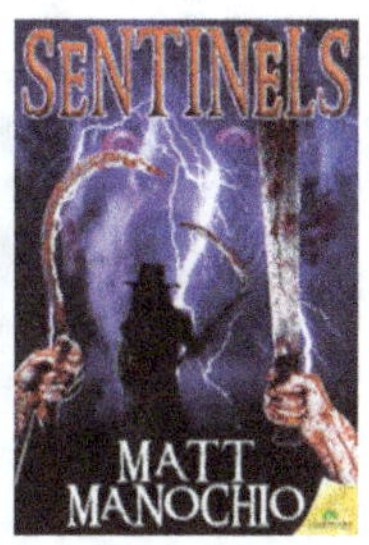

Sentinels
Matt Manochio
Samhain Publishing
November 3, 2015
Reviewed by Tim Potter

Matt Manochio's upcoming novel *Sentinels* is a relentless, action-packed and almost entirely successful novel of historical horror. The story is set in 1873 South Carolina, a small town called Henderson, and focuses on the all-too-real horrors that plagued the southern United States in the years after the Civil War and Reconstruction. The terror that centers on the real world does eventually spin into the supernatural, but never at the cost of derailing the book's moral and ethical foundation.

Racism is at the center of the plot, with former slave and current land owner Toby, his wife and their infant son drawing the ire of white landowners and the Ku Klux Klan. Toby can't rightly be called the hero of the story because he's too complex for classification, which results in him being a character of great depth. His connection to the land he rightfully owns and will do anything in defense of is the central conflict of the novel. Another local landowner will stop at nothing to acquire Toby's land, starting by offering to buy the land (an offer that is flatly rejected) to physical coercion and attempted murder.

Noah is the story's main character and lead protagonist. He grew up in Henderson but moved north in his pursuit of an education that will make him a lawyer and as he is living in the north, he becomes a member of the Union Army during the Civil War. His brother, who never left Henderson, is fighting in the War also, though on the side of the Confederacy, which leads to one of the book's only faults. Not only do the brothers meet on opposing sides of the battlefield, but come face to face as Noah is gravely wounded and his brother is killed. It an unnecessary cliché that does nothing to advance the plot of the book. Without any brother Noah would still have had ample motivation for his actions.

Having returned to his hometown after the War, Noah decides to become a deputy to the sheriff in an attempt to help his hometown. This brings him together with Toby in opposition of the KKK and entwined in a conspiracy with roots deep in Henderson society. While putting their respective families at risk, Toby and Noah work to understand the convoluted politics and social institutions that are threatening Toby, other Freedmen and Freedwomen and the soul of Henderson.

The story is set a few years too many after the Civil War. It's a small criticism, but an important one from a historical perspective. The power of the Klan and the presence of the army of the Union was much greater in, say, 1870 than 1873. Luckily it's an issue that doesn't interfere with the reader's ability to enjoy the tale.

The setting in place and time (give or take three years) is very successful in all other levels. The reader is easily transported to Henderson, South Carolina in the years following the Civil War. The book's greatest achievement though is in its pacing as it seamlessly blends characterization, suspense, mystery and almost non-stop action. From the gritty realism of the beginning of the book to the climactic supernatural showdown, *Sentinels* is a novel that never lets up, always delivers on unfolding mystery and is suspenseful to the last page.

◇◇

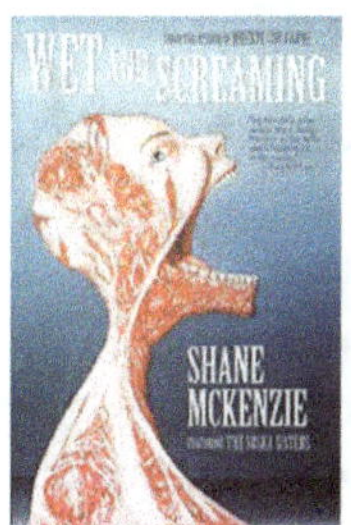

Wet and Screaming
Shane McKenzie
Deadite Press
June 12, 2015
Reviewed by Marvin P. Vernon

In Shane McKenzie's first collection of short fiction, *Wet and Screaming*, we get what we expect from a book by that title. McKenzie writes bizarre fiction that isn't nice and doesn't open the door for you. If it does open the door for you, expect to be kicked in the rear when you enter. The author's fiction is the epitome of hardcore horror yet there is something natural and casual about the way he tells his stories even while they soar over the top in disturbing and shocking images. This is the sign of a natural storyteller.

Wet and Screaming offers 11 short stories by the author. In a strange move, there are also two stories by *American Mary* directors the Soska Sisters, but for this review I will concentrate on just the fiction by McKenzie.

A less strange and welcome addition are introductions to each story, which are not just informative but very entertaining. The first tale, "Fat Slob," serves as a warning to the neophyte McKenzie reader that squeamish stomachs need not apply. "Ed Gein's Garage Sale" is a particular favorite of mine. As I read it I can see *Psycho* author Robert Bloch smiling down on the pages. "He's Just a Baby" suggests that even a burglar can develop a fraternal instinct. "I'm on my-" has nothing supernatural about it but for my money, it is easily the most disturbing piece in the book. "Red Asphalt" reminds me of what I learned in my therapeutic practice: anything can become an addiction and anything can be taken to extremes. "So Much Pain, So Much Death" is another disturbing story where, during the introduction, the author explains his reason for writing it. The piece itself evoked equal parts of *The Omen* and the story of Abraham and Isaac.

Those are some of the highlights but there is not a weak story here. However I would feel amiss if I didn't mention my pick for best tale of the lot, "Stab the Rabbit." While the author is sometimes mentioned as a prominent Bizarro writer, I have always thought of him as more straight hardcore horror. "Stab the Rabbit" really brings out the Bizarro in McKenzie while still being a disturbing and scary work of horror. The author states the influence for the story is Jessica Rabbit which may help you understand the bizarreness but, believe me, doesn't even come close to how weird and horrific it really is.

So this is an excellent collection yet, to be honest, if I were to recommend a first read of this author it would be one of his novels, particularly *Muerte Con Carne* or *Mutt*. That isn't to trivialize his short fiction but McKenzie has a real talent for creating characters that involves the reader and leaps off the pages. Short fiction doesn't do that in most cases, yet even here it happens. "Stab the Rabbit" presents two brothers who are very real but different, making the story not only delightfully gross and weird but an insightful look at sibling conflict. Most of these stories set up a plot and takes you to the punchline. There is nothing wrong with that. In fact, it is a strength to be able to do both so well. In these stories, McKenzie reminds me a lot of my favorite short fiction horror writer, the aforementioned Robert Bloch. No one is as good as setting up the story then throwing in the shocking twist as Bloch. Yet McKenzie is certainly nipping at his heels to take away that title.

If someone wanted a "sampler" of what this author can do, or if you are just one of those readers who prefer short fiction, *Wet and Screaming* would still be a fine and perhaps essential choice. But let the "Not For Everyone" banner be waved. For the horror reader who digs the weird, explicit and hardcore, Shane McKenzie's *Wet and Screaming* is a must read.

◇◇

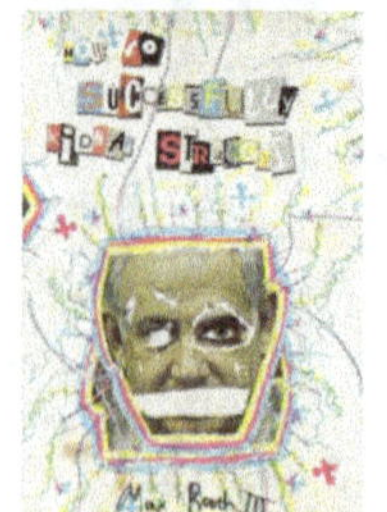

How to Successfully Kidnap Strangers
Max Booth III
Bizarro Pulp Press
July 20, 2015
Reviewed by Tim Potter

Max Booth III's compulsively readable new novel, *How to Successfully Kidnap Strangers*, is an anthem for small, independent book publishers and authors. The novel is well constructed with a tight plot and solid, unique characters. Its story is a warts-and-all depiction of what goes into running a small press, though in this case readers will want to know what goes into the literary sausage. There are twists and turns that no one will see coming, because, really, when an angry (and likely quite intoxicated) author kidnaps a reviewer as revenge for bashing his books, where can things possibly go? For all its literary merit, sharp characterization and informative nature about the publishing game, the main selling point of *How to Successfully Kidnap Strangers* is that it just a great, fun read.

The relentless pacing of the book is its biggest success. There are no peaks and no valleys, just an explosion of an opening that keeps burning until the last words are read. A disgruntled writer makes the most of a chance encounter with a reviewer who hates his books by kidnapping the reviewer. It should be simple, but one kidnapping leads to a second kidnapping by way of grand theft auto. People die, books are pimped on street corners as though they were hookers or drugs. There are severed heads, weaponized dildo crucifixes and possible salvation through two books chronicling the erotic adventures of Jesus.

The characters are fantastic and loveable, the type of people you probably know in the real world if you've been making poor life choices. Harlan Anderson reads books, always illegally downloaded, and always with one purpose: to write bad reviews of them online. Nick is the editor-in-chief of the publishing company the group of friends works for, in varying capacities. BILF, or Books I'd Like to Fuck, publishes extreme fiction from little known authors, including Sergio Placid, who is something of a big name in a small world. Sergio has written dozens of books, despite being in his mid-twenties, and has had one real success, *The Cumming of Christ*. (Sorry. That is not a typo.) Sergio, along with Nick, have great character arcs and evolve with the plot and have very satisfying conclusions to their parts of the tale.

This is a book about revolution. Revolution against the mainstream publishing industry, against the traditional literary community, against any restrictions on authors and the work they create. But it's also about revolution against responsibility, sanity and sobriety. Funny lines like "fuck James Patterson" or "fuck genre delineation" are actually backed with solid commentary and important, subversive ideas.

Written in such a clean, sharp style of prose, it's like the words in the book are speed, they shoot directly to the pleasure center of the brain and make everything that follows faster, more intense, more pleasurable. The chapter breaks are an almost physical relief as they provide a short period of rest before the next hit of prose begins. Readers will wish that BILF was a real publishing house and that titles like The Trampoline Incident, Cock Mutants, Attack of the Chlamydia Kamikazes and even Harlan's That's What She said were sitting on their shelves waiting to be read. *How to Successfully Kidnap Strangers* is most certainly a BILF.

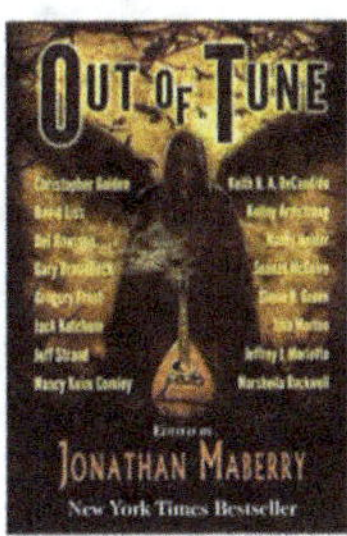

Out of Tune – All New Tales of Horror and Dark Fantasy
Edited by Jonathan Maberry
JournalStone
2014
Reviewed by David Goudsward

Out of Tune is collection of new dark tales inspired by traditional folk ballads. Ballads, much like pre-Disney fairy tales, range from the unpleasant to the gruesome. It's a perfect match to the modern masters of horror. Jonathan Maberry has pulled out all the stops and assembled a choir of the macabre, each reimagining an archetypal ballad and yet keeping the distinctive voice that makes each author memorable.

This is a stunning array of 14 authors, each reveling in the material. Christopher Golden returns to his beloved Peter Pan motif, using it to tell a disquieting tale based on the infanticide ballad of the Cruel Mother. On the opposite end of the spectrum is Jeff Strand, the master of gallows humor and his version of John Henry's determination to win a race against a steam engine, even if it kills him a few times. In between are a variety of stories by best-selling and award winning authors such as Nancy Holder and her take on Edgar Allan Poe in Lovecraft's Arkham, Jack Ketchum's tale of a relationship gone bad, and Gary Braunbeck's modern version of The Streets of Laredo. Each story is followed by commentary about the original ballad by folklorist Nancy Keim-Comley.

This is simply one of the most elegant and brilliant concepts for a themed anthology to come around in years. My major complaint is that no one thought of it before now.

Pixu: The Mark of Evil
Written and Illustrated by Gabriel Ba, Becky Cloonan, Vasilis Lolos, Fabio Moon
Dark Horse Comics
September 9, 2015
Reviewed by Elaine Pascale

Award-winning artists collaborated on *Pixu*, the story of haunted apartment dwellers. The images throughout the story depict a dark mark in the building: a mark of evil that spreads, causing violence and insanity.

The artwork is meant to carry *Pixu*, and largely, it does. The four artists are fantastic and their black and white drawings blend well and give *Pixu* a solitary feel. The book is largely a showcase for the art, which is very frightening and contains staples of the horror genre. *Pixu* begins with a visual feeling of dread, which blossoms into nightmarish and terrifying images.

While the artwork is impressive, the story is vague. I know that one picture is worth a thousand words, but the individual panels leave gaps in the narrative. There were characters that I really could not get a handle on, even after additional readings. That might be because the main character is the "mark of evil," but even that dark mark is largely undefined. *Pixu* contains a wealth of creepy stuff, I simply wanted it to be more cohesive.

I also wanted more of a backstory. For example, is the landlord aware of the mark and is he using it in some nefarious way? Each individual apartment's story begins in media res; perhaps the clues were too vague for me to craft a plot from the images and very sparse text.

Pixu is an adult only graphic novel. There are disturbing visuals, as well as a story line that suggests child molestation and pedophilia. If you enjoy a minimalistic plot that is open to many interpretations, then *Pixu* is a good match for you. Likewise, if you are a fan of any of the four artists, you will not be disappointed.

Spore
Tamara Jones
Samhain Publishing
June 2, 2015
Reviewed by Tim Potter

Tamara Jones's new novel *Spore* is, at first glance, a pretty standard looking zombie novel. When the reader gets into the story, which takes no time at all, it becomes clear that this isn't necessarily a zombie novel at all. Sure, there are people rising from the dead, but not in ways that populate so many novels in the subgenre. Jones uses the zombie and pandemic ideas of horror to create something unique, a novel of pure horror that stays away from cliche and never lets up on the suspense until the end.

Spore succeeds mainly on the author's commitment to keeping the story about the small town and the few main characters that the reader really gets to know. Stories like this, dealing with the undead or spreading infection, tend to have a sprawling plot and cast of characters that may come together at the novel's end. That's not the case here, as the story never loses its focus on just a few characters in a small town. This allows for the realistic human element to shine through the fantastic elements.

The lead character is comic book creator and artist Sean Casey, a good man working to have a happy life and escape a troubled past. The tale opens as a number of naked people walk through the treeline at the end of Sean's property, likely having come from the cemetery on the far side of the trees. It takes very little time for it to become clear that these are not run-of-the-mill zombies.

Actually, they may not be zombies at all. These "Pine People," or "Spores" as they will come to be known, are fully functional, aware people. Their shared trait is a lack of memory, some for weeks, some months and some for decades. They can remember everything about their lives up to a point and then they find themselves naked at Sean's house.

Sean's reaction is unexpected and perfect, and sets the tone for the remainder of the novel. He talks to the Spores, realizes that they are people like himself and he helps them. He invites them into his home to cover up and try to contact family as he calls the local police for help. The police arrive, one of them a friend of Sean's, and they take the Spores to the hospital where the staff tries to figure out what is causing their strange circumstance.

This is the strength of the book—its reliance on the characters and what the human reaction to such a situation would be. In a genre where the focus is often on the situation, the cause and result of the horror and the gore, Tamara Jones has written a book that is about the people. It never comes at the expense of the gore and situation either, as both are present and well done. In focusing the story on the micro instead of the macro, *Spore* elevates itself to the level of a superior novel.

◇◇

Flesh Like Smoke
Edited by Brian M. Sammons
April Moon Books
July, 2015
Reviewed by David Goudsward

The conventional wisdom is that the werewolf trope is played out—that *Twilight* was the final silver nail in the wolfsbane coffin. The moon beast has become mundane since H. Warner Munn reinvented the genre in *Weird Tales* back in 1928; the ravenous killing machine is today more prone to teen angst than bloody carnage. Well, hang on to your Lon Chaney underoos, there's good news gleaming in the moonlight!

From April Moon Books comes *Flesh Like Smoke,* a new anthology of shapeshifters for the lycanthophiliacs in your life. Brian Sammons is rapidly developing reputation for his almost supernatural ability to find and juxtapose stories that make even old tropes new and exciting.

Sixteen new stories of varying degrees of spilled sanguinity, and not one angst-filled, pretty boy, werewolf sex symbol in the book. All feature mutable monsters, all radically different from each other. As well it should with a solid roster of authors with diverse reputations of their own—Tim Waggoner, William Meikle, Pete Rawlik, Cody Goodfellow, and Don Webb just to name a few.

It is not a one-sitting read. This is one you'll want to stop between stories and savor the experience before plunging into another tale. Indeed, it's almost advised—the stories leap from place to place and time periods. Stories jump from modern day South Boston to the Reign of Vikings to a Cyberpunk future with Indian legends, folk legends, and pure sci-fi along the way.

I hope Sammons considers reinvigorating other old monsters in need of a transfusion of fresh blood—and I don't necessarily mean just vampires.

◇◇

The Dark at the End of the Tunnel
Taylor Grant
Cemetery Dance Publications,
November 2015
eBook, $4.99
Reviewed by Michael R. Collings

In "Gods and Devils," the fourth of ten stories in Taylor Grant's exceptional collection of short fiction, *The Dark at the End of the Tunnel,* Captain Vega considers his susceptibility to "Solipsism Syndrome" following months as the only fully conscious human onboard his space ship. The condition, the narrator notes,

> ...was a serious risk for anyone who spent long periods alone in space. It created the overwhelming feeling that nothing was real—or simply a dream. Sufferers had been known to feel so lonely and detached from the world they became utterly, and terribly indifferent.

As I read that paragraph on my Kindle, I highlighted the words; I was only about one-third of the way through the volume, yet already I recognized a key thematic element that, as strongly stated as it was, might ultimately connect all of the stories. Reading the final words of the capstone piece, "The Dark at the End of the Tunnel," confirmed that sense.

Regardless of the convolutions and reversals each might take, every story dealt on some level with an "overwhelming feeling that nothing was real—or simply a dream." For every character, that feeling leads to horror, death, and beyond. And in these stories "beyond" might entail gruesome and appalling visions of the transitory nature of life... and the terrors of dark eternities.

"Masks" opens the book with a powerful portrayal of a man whose inner and outer lives begin to open on unwanted, almost indescribable vistas of pain and torture. As those images increasingly intrude into his relationships with others, he changes, at first subtly, then so radically that he no longer recognizes his own self and begins to understand that within—beneath the mask of humanity—lies horror.

"The Silent Ones" is among the most effective of the stories (although saying that suggests that some are ineffective—definitely not the case here). The narrator suspects that something is wrong when people seem not to notice him, and people he knows well forget him. Step by step—quite literally through much of the story as he wanders streets looking for something "real"—he is removed farther and farther from touch with humanity. For me, one of the most telling scenes occurred when he enters a late-night bar and realizes that the people there actually *see* him... because they have already become as invisible as he. Some years ago, I spent a number of evenings at a fast-food restaurant nearby, writing. Only gradually did I see that the same people were always there, often just sitting, rarely eating. And *I* had become one of them! Coming across an analogous scene in a horror story was startling—but that was not the end of the surprises.

"The Vood" carries the image of isolation and self-abandonment to a hideous extreme. Grady lives—if it can be called living—in mortal terror of the Vood. The only protection he knows is light: If he is surrounded by light, the Vood in the shadows cannot devour him, as it had his mother years before. Grant carefully withholds information about who and what the Vood is, delivering it in packets that move the story inevitably forward to the moment of discovery, an un-covering in more senses than one.

In "Gods and Devils," an alien parasite has transformed almost all of humanity into *Homo Hirudinea,* human hosts who either carry and spread the parasite, or feed it. Captain Vega is brought out of sleep stasis to face a crisis: One of the several hundred passengers aboard, who constitute the remnants of the human race, has awakened and, infected and hungry, threatens the lives of all aboard.

"Dead Pull" focuses on Brennan, a pet-store employee, a sadist, and—we discover almost accidentally—a murderer. By brutally wielding his presence and his life-or-death power, he has terrorized every animal in the shop into submissive obedience. But when he uses his authority to maltreat a young intern... well, things don't go quite as Brennan anticipates.

In "Show and Tell," young Jacob Campbell decides to explain to Mr. McDaniels why he had drawn the highly realistic—and horrifically detailed—pictures his teacher had confiscated. When he begins to open up about himself, his family, and his past, the counselor is at first mildly interested, though disgusted; as the story proceeds, Jacob pulls him into a story that ceases to be a story and leads—no surprise—to revelation, destruction, and death.

"The Infected" is the almost obligatory story of a writer whose story comes to mean more than he anticipates. In some ways it parallels and completes the depiction of isolation in "The Silent Ones," only here the progression is slower, more cautious, and more devastating. Opening a Vietnam-era footlocker of his fathers, the character discovers an unfinished novel—unfinished by his grandfather, resumed and left unfinished by his father. If he can finish the novel, it will be the answer to financial and family troubles, if only the couple can survive the next little while. An opportunity for temp work arises—through the Tempting Agency—and life begins its inexorable assault on dreams.

"Whispers in the Trees, Screams in the Dark" is a neat modern recreation of a familiar folk-tale. Grant studs the backstory with clues, so it comes as no surprise that Blake must confront the ultimate wicked stepmother, in fiction and in life. It is a dark, finely honed story, of a loner so desperate to be part of something—*anything*—that he is willing to bet the one thing most precious to him. He just doesn't know that his life is also on the line.

"Intruders" focuses on Mason, another character convinced that life does not reveal all of its horror easily. He has become convinced that the "crazies" on city streets—the ones talking to themselves, arguing with themselves, gesturing to nothing at all—truly hear voices, not because they are schizophrenic but because there are creatures out there, out of dimensional sync with most human vision and hearing. In desperation, he seeks out an old lover and pleads for her help. She gives it. Sort of.

And finally, "The Dark at the End of the Tunnel." Matt Jackson awakens from a decade of brain death to find himself ultra-rich, with a magnificent home in Malibu, a dream car in the garage, and the wealth to go anywhere and do anything he wants. But what he wants is to discover who he was *before*... before whatever made him go into cryogenic sleep. His physician assures him that full memory will resurface in a month or so, but Matt can't wait. And in this case, he should have.

I've no doubt done the stories a disservice by compacting them to near bumper-sticker length. They are beautifully constructed and in the largest part well written (My only quibble with the collection is an occasional word choice or phrase—occupational hazard with being a retired English professor and an active editor). The stories read smoothly, as they should, since they deal mostly with twists on and distortions of reality, objectivity, perception, and individuality. There are, of course, scenes of gore and blood-letting and monstrous transformations and some that are not monstrous but manage to seem even worse: yet there is also humanity, even it if is only described by its increasing absence. Much is at risk in each story—not only a characters' physical beings, but their hearts and souls as well... with emphasis on *soul.* ◆

www.ingramcontent.com/pod-product-compliance
Lightning Source LLC
Chambersburg PA
CBHW081137300726
48982CB00005B/979
9781940161594